Please return this book on or before the date shown above. To renew go to www.essex.gov.uk/libraries, ring 0845 603 7628 or go to any Essex library.

Essex County Council

# AUTHOR NOTE

I want to say the inspiration for Mairead and Caird's story came from a fateful trip to Wales. But it didn't. Not really. Caird is brother to Gaira, who is wife to Robert, who I saw grieving under a tree in Wales (long story). But that doesn't explain much. Except that there are people in my head, and those people want their stories told. Now and all at once. So, although I intended to write about Robert's friend Hugh, from *The Knight's Broken Promise* (stay with me on the people!), I couldn't ignore Mairead, who was about to do something mad.

Well, mad for the rest of us. Not for Mairead. She's impulsive, she makes mistakes and she's reckless. When her brother was killed she chased after the murderer. Since she was by herself, I rushed to tell her story in case she got hurt. When Caird showed up I thought, *Oh, good, he'll rescue her*.

Unfortunately he hates Mairead, he is controlling and he only plays by the rules. When Mairead realises that Caird is just as insufferable and arrogant as the rest of his clan I knew Caird needed rescuing from Mairead.

Then they kissed. They *kissed*! At that point I gave up and told them to write their own story. I think they did. I don't know; I'm afraid to look.

# HER ENEMY HIGHLANDER

Nicole Locke

Published in Great Britain 2015
by Mills & Boon, an imprint of Harlequin (UK) Limited,
Eton House, 18-24 Paradise Road, Richmond, Surrey, TW9 1SR

© 2015 Nicole Locke

ISBN: 978-0-263-24805-0

Harlequin (UK) Limited's policy is to use papers that are natural, renewable and recyclable products and made from wood grown in sustainable forests. The logging and manufacturing processes conform to the legal environmental regulations of the country of origin.

Printed and bound in Spain
by CPI, Barcelona

**Nicole Locke** discovered her first romance novels in her grandmother's closet, where they were secretly hidden. Convinced that books hidden must be better than those that weren't, Nicole greedily read them. It was only natural for her to start writing them (but now not so secretly). She lives in London with her two children and her husband—her happily-ever-after.

**Books by Nicole Locke**

**Mills & Boon® Historical Romance**

*Lovers and Legends*

*The Knight's Broken Promise*
*Her Enemy Highlander*

**Visit the author profile page at millsandboon.co.uk**

To my husband—
you know what you did.

To my children—
who seriously should have known better.

# Chapter One

Scotland—September 1296

Mairead Buchanan tried to calm her heart and failed. She didn't even know why she tried. She knew it wasn't possible. It had been pounding like this for over a fortnight and now it was only worse. Inside her thumping heart, grief clawed sharp.

But she didn't have time for grief, didn't have time to be reasonable, or to think. She was about to break; she just needed to *do*.

This nightmare had to end. And here, tonight, where she stood observing the shadows of a disreputable inn and freezing in the night's damp cold, it would.

The candles on the inn's ground floor were finally extinguished. The windows were black; the main shutters were closed. Not even a woman laughing in the distance marred the soft rustling of the night breeze. It was late; it was time.

Yet even now she fought what she had to do. Even now, she wanted to shake herself, to run in circles like a madwoman trying to escape what she had seen, what she had done. What she could not ever repair. Her brother, Ailbert, collapsing to the ground. His eyes going vacant, losing their sight. She clenched her eyes shut. Grief clawed. She clawed back.

It wouldn't do to think of Ailbert now. Her anger or her pain. She must still her heart and retrieve what was stolen from him. It was the only way to save her family from Ailbert's recklessness. If she didn't retrieve the priceless dagger, the laird would certainly punish her family.

Scotland was being ravaged by war and conflict. Her mother and sisters would never survive the humiliation or the certain banishment from the clan. Without the clan, there was nothing to protect them from the English. They had nowhere else to go. No other family to turn to.

For her family's sake, she followed Ailbert's murderer to the inn. The man had actually paid for a room. Had probably eaten his fill and was now sleeping soundly. Ordinary actions her brother would never do again. Fury swamped Mairead's grief and she welcomed it. Grief and desperation consumed her, but only anger would get her through this night.

Looking over her shoulder and into the gloom

of the evening, she took a big breath. There was no one behind her and she had had enough of waiting.

Silencing her breath, she opened the door and let herself in. It was darker than she imagined; the shadows blanketed furniture and walls. It was unnaturally quiet and she concentrated on the sounds she could hear. The hammering of her heart, the air as it left her body, the creak of the boards as the night wind buffeted the old building.

Nothing else.

Swiftly and nimbly, she weaved through the benches and trestles on her way to the stairs. She wasn't certain which room the murderer occupied, but she'd give herself no more than an hour to search the rooms for the stolen dagger. Any more time and travellers would be likely to stir.

She had to have—no, needed that dagger. She'd lie and steal if she had to. She'd even go into strangers' rooms and risk her life. The dagger's large handle was made of finely decorated polished silver and was inset with two rubies. If she could sell it, like Ailbert had intended, the debt he'd incurred could be repaid. Everything would not be lost by his reckless gambling and then, only then, could she grieve.

Walking down the small hallway, she stopped at the first door and eased the heavy iron latch open, only to find the room empty. Gently closing the door, she peered over her shoulder. She was alone.

Mairead crept to the next room and winced as the door clicked loudly. A narrow window on the opposite wall provided the light needed to illuminate an occupied bed.

From the size and shape of the lump, it looked to be a man. Her brother's murderer was large and this man looked large, but she couldn't tell whether the bed linens gave him the breadth or if it was the man himself.

Reminding herself she needed the bed occupied, she released her breath and entered the room. Clothes were strewn over a stool at the foot of the bed. A pair of boots sat nearby. Perhaps the dagger was here. Grateful that the floorboards did not squeak, she knelt on the floor.

The dim embers in the fireplace provided little light, but the unshuttered window gave plenty. His clothing consisted of a cloak, braies, dark leggings, a whitish tunic, boots and a pouch.

The man in the bed was naked.

The bed creaked as the man shifted and gave out a heavy breath. Mairead tensed, ready to run, until he stilled.

Her heart wasn't so accommodating and continued to hammer in her chest. Trying to steady her nerves, she continued her search, but her fingers trembled as she felt along his boots. There was no dagger placed deep in the feet. Careful of the attached belt, she pulled the pouch off the stool and on to her lap. A slight jangle of coins made her jump, but the man remained still. The bed linens continued to rise and fall with each steady breath.

Not bothering to open the pouch, she felt along the fine leather. No dagger. She felt the tunic, the braies and the thin leather leggings. Nothing. That left the cloak.

Gathering it in both hands, she was instantly aware of the fine soft wool. Never having felt such a cloth before she reveled in its feel as she pulled on the immense amount of fabric. The stool up-ended, and she made a grab for it. Too late. It fell with a dull thud to the floor. The man's deep breathing stopped abruptly.

She froze.

'Who's there?'

His rough voice commanded the little room. She didn't answer. Maybe it was too dark for him to see. Maybe if she didn't make a noise he'd go back to sleep.

The man rose in a half incline. Though she willed her body to remain still, slight tremors began in her legs and arms. If possible, her breathing grew louder.

The bed linens did not make him look large. He *was* large. His chest was bare of any ornament. She could not see the texture of his skin, but could see the ripples and curves of deeply embedded muscles coursing from his wide shoulders down his arms. His long loose hair gave his dark face a wild and untamed look. The rest of him was partially concealed by the bed linens, but not the glint of steel he held in his hand. This was a man who slept with weapons.

'If you…think I cannot see you, you forget you sit within the light of the window.'

This was not the murderer. His voice was too calmly masculine, too reverberating, too…slurred. He was drunk!

Relief skittered through her. Thinking only of slow responses from a drunken man, she leapt for the door.

Her eyes did not register the blade flying past her arm. But she heard the sharp slice it made in the oak door, mere inches from her outstretched hand.

# Chapter Two

Mairead's hand froze along with the rest of her body. But her eyes blinked rapidly as she tried to focus and comprehend.

Had he thrown a dagger towards her? She peered closer. It was only a small boot blade, and not the dagger she wanted.

What kind of man slept with a small blade and a sword in his bed? Her hand could have been cut, or worse, sliced in two!

She whirled around. 'How could you throw a dagger at me?'

'You're a woman?'

'Ach, of course I'm a woman. Even in this dim light you must see I'm wearing a gown!'

He made a noise, somewhere between a huff and a groan, as he shoved the linens away and swung his legs over the side of the bed.

He was not just a large man, he was huge. He carried his sword loosely at his side. She didn't

care about his sword. She cared about his nakedness walking towards her.

'Who are you?' he demanded.

The dim light wasn't going to hide him much
longer. She could not only see the size and shape
of him, but also—

He was magnificent. Just stunning. It was as
if he reinterpreted everything she'd ever known
about the opposite sex. There wasn't a Buchanan
man built like him. She didn't even know men
were made like this.

She couldn't tell the colour of his hair or eyes,
but the light did not hide the hard slant of sharp
cheekbones, the bold line of a straight nose. And
lips beautifully curved, shaped full underneath.

Her eyes didn't want to blink. Her chest felt
light and constricted at the same time. Her breath
came in short gasps. Was she going to actually
giggle?

He walked nearer. He was naked. Utterly naked.

Revealed to her were the defined curves of
powerful shoulders and arms, the very masculine breadth of his chest, the fluid movement of
muscles tapering slightly to a rippled stomach.

She should have turned away, but she couldn't.
Maybe it was the darkness making her bold.
Maybe it was her impulsiveness, a trait her mother
lamented, stopping any maidenly blushing. Or
maybe she looked because she couldn't help herself. Aye, that was it.

Her eyes dropped lower.

Her mouth became dry, her lips parched. Fearing her mouth hung open, she licked her lips, only to feel the moisture evaporate like all the thoughts in her head. Her legs suddenly felt like tall reeds of grass swaying in the wind. Try as she might, she could not lock her knees.

He growled, low, almost a purr except for the fact it was so masculine. So predatory. She didn't know how to interpret the sound and couldn't seem to look to his eyes for any help.

'Do you like what you see?' He set the sword against the bed. Her eyes thankfully followed the movement. But averting her eyes did not give her balance and she looked back up.

'I like what I see.' His eyes were too intense, too penetrating and held her immobile. 'I like what I see very much.'

Where was her anger and fury? Gone. Just like her ability to move. He was so close to her, she felt the heat from his skin. Despite his nakedness, he smelled like warm leather, cold steel and a scent she had never encountered before. Something so tempting she inhaled it greedily.

His eyes continued to hold hers and she did not break that hold. So she felt rather than saw the caress of his fingers stroking from her temple, along her jawline to the cusp of her lower lip.

'So-oo bonny even though you're not talking,' he purred. 'Did my brother send you to me? Was that why you were by my bed?' He cupped her chin, tilted her face up to his. 'I didn't think I'd have the strength for any lass this eve, but I'm glad to be proven wrong.'

Reeling, Mairead felt the heat of his hands as he seized the sides of her face. She tasted the ale warmth of his breath, the restrained caress of his fingertips as he brought her lips to his.

When he coaxed hers to part, when his tongue teased along their seam, she knew this was more than a kiss. It was something altogether different—just like the man.

He cradled her face, but it was neither his lips nor hands holding her captive. Instead, she was bound by the potency and response of her body against his.

He released their lips, only to draw her more fiercely against him. His arms wrapped low around her, his hands cupped and lifted. No longer on her feet, she was kept in balance by the breadth of his body and the strength of his hands and arms.

Then he tilted her head, exposing her neck to his lips, to his kisses.

Suddenly, she spiralled as desperation and anger returned to her, but now the emotions changed, turned darker, more volatile, wanting something else, something she didn't understand even as her hands went to his shoulders. Her fingers tugged, kneaded, trying to draw the great bulk of his body closer to her.

He groaned, shifted. Not enough. Not nearly close enough. Mairead pulled harder and the next step he took made him stumble and bump her against the fireplace behind her.

The sharp jab of pain in her back and his gentle oath broke their contact, pulling her back to reality. And the reality was more painful than the fireplace, mortifying even.

She was kissing a man. A *naked* drunk man she didn't know! Her eyes flitted from the door to the open shutters and back again. She looked anywhere but towards him. He had regained his balance, but his oath made her tingle and reel almost more than his kisses.

The room was dark. That fact was important, but she couldn't remember why. The dagger!

He crooked a finger under her chin. 'There now, where did you go?' he teased.

His head was tilted down to catch her gaze. His eyes were still dark with desire, but amusement made them sparkle. He was pure masculine temptation and completely focused on her. What was she doing?

She had to make a run for it, but it wouldn't be easy. He was a large man with a sword. There would be no reasoning with him. The only advantage she had was surprise and his nakedness. Her eyes shifted to the door again.

His eyes narrowed and he straightened cautiously. 'You're not going away…now are you, lass?'

'There's been a mistake,' she said, her voice unsteady, just like her thoughts. 'I'm…in the wrong room.'

Though he didn't move any closer to her, and his caress on her neck was light, she wasn't free of him.

'There's been nae mistake. You came to my room. You let me kiss you.' His fingers made gentle circles, skimming down her neck to her shoulders and back up. 'And before I was clumsy, you wanted me to kiss you…more.'

So true. All so confusingly true, but she needed the dagger, not this man who caused her to want to go and stay at the same time. How was this possible? How could she be here like this?

'I mean nae harm,' she said, willing her heart to stop fluttering inside her chest so she could concentrate. She was Buchanan, lying was her greatest skill. But she'd never be convincing if she was trembling with this *need*.

'I have to go,' she continued, pleased her voice was growing steady. 'My friend will be looking for me.'

'A friend?' He snatched his hand away and his brows drew together. 'A male friend?' The tempting mouth turned fierce. The change was so sudden it would have been comical, if not for the fact he looked a bit frightening.

'You're here with a *friend*?' he said, the last word a growl. 'My brother did not send you to me?'

There could be only one reason his brother would send a woman to his bedroom. If she'd had any modesty left, she would have blushed with embarrassment, not with desire as she thought of their kiss.

Shaking her head to dispel the images, she replied, 'Nae, I doona know your brother.'

He pursed his lips. 'A neglect of my brother and of mine. If I had seen you serving downstairs, I would have stopped my drinking to be with you. Do you belong to your friend for tonight only?'

'Nae! I just need—'

He grew angrier. 'You belong to him for life? You are married!'

Her mistakes just got worse and worse! She was either a whore, a cheating wife or she could tell him she was a thief. He now stood too close for her to escape or to think clearly.

'Nae, nae,' Mairead said. 'I am not married. You doona understand. I entered this room by mistake.'

A wolfish grin replaced his frown, but it did not erase the traces of anger furrowing his brow. It was as if he was angry, frustrated and filled with some fierce determination all at the same time.

'I may be slowed by drink, lass. But there is nae mistake you entered my room. You have been conjured by my very dreams.'

Her gestures were restricted by his presence looming over her. 'I will blame it on the drink, but you are not getting my meaning. I'm not supposed to be here. I didn't mean to kiss you. You must let me go.'

He shook his head as if he just didn't understand. 'It was my clumsiness startling you. Please forgive me.'

Inclining his head, he continued, 'My name is Caird. I'm here celebrating my sister's wedding you see, and I've done a bit too much of that celebrating. It's made me clumsy on my feet, and in my manners.'

He smiled. 'Or maybe I'm clumsy because a bonnie lass...with curly hair...entered my room. But I promise if you lie with me on that there bed, I won't be a clumsy lover.'

With the tips of his fingers, he started caressing her skin again. Behind her ear, down the cords of her neck, then across her shoulder, then up again to repeat.

Caird. He had a name. Not so much a stranger any more and his fingertips were doing strange things to her again.

'If you lie with me, I promise to be the most skilled lover who has ever taken you.' His voice was a low purr of pleasure. 'My lovemaking won't be fast. Urgent, aye. But I'll take my time with you, lass. I'll make sure my body moulds to yours so you won't feel the chill of the night's air.'

She could feel the roughened surface of his fingers, the heat from the palm of his hand. She felt naked under his gaze.

'My hands will caress you. With heat, my tongue will taste your breasts. Ah, to see them, to feel how they'll tighten.'

His words seared through her. She should have been shocked or at least offended by his intimate words. But instead she was captivated. Enticed.

'I'll make you crave my hands and my mouth as I stroke across your stomach.' He flattened his hand until his entire palm slid low at the base of her throat. 'Your legs will spread and my mouth and hands will move lower still.'

He must have loosened her ties or her thin gown was no barrier to his ministrations. He was pushing her gown down from her shoulders. The bodice loosened above her breasts and the sensation of the air's coolness was nothing in comparison to the heat of his hands. She parted her lips to let in more air and didn't mistake the look of triumph in his eyes.

What was she doing?

'Nae!' Swiping her arms to break his contact, she ran to the door and wrenched it open.

# *Chapter Three*

Blindly, Mairead entered the hall and rammed into a man heading towards the stairs. The impact knocked the wind from her and threw her back against the wall.

The man's cloak loosened and his hood fell. She saw his face and the flash of a silver dagger tucked into a belt around his waist.

'You!' she cried.

Turning suddenly, the man took a moment to register who she was. His surprise held him still.

She found her tongue. 'You thief! You murderer. Give me my—'

'What's going on here?'

Caird entered the hall. His loose tunic just covered him, but didn't hide the sword he carried.

Mairead blinked. Had he grabbed the sword before or after she cried out?

The man adjusted his cloak. His eyes turned calculating. With Caird here, she didn't know what to do. If she made accusations, the questions would be numerous. Kissing Caird didn't mean she trusted him. The dagger was too valuable.

Even lunging for the dagger would be futile. She had no weapon with which to fight. At best she'd get hurt. At worst, killed.

Her plan of stealing the dagger and returning home was now impossible. Her hands were tied. By the look of the gleam in the man's eyes, he had come to the same conclusion.

The man inclined his head; his lips a smirk. 'Pardon, wench. I see you are already detained for this evening. I meant nae harm.'

'What's this!' Caird indicated with his sword. 'Is this your friend?'

Mairead didn't even think. Caird seemed…uncontrolled. His stance widened, his tunic not covering the aggression and tightening of muscles in his legs. He looked like he was about to spring. Maybe she did have a weapon she could use. Her practised Buchanan lying would come in handy.

She nodded haughtily. 'Aye, and now he leaves like a thief in the night.'

'A thief?' Caird looked at her closely. His eyes narrowed, his posture becoming even larger. 'He's ripped your gown!'

She looked down. Somewhere between Caird's expert hands and the impact with the murderer, her well-worn gown had torn. Horrified, she frantically adjusted the thin strips of cloth covering her breasts. It was useless and she kept her hands across her chest.

The murderer sensed the change in the air and attempted to put up his hood. 'I never touched the wench! This is all untoward; I bid you both goodnight.'

The swift whip of air was all she heard as Caird's sword came up in front of the man. He could move, but only if he wanted to be cut in half.

'She called you thief,' Caird said. 'Exactly what were you thieving?'

'Nothing, the wench—'

'Stop…calling her wench; she's a lady compared to the likes of you.'

The man's entire demeanour changed from umbrage to overly pleasing. He raised his hands, and shrugged his shoulders as if in defeat. 'You are welcome to the lady. It was an accident. She bumped—'

'It wasn't an accident!' she interrupted. Mairead wouldn't let the man's false humbleness ruin her only chance for retrieving the dagger. 'This is the man I was to meet. But he saw me come from your room and in a rage he tore my gown!'

The man's eyes widened in fright; if it wasn't dark, she'd swear she saw sweat break over his brow. Even better, he looked guilty. Good, he should feel guilt. Especially since she was wishing him dead.

Caird's sword sliced the cloak's tie under the

man's chin. The cloak billowed to the ground, revealing her dagger and a sword strapped to his belt.

'You need to apologise to the lady,' Caird said.

'But I didn't—'

Another slight movement and this time the sword neatly slashed the man's tunic. Right across his heart.

Mairead bit her lip to hide her reaction. Grief, desperation, anger…and now this?

Caird did everything she wished to do, but it wasn't enough, not for what this man, this thief, had taken from her. She wanted to swipe the sword and slice the black heart of her brother's killer.

The man's eyes grew wide. There was no calculating gleam there now. His eyes darted to the sword, to Mairead and then to the staircase; his right hand visibly twitched. Was it because he feared Caird? She hoped so.

Being half-undressed didn't make Caird look vulnerable. In fact, his well-muscled, well-trained body looked more formidable than the sword he held. She couldn't believe she had curled her body around the man as if he was safe. Right now, he looked anything but safe.

A flash of movement.

'The stairs!' she yelled.

Caird lunged, but the murderer wasn't planning escape. He had the dagger in his hand and he swung it around. Moving his sword and body to the side, Caird pounded his great fist on the man's head.

The murderer teetered on the edge of the stairs. Caird clutched the man's shredded tunic. It tore and the murderer tumbled down the stairs like wet clothes in a river.

A door opened behind them and a tall lean man stepped out. His short dark hair was tousled, and a lock fell over his forehead. A recently healed scar ran the length of his left cheek and down across his bare chest. He looked menacing even as he carelessly leaned against the doorframe and looked pointedly at Caird, Mairead, then the man crumpled at the bottom of the stairs.

His lips quirked before he burst out laughing. When he was done, he pretended to wipe his very green eyes and asked, 'Need any help?'

'You took your sweet time, Malcolm,' Caird said.

Malcolm shrugged. 'I was occupied. You left me with two of them.' He pointed to Mairead. 'Who's this?'

Caird frowned.

Malcolm laughed again. 'How about that down there?'

'I doona know about that either.'

'Well, you've certainly kept yourself entertained.'

Giggling floated out of Malcolm's room and he closed the door.

Mairead desperately wanted to run down the stairs, grab the dagger and escape. But now there were two of them. She must keep lying.

Trying her best to look worried for the murderer, she asked, 'Shouldn't we see if he is dead?'

Caird's eyes narrowed on her. To avoid his stare, she looked down the stairs and bit her lip.

'I'll go.' Malcolm's mouth lifted at the corners. 'Out of the three of us, it seems I'm the only one decently clothed.'

Mairead snatched her hands to her breasts again. She'd forgotten about her gown.

Malcolm went down the steps and checked the inert body. 'Not dead,' he whispered up.

Her immediate relief surprised her. She'd thought she wanted him dead.

Malcolm ripped the torn tunic and tied the murderer's arms behind him. He then searched the man's pouch and boots before he ran up the stairs. 'His pouch held a few coins, but nae seal or any identification.' He pulled his hand from behind his back. 'He did have this in his hand.'

Malcolm held Mairead's dagger. The rubies winked.

She tried not to gasp, but part of the sound escaped. Caird's eyes went to hers briefly and she quickly lowered her gaze. Now what was she supposed to do? Say the dagger was hers, and that she'd be on her way? They wouldn't believe her. She'd have to stay quiet.

Caird took the dagger, his fingers caressing the decorative handle. When he looked again at Mairead, his eyes were no longer soft from desire or drink. Instead, they were as cold as the dagger in his hands.

'The man's clothes are too poor for such a fine piece,' he said.

'I agree,' Malcolm replied. 'Most likely it is stolen.'

Caird nodded. 'Aye, a thief.'

Was it her imagination, or did Caird emphasise the word *thief*? Feigning nonchalance, she fiddled with her bodice.

'Doona harm the man,' Caird said. 'Leave him his coins and sword, and take him outside the town's gates. Preferably further than that.'

'Off the land?'

'I wouldn't burden you that distance.'

Malcolm nodded his head towards his room. 'I'll grieve enough for leaving those two.'

Caird shook his head. 'Do you think of anything else?'

'Aye, food.'

Caird hesitated, looking as if he wanted to say something more.

Malcolm lifted his eyebrow. 'Worried for me again, Brother?'

Caird huffed and shook his head. 'I'll keep this

dagger. I must think. See that he continues away from our land.'

A groan and movement from below caught their attention.

Malcolm ran down the steps and roughly pulled the murderer to his feet. The man stumbled, clearly not ready to rise.

''Ere, now, where's my sword?'

'You'll get it soon enough,' Malcolm replied.

The man acted resigned, but then in a struggle, he wrenched his arm free. 'The dagger. Where is it?'

'Here,' Caird called out.

Malcolm resumed his hold and the man struggled to remain upright. 'The dagger's mine,' he argued. 'Surely you wouldn't take that. A man's got to have some defence.'

Mairead stayed silent and dug her fingers into her bodice. She glared all her hatred at him. She'd never forgive or forget what he did.

'You have the sword,' Caird replied. 'The dagger's not yours.'

The man tugged uselessly to free his arm. 'I've got to have the dagger. Take my pouch, take my sword, but the dagger holds sentimental value to me.'

'Nae.'

The man stopped his pleading, his movements frantic now. Anger and fear flashed in his eyes as he pierced them on Mairead.

'You stupid wench. It wasn't me who did it. If you—' The man tried to butt his head against Malcolm, but Malcolm cuffed him on the jaw and the man slumped heavily in his arms.

'I may have wanted to hear the end of that sentence,' Caird said drily.

Malcolm shrugged. 'His head must have still been ringing.'

Caird looked at the dagger again. Mairead did, too.

'Take him away,' Caird demanded.

'Nae, wait!' Mairead said. 'Shouldn't we wait until he wakes to see what he was going to say?'

'Too late. I'm missing my sleep,' Caird said.

Oh, but she needed to hear what the man was going to say. It had all happened so fast when Ailbert was killed. She had only seen the one man running away. This man. Had there been another? If this man was only a thief, then who was the murderer?

'But he should at least be awake for his journey,' she argued.

'I think not,' Caird replied. 'I ask my brother too much as it is. An unconscious burden will be easier for him.'

Malcolm's door flew open and two dishevelled women came out. They clutched one piece of bed linen and each other with equal amounts of clumsiness. 'Malcolm,' one of them trilled. 'Malcolm, come back. Where are you?'

'Oh!' The brunette stopped so suddenly the red-haired one stumbled and lost her share of the linen covering her naked body.

'Look at this one here, Annie.' The brunette pointed to Caird.

'Oooh, now he's a triumph,' slurred the red-head, trying in vain to reach for the corner of the linen. She curled her lips at Caird. 'Come with us, pretty.'

Caird, clothed only in his tunic, lightly held his sword to his side. He was covered, but barely. Mairead's anger switched from Malcolm for hitting the thief to Caird for having no modesty. Did he intend to parade around for all the women of Scotland and why did she even care?

'The man you want is downstairs,' Caird began, 'and, as you can see, I'm well taken care of by a friend of yours.'

Mairead wanted to punch him in the stomach.

'Oh, she's nae friend of ours,' said the brunette.

'Never seen her before in my life,' said the red-head. 'Malcolm's downstairs?'

'Lasses!' Malcolm cried jovially.

They stumbled towards the stairs.

Caird didn't watch the women, he watched Mairead. From the look in his eyes, he wasn't surprised the two women didn't know her.

She was right in thinking he was too intelligent. If she wasn't careful, he would link her trespass in his room with the dagger and the thief.

But she couldn't just leave. Caird had the dagger. So how was she to get it and keep his mind from making the correct assumptions? The only way she knew how.

Mairead dropped her hands from her gown. His eyes flickered to her chest. But they didn't stay there.

Instead his eyes narrowed, his cheeks hollowed and his lips pressed tight together.

'Get in my room,' he said.

## Chapter Four

Mairead mostly prided herself on her impulsiveness, but right now she felt no pride. Right now she was in danger. Especially when she had no plan and there was a well-armed, vexed stranger following behind her and closing the door.

Her anger and fury had disappeared and her legs didn't feel as if they would hold her much longer.

In the dark and quiet room, she could almost hear his mind making connections between her and the thief.

If it wasn't for her family, she'd have run. They needed the money that dagger represented. Not that her mother and sisters knew about their predicament, but Ailbert had known. Ailbert had... Oh, she didn't want to think about him. Not now. There was no time.

She had to choose: humiliate herself here, or in front of her entire clan. She'd prefer to do it here.

Straightening what was left of the top of her gown, she took a candle and walked to the fireplace. The fire was dim, but enough to light the wick.

'Not now.'

'I was just lighting it. It's dark.'

'We doona need light to sleep.'

But she did. She needed the light to see if his expression matched the biting tone of voice. Setting the unlit candle by the table, she turned towards him.

He had rested the sword by the bedside and was right behind her. Quickly, he took his tunic off. 'Here.' He gestured with the tunic.

As she tugged on the fabric of her hopelessly torn gown, she tried not to look at him. 'What will you wear?'

'I'm not going anywhere.' He shoved the tunic into her hands and turned towards the door. 'And I'll not be doing any more thinking tonight.'

She clutched the tunic and tried to think of an excuse to stay. But instead of opening the door and demanding she leave, he retrieved his boot dagger still embedded in the thick wood.

Her fingers eased on the fabric, but she wasn't completely safe. He turned around and gazed pointedly at the tunic still in her hands. Walking past her, he placed his boot blade on the windowsill.

She wanted to say something, anything, to ease the tension. But he acted as though he felt none and he was still…naked. He might be comfortable, but his state of undress played havoc with her emotions.

Even thanking him seemed moot as he straightened the bed covers and lay down. Just above his head, he placed her dagger.

Not only was she mute, but she didn't know what to do. It wasn't only his tone of voice that was different. He was different. His speech was shortened. The warm lilting voice that made her limbs go heavy was gone. He wasn't even looking at her any more.

So she just stood there.

'My head's aching and I'm tired. You can either put that tunic on or not, climb into the bed to sleep or not, makes nae difference to me.'

Feeling helpless, Mairead stared. The bed creaked as Caird adjusted himself. His back was to her now and he was partially covered with the thin blanket he pulled up around him.

It wasn't daylight yet, but it would come and soon. There was still a chance to get the dagger, but only if she stayed. Pulling on the tunic, she climbed into bed. It wasn't a large bed and she adjusted her position so as not to touch him.

He might be a heavy sleeper. If she hadn't upended the stool and made a noise, she might have made an escape, but it wouldn't do to think of her mistakes.

For now, she'd just have to wait until Caird fell asleep.

Mairead woke with the sudden awareness of the sun rising. The room was just growing light, but she did not need the daylight to see her impulsiveness had landed her in danger. Again.

She didn't need to see at all. All she had to do was feel.

Her upper body was still contorted away from Caird, but her legs were wrapped neatly under his. Her feet were warm, which was probably why she'd slept. Her feet were never warm.

She kept still, waiting to see if Caird woke as well, but his breath remained steady and his body relaxed. He still slept.

The dagger still rested above his head.

To keep silent, she held back her sigh of relief. There was still a chance to get the dagger and walk away. Then she could grieve. She needed to grieve. Her nerves frayed more with every delay.

Carefully, almost painfully, she reached for the dagger.

'Oomph!'

A fierce grip on her wrist, a twist of a large body and she was on her back, hand above her head, her fingers wrapped around the dagger.

'Admiring its beauty?'

His tone was calm, but not idle.

And he was heavy. She couldn't breathe to protest. She shoved her legs up.

'You're...' She huffed.

He eased his weight, but not his hold on her wrist.

His loose hair fell forward. A long scar curved from his right shoulder into the splattering of dark hair on his chest.

And his eyes were a changeable shade of grey.

'Answer me!' He shook her wrist.

Caird hadn't been thinking last night. The fact he could even remember last night was a miracle after the amount of ale he and Malcolm had drunk.

The woman lay absolutely motionless beneath him and she hadn't said a word. But she didn't need to.

Her dark-brown eyes were wide with fear and something else making them darker still. Her cheeks were flushed from sleep and her lips were full and impossibly pink. Beneath his hips and legs, he could feel her ample hips and buttocks cushioning him.

He had not dreamed of this woman beneath him, or the effect she had on him. She was not some fantasy conjured from the wedding celebrations.

She was like having Spring's first ripe berry after a hard winter, and just as tempting.

'What do you want with this dagger?' he repeated.

'I...was looking at it.'

It was more than that. There was the admiring gleam in her eyes, but also one of intent. 'You were doing more than looking.'

'Nae, it was just there. I picked it up. That's all.' She shook her head. Her abundant dark brown curls bounced like a tarnished halo around her head.

But she was no fallen angel. She was in his room last night. If he hadn't been so drunk, so tired and so stupid, he wouldn't be having this argument with her.

Instead, she would be fully and completely underneath him. Or he would have thrown her from his room and been done with all the temptation and trouble.

He might not have been thinking straight last night, but he was this morning. Now, he needed to solve the problem of why she was here. 'Why were you in my room?' he demanded.

She looked down, but her eyes widened and her eyes flew back to his. Her flush deepened, too. He was still naked, the thin blanket inadequate covering.

Perhaps he wasn't thinking straight after all. He prised her fingers from the dagger and stood from the bed. Keeping his eyes on her, he set the dagger on the table by the fireplace and reached for his braies.

Mairead tried to keep her eyes trained on the man, not the dagger. What she had come for was now almost within her grasp and she felt a mixture of relief and tension. She knew all she had to do was either lie for or steal the dagger. Now was her time. Just a little longer and she'd be done with all of this.

She sat up. 'I told you it was a mistake.'

Finishing tucking the braies, he said, 'The room's a mistake. Not the reason why you were here.'

This man was too intelligent to fool and too fast and strong for her to make a run for it with the dagger. A little bit of truth wouldn't hurt.

She gave a sigh as if she couldn't hold up the pretence any more. 'The dagger belongs to my family.'

'How convenient.'

Never taking his eyes from hers, he reached for the brown leather leggings.

'I knew you wouldn't believe me. It's why I didn't say anything before.' She pushed the cover away from her legs and stood. 'Why would you believe me? We're strangers; the dagger has some value. But I ask, why would a lone woman enter an unknown inn at the dead of night if not to retrieve something of great value to her?'

'To steal.'

Too true. Lowering her eyes, she rubbed her hands down the tunic to ease the creases there. 'If I was such an expert thief, I could do it in broad daylight, within the comforts of safety. What I did was anything but safe.'

'Maybe you're not a good thief.'

'Exactly!' She looked up and gave him a wide smile.

His only response was to raise one brow.

She continued, 'An inept thief, who doesn't know any better or have the sense not to search rooms in the dead of night.'

The last line took a dent to her pride, but it worked. He was starting to believe her.

He pulled the leggings up over his braies until everything fit properly. Without a tunic, it didn't hide the muscles and scars on his arms and broad shoulders.

'How did the man steal it?' he asked.

Flashes of memory. The sudden shock, the man running away, her brother collapsing to the ground. Ah, the grief.

'I doona know.' She held up her hand when she saw him begin to doubt.

'The dagger isn't mine, but my brother's,' she said. 'I was there when it was stolen, but didn't see what happened. My brother told me and said he would get it back.'

'Where's your brother?'

Crumpled on the ground. Her call for help. Her mother's scream.

She wrinkled her nose, trying to stop the threatening tears. 'He thought that man in the hallway, that thief, went west and decided to pursue him.'

'And he sent you east.'

She shifted and tried to look guilty. 'Nae. I came this way on my own. He described the thief to me. I thought I'd help.'

He huffed.

'I wasn't confronting the man on my own, just getting the dagger back. It's the reason I searched the room at night.'

He straightened the upended stool, sat on it and proceeded to put on his boots. 'The thief seemed to know you.'

Despite being drunk, he had too good a memory.

'Did he?' she said.

'He said it wasn't him.'

She acted like she couldn't remember. But she did. Vividly. If only Malcolm had not hit the man, she'd know what the thief meant to say!

She shrugged. 'I didn't ken his meaning. He had my dagger.'

Caird bent and picked up his pouch. Without attaching it, he stared at her. She kept her eyes straight on him. He almost believed her, but something was bothering him. She'd have to make certain he had no doubts.

He nodded. 'You were lucky.'

Only if he believed her.

He wrapped the belt with the pouch around his waist. 'You could be dead.'

Ah, gratefulness and flattery. Those were easy emotions to fake. 'I know. Strange as it may seem, I am glad I came to your room.'

Something besides doubt flitted in his grey eyes, making them almost green. Something like…heat.

He took a step towards her. She had risen from the bed and straightened her clothes, but she hadn't gone any further. If she had, she'd have somewhere to move. As it was, she was stuck between Caird and the bed.

He was measuring her again, weighing something. His eyes moved from hers down her cheeks to her lips. Between her torn gown and his deeply cut tunic, her neck and most of her shoulders were bare. There, his eyes stilled and her bare skin felt even more exposed.

'Me, too,' he said as his eyes caught hers. His voice had lowered, softened. The beautiful lilt of last night wasn't there. He wasn't talking enough for that.

Which was probably good because just the tone of his voice was causing her to remember last night. Before the thief. The darkened room and their kiss.

She swallowed, trying to moisten her suddenly parched mouth. 'I woke you, caused you trouble.'

His mouth quirked and he took another step. 'Nae trouble.'

What was wrong with her? She needed to get out of here. She needed to keep lying like she always did with the Buchanan men.

But this man didn't affect her like Buchanan men, and she couldn't think fast enough. 'I...' she started, then licked her lips.

His breath stopped, released.

For some reason, her breath did the same.

'I should thank you,' she said, her voice catching.

Slowly, so slowly, she felt the heat of him as he leaned towards her.

Oh, he was going to kiss her. Again.

And she didn't want to stop it. Didn't want the heat of him to go away or the heady scent of him to vanish. All she wanted—

Her stomach growled.

His mouth twitched and his eyes flashed with more green than grey.

If she thought herself incapable of moving before, she was wrong. Now, her very feet were nailed to the floor. How did *eyes* do that?

'Trestles are being moved for breakfast.' Turning rapidly, he looked around the room. 'I'll see about a gown and food.'

Her knees shaking, she sat abruptly on the bed. 'I have nae coin to repay you,' she said.

Shaking his head, he said, 'A gift.'

'Thank you,' she answered. He was being generous despite the trouble she'd given him. She didn't feel guilty for tricking him, but she wished she could repay him. He truly was different from any Buchanan man she had ever known.

He was too breathtaking, too honourable and now kind as well. A Buchanan man wouldn't have believed her. They would have shoved her out of the room and kept the costly dagger. Instead, he was giving the dagger to her, feeding her, clothing her.

She tried not to think about the kiss he hadn't given her. He was still walking around the room. 'Where's my small blade?'

She smiled. 'The one you threw at me? You left it over there.'

Following her arm movement to the window, he reached for his dagger on the windowsill.

The bright morning light shone against his still loose hair, making the red hidden in his brown locks glow. Odd, how she hadn't noticed he had red hair before.

Red.

'You're a Colquhoun!' she gasped, too surprised to stay quiet.

He turned around. 'Aye, I am, but that wouldn't

matter unless…' His eyes narrowed, and took in her every feature.

Hell and damnation.

Mairead leapt for her jewelled dagger on the table by the fireplace. She didn't know who was quicker, but Caird was bigger and already standing. He had the advantage.

He pushed her towards the bed, his body already blocking her.

Determined, she ducked underneath his outstretched arm, and her hand grasped the table. Just a little further—

He dropped his weight on her and the table. She was flattened and the table overturned.

The dagger skidded across the floor. Scrambling, she lunged, but Caird dived over her and grabbed the dagger with his fingers. Rising up, she clasped her hands together and rammed both elbows into his back. He lost the grip on the dagger, and it flew against the opposite wall. The dagger broke.

Out of the handle, a green stone slightly larger than a duck's egg skidded towards them.

## Chapter Five

Snatching up the gem, Caird watched emotion after emotion flit across the woman's face. She certainly looked surprised. But she was a thieving no-good Buchanan and they were all well practised in the art of lying.

'Explain.' Anger scraped the edge of his word, making it rough and barely controlled.

She didn't stop staring at the green gem and he clenched his fingers around it, moving it up to his face.

Like a cat focused on its prey, her eyes followed the gem. They remained almost unfocused, as if her thoughts couldn't catch up with her action.

Then her eyes skidded to his.

Oh, she was a master at lying. He could tell. Even now, she faked astonishment. As if she didn't know the gem was there.

A Buchanan was right before him. He had shared his room, his bed, with her. Disgust slithered fast through his veins and his stomach recoiled.

Last night, his drinking had dimmed his ability to think. Now, his absolute anger at being tricked was blinding him. For years the Buchanans had bordered with the Colquhouns. For years the Colquhouns had endured the thieving, lying, murdering ways of the Buchanan clan. And here he was, stuck with a Buchanan, and he held a lie right in the palm of his hand.

But no more lies, nor more prevarication. He would have answers and then he would have his revenge.

Staring at the gem, Mairead sat up. Even in Caird's hands it was large. The cut facets were shining, twinkling, laughing at her.

'I didn't know it was there,' she answered. She couldn't think of a lie fast enough. Couldn't think at all.

The dagger had been the answer to all her prayers. However, next to the startling beauty of the gem, both the dagger's silver ornamental handle and the two inset rubies looked fake. She just couldn't believe something like the gem existed.

It was oblong, cut on one side, and rough on the other. Some facets showed the gem bright green, but the rest of it looked like a rough river, and almost blue.

The gem was stupendous, magnificent and unbelievable. Enough to get the family out of debt, maybe enough to spare them humiliation.

He glowered. 'Give me true answers, Buchanan!'

'I doona know—'

'How to keep your story straight? Tell me. Either the dagger is yours or not. Likewise this gem. You cannot have it both ways!'

The door banged open and Malcolm stared at them both on the floor. He didn't try to contain his look of amusement.

Mairead hastily pulled up Caird's gaping tunic and stood.

'What is it?' Caird closed his hand around the gem.

'It's about my nightly package,' Malcolm replied, his voice laced with humour. 'But I can see you're occupied at the moment.'

Caird stood, but anger still bit into his words. 'Where is he?'

Reading his brother's mood, Malcolm's grin abruptly vanished. 'We went south several miles. The further we got, the further agitated he became. When he finally co-operated, I set him free and gave him his horse. I watched him, but he continued south, so I returned.'

Brows drawn inward, Caird made some sound in his throat. 'The river's south.'

'It was that or east. Since it was dark and rain-ing again, I took him the way I knew to not risk the horses.'

Caird's brows eased and Malcolm's smile returned. 'So, I had a miserable night and you still have the bonniest lass in Scotland in your room.'

Mairead waited for Caird to mention who she was, but instead he ignored her and stepped towards his brother.

'That's not all I have in my room.' Caird opened his hand.

Malcolm picked up the gem and turned it in his hands. 'This is unbelievable.'

'Aye,' Caird replied.

'Where did it come from?'

'The dagger,' Caird gestured to the floor where the dagger still lay in two pieces.

'Nae wonder my package was agitated the further we got from this gem. It's unusual, and valuable.' Malcolm handed the gem to Caird, who put it in his pouch around his waist. 'But the man was poor, a thief at best.'

'There is more to this.' Caird glared at Mairead.

Malcolm's smile didn't reach his eyes. 'Aye, you'll want to say your goodbyes before we leave.'

'She's coming with us,' Caird answered.

Mairead didn't like that they talked around her. She especially didn't like being told what to do. But what else should she expect from an arrogant Colquhoun? Their entire clan was smug in their supposed superiority. It was the reason why for years her clan had loved stealing and borrowing from them. Colquhouns deserved the humiliation of being robbed.

'I'm not going anywhere,' she said. 'I'll take my dagger and that gem and be on my way.'

'They are yours?' Malcolm said, his eyebrows raised.

She owed this brother no explanations, but if she could persuade him, then he might have some sway with Caird. 'The dagger, and what it hid, is my brother's,' she continued. 'You are both right that the thief stole it. He stole it from my family.'

Caird huffed.

Malcolm looked intrigued. 'But you didn't claim it last night.'

'And her gown is heavily worn and frayed,' Caird added.

She turned to Caird. 'What my family spends their money on is none of your concern. This might not even be my real gown.'

'Imagine my not knowing what's real,' he replied.

'And I thought last night was interesting,' Malcolm drawled. 'My brother clearly does not believe you and this is nae ordinary gem.'

She felt like roaring in frustration and helplessness. She wanted the nightmare over and these Colquhouns were making it worse. 'It matters not if you won't believe—'

Malcolm shook his head. 'But it seemed the thief knew you.'

Caird folded his arms across his chest and nodded. 'Aye.'

'So, who is she?' Malcolm pointedly asked Caird.

Expectantly, Mairead looked at Caird; surely he'd reveal her clan identity now. But Caird stayed quiet, his expression only darkening.

Malcolm smirked. 'She spent the night and you still doona know her name? Brother, you have always been a man of few words, but I think one or two to ask this lass's name wouldn't have been untoward.'

Hating the conclusions Malcolm was making, she threw a knowing smile at Caird. 'Mairead of Clan—'

'Enough introductions,' Caird interrupted. 'We need to find this thief.'

Malcolm's brows rose as he noted Caird's interruption, but he didn't comment and neither did she. If Caird didn't want Malcolm to know who she was, she didn't need to know these Colquhouns either.

She just needed to return home. For a moment, she was tempted to find the thief on her own. Her grief was once again scraping across her skin, demanding she confront Ailbert's killer. But she had to focus on the dagger and return with it before the Buchanan laird realised her brother's debt.

Unfortunately, it was in the hands of self-righteous Colquhouns. As much as she would love the gem as well, she had to fake a compromise.

'Ach!' She swept across the room and picked up the dagger and handle. 'Keep the gem, do with it what you may, but this I'll keep.'

''Tis broken,' Malcolm said.

Mairead didn't reply. There was something odd about the dagger. The blade was still attached to its handle. The second piece was smaller, and she realised it was the handle's tip. Carefully, she put the pieces together. They fit. The dagger had a hollow handle and the lid to the handle had come loose.

'Give that to me,' Caird said.

She hugged the dagger to her chest. 'Nae, it is mine. What do you care for this dagger when you have the true prize?'

'Do we?' Caird replied. 'And you will go with us.'

'I'll go nowhere with you.'

'The thief,' he said.

'Is free and going south, aye, I know and doona care,' she lied. 'I have what I came for.'

'I think my brother meant you'll need to come with us,' Malcolm said.

'And I told you I won't.'

'The thief was going south, but he didn't like it,' Malcolm continued calmly. 'He knows the dagger is still here.'

She'd go nowhere with a Colquhoun. She went around Malcolm. He didn't stop her from reaching the door.

'He could be outside the door,' Malcolm continued.

'With sword drawn,' Caird added.

## *Chapter Six*

Mairead halted. They were right. But she wasn't done with them. She whirled around. 'He wouldn't have a sword if you hadn't given it to him.' She pointed at Malcolm. 'And he wouldn't be anywhere near here if you hadn't just set him free!'

'Enough,' Caird said. 'You'll go with us. We'll find the thief and who truly owns the dagger and gem.'

Oh, she was angry now. 'Because you think that's right. Because you think you're correct. But you're not! This dagger was my brother's.'

'Was?' Caird walked to the bed and grabbed his sword. 'Perhaps we should talk to your brother first.'

She didn't want to think of her brother. She didn't even want these arrogant Colquhouns to mention the *word* brother.

'The devil have you!' she yelled. Yanking the

door open, she flew out, satisfied by the crash of the door against the wall.

She had barely reached the second stair before she was lifted off her feet and tossed over a shoulder. It was Caird. She hated the very sight of his bare back. Almost as much as she hated how she recognised him just by the width of his hands on her waist.

'Release me!' she demanded.

He huffed and started to return to the room. She raised the dagger, blade pointed at his back.

He suddenly pivoted and flung her against the wall. She dropped the dagger.

'Owwww!' She pounded on his back and tried to twist out of his grasp.

Her head and arm hurt, but not as much as her pride. 'Put me down.'

Malcolm grabbed the dagger.

'That's mine!' she cried.

'Stop yelling,' Caird said.

'I will when—'

Whoosh. She hit the stairs so hard her teeth clacked together.

'Better,' he said, grabbing her arm and hauling her to her feet.

She reached for the dagger, but Malcolm took a couple of steps back.

'I hate to break up this little dance, but Caird, what are you doing?'

'Catching a thief.'

'What of Gaira's wedding celebrations?'

Caird stopped so suddenly, Mairead tripped and he tugged her arm to keep her upright. She tried to tug back, but his fingers dug into her arm and he drew her up against him. She pushed, but it was like pushing against a mountain. A very stubborn mountain.

Looking back at Malcolm, Caird said, 'Who's still here?'

'Pherson and John returned for the feasting and games yesterday, but the rest are here.'

Caird lowered his head and pinched the bridge of his nose.

'They'll expect our presence for our sister's wedding feasts,' Malcolm continued. 'And I should probably mention the innkeeper is quite annoyed. It seems our activities last night woke his wife.'

Caird stared at the floor and spoke low. 'Pay the innkeeper extra and make ready the horses.'

'What'll you do with—?'

'Avoid them.'

'Nae, I meant her—'

'Who are you avoiding?' A deep voice came from the bottom of the stairs.

Mairead gaped. Two men, with smiles wide and arms crossed, stood shoulder to shoulder.

Two men. Exactly the same. Rich brown shoulder-length hair and light hazel eyes that sparkled with mischief. Curved lips, broad chests, bared arms, stances wide. All the same.

Mairead stared hard and blinked. But her eyes didn't clear the vision. She was seeing double.

'What did you do to me?' she said. 'You dropped me too hard.'

Caird's grip on her arm tightened.

'Ow! Let go! Something's wrong with my—' She stopped trying to prise his fingers loose. There was only one of Caird's hands. She glanced up. There was only one of Caird. Nothing was wrong with her eyesight. She stared downstairs again.

There were still two identical men and as fine as any she had ever seen. They were not quite as tall as Caird or Malcolm, but they were broad. What was it with these men? If she knew men here were fair of feature and broad of shoulder, she would have left Buchanan land long ago. Of course, if she had, she'd be no better off than her giggling sisters.

Malcolm quickly sheathed the dagger under his cloak and took the remaining steps downstairs. Mairead couldn't hear Malcolm's whispered words, but both men laughed.

Mairead felt a hysterical bubble in her throat. She had been worried about retrieving the dagger from one man, now there were four. Her nightmare had just got worse.

'Caird! You're standing fairly well despite the drink.'

'Camron, Hamilton.' Caird nodded to each man. She didn't know how he could tell them apart. 'I stand as much as ever I did.'

'Slept in a bit though, didn't you?' Camron said. 'Looking a bit flushed, too, I see.'

'Never bet a Graham on drinking.' Hamilton laughed. 'Our mother's milk is stronger than any ale made.'

Camron peered around Caird's shoulder and raised his eyebrows. 'But it looks like the ale got our silent cousin's words a-going again.'

Hamilton elbowed Camron as his eyes alighted on Mairead. 'Ha! Who's this?'

'She's Caird's,' Malcolm said. 'He may have shared his drink, but he won't share her.'

'Two not enough for you, Malcolm?' Camron said.

Malcolm grinned. 'Such a bonny lass, I couldn't help but ask.'

'Looks like Caird did share something, though,' Hamilton said. 'His clothes.'

Caird cursed.

Mairead gasped and quickly moved behind him. She had fled the room wearing her ripped gown and Caird's tunic. She wasn't decent to be around her own family, let alone complete strangers.

'Bit rough of you, cousin, if her clothes are

torn,' Camron said, all joviality gone from his voice.

'Are you hurt, lass?' Hamilton asked, his hand reaching to his hip where a knife was kept.

She couldn't tell him. If she did, there'd be a fight and Malcolm still had her dagger! But what could she say to them?

'Nae, I'm—'

'Too intent on my brother to remember her surroundings,' Malcolm interjected. 'I was just coming down the stairs to stop them when you arrived.'

Camron looked at Caird's hand wrapped around her arm. 'His grip is too tight.'

Caird did not release her. 'She slipped,' he said as if that would satisfy his cousins.

Could the man not even come up with a little lie to get them out of trouble?

'On the stairs,' she added, and peered around Caird to give his cousins a smile. 'Silly of me. So kind of you to block our way and stop me from showing myself to all of Scotland.'

Camron released his eyes from Caird's. 'Our pleasure, lass, if that's the truth of it all.'

Why would the truth be important now? 'Other than shamed to supper, I'm unharmed.' She patted Caird on his bare shoulder and felt him stiffen. What did she care if he didn't want her touching him? She was getting them out of trouble. Lowering her voice, she added, 'Cannot think of what it was that distracted me is all.'

Hamilton gave a short chuckle, but Camron didn't look convinced.

'And you forgot her state of undress?' Camron said to Caird.

'Aye,' Caird replied.

Camron frowned even more. Hamilton, sensing his brother's displeasure, lost his laugh.

Caird wasn't helping their cause at all and she wanted to kick him. Certainly his glowering expression wouldn't convince them that he enjoyed her presence.

She draped herself more heavily against Caird. If possible she felt him stiffen even further. 'Must have been that wee bit of ale being poured,' she added.

'Hah! I knew it!' Hamilton laughed and hit Camron in the chest with the back of his hand. 'Caird never could hold his drink.'

Camron's expression eased and his grin returned. 'But Colquhouns can hold their women.'

'Ah, she is a bonny lass, cousin,' Hamilton said. 'Where'd you find her?'

'In my room,' Caird replied.

Hamilton's eyebrows rose. 'Nae wonder you wanted to stay here and not hurry to the keep. Of course, if you had hurried, you'd have had—'

Malcolm moved forward, 'Well, cousins, we

should set off for your home. When do the games begin?'

'Tomorrow. It's why we were coming to fetch you,' Camron replied. 'We'll be late for the start and John owes me some pride.'

'Help me saddle our horses while my brother finds a gown and pays our bills,' Malcolm said.

'He'll be paying mine as well,' Camron said.

'Mine, too,' Hamilton added. 'And I drank a wee bit more after you left, cousin.'

'Nothing more than a flagon or two,' Camron added.

'Or three or four.'

'Ah, to have such rich, generous cousins,' Camron said.

'Aye, does a belly and a coffer good.'

Caird huffed, reached into his pouch still carrying the gem and pulled out several coins. Malcolm bounded up the stairs to take them. 'You get a gown,' Caird said. 'We'll wait.'

Malcolm dropped the money into his own pouch, making the coins chime and clank.

Hamilton sighed dramatically. 'That is too much money by far.'

Malcolm took the steps down to slap Hamilton on the shoulder. 'There'll be time to remedy that at the games.'

Caird waited until the three other men were out of sight before he pulled her into the room and closed the door.

Rubbing her arm, she stumbled to the window.

Caird stood by the door and didn't move. She didn't know how long Malcolm would be, but she wasn't wasting a moment.

She turned to him. 'Getting me a gown doesn't make us even.'

He didn't say anything.

'Despite what's in that big fat head of yours, the dagger is mine and I will take it back.'

He ignored her. No. It was more than that, he just stared straight through her. She knew he was alive by the slight rise of his chest and his occasional blink, and the fact that he opened the door when they heard the two quick knocks.

Malcolm didn't step in, but pushed a yellow gown and the dagger through the slight opening. Caird threw the gown at her feet.

It was a bright, deeply coloured yellow. With her dark hair she could never tame, she'd look like an overused broom.

She picked it up. The length was good, but it'd be too tight around the bodice. The person who wore this didn't like food as well as she. There was no hope for it.

'Will you turn around?'

Caird didn't acknowledge her question. Instead he secured the gem inside the dagger and placed them both in his pouch.

Watching avidly, Mairead couldn't believe how

close and yet how far she was from the means to end the nightmare she was in.

When he was done, she waited several heartbeats for Caird to turn around; instead, he crossed his arms and raised an eyebrow.

Glowering, she turned her back to change. In her haste, the torn gown ripped further. She'd have to repair it when she returned home. Shoving it to her feet, she pulled the new one over her. It caught on her breasts and hips and was altogether too tight to quickly tug over her and tie the cords around her. No matter, though her chemise was threadbare, it provided enough cover until she could get the fabric over her. She had too much pride to beg a Colquhoun for her privacy.

Still, his presence, and his silence, made her feel like elbowing him in the stomach.

Losing her temper wasn't anything new to her. Wanting to harm another person was. But nothing had been normal since she'd met Caird. Her reaction to him was... No, she didn't want to think of her reaction to him. It wasn't Caird making her crazy with desperation and anger and...everything else, it was the dagger.

'I know you believe you're right,' she said, tugging at the yellow fabric in the vain hope that it would cover more. The colour was beautiful and probably had cost its original owner some coin. 'But you must see reason on this.' In their haste, she was sure Caird's brother had paid too dear for it. If he thought to bribe her with the cost, he was mistaken. Turning to face him, she continued, 'We must talk—'

She stopped. Caird's face was no longer impassive. His face was pained, as if she had indeed jabbed him.

He held just as still as before, with his arms at his sides. But he flexed his left thumb and his eyes no longer looked through her.

They consumed her. Wrath, heat and frustration warred in the weight of his grey-green gaze.

She felt his eyes, everywhere. They trailed up her legs, slowly, so slowly that her skin flushed. She'd swear his eyes tore through her gown, sought under her chemise—

Her chemise. Oh, the window. Of course she felt his eyes; her worn chemise hadn't covered her. Not when she stood in front of the window. The light would have made the thinning fabric transparent. She had not been covered at all. Just outlined and bared to him.

He hadn't turned around like she'd asked; neither did he lower his eyes.

She tried to calm her tangled emotions, but the gown, too tight by far, constricted her breathing. And he dared to be angry with her?

'Doona watch next time,' she scorned.

She picked up and threw his tunic as hard as she could at him. It billowed to the floor slowly, which didn't help her mood.

He snatched up the fabric at his feet, removing his gaze and releasing its hold on her. 'Doona want to ever look at a Buchanan.' Without turning around, he unwrapped his belt. 'Tell the truth and you can leave my sight.'

His animosity seared her, but she wouldn't cower before him. No, she would turn the tables. Since he hadn't turned his eyes whilst she dressed, she wasn't turning hers.

But she wished she had. Oh, she truly wished she had because the moment Caird reached for his tunic and began to put it on, her stomach changed places with her knees and she felt the need to sit.

As she watched, shock and something she didn't want to guess at flushed her skin.

She knew he roughly pulled on the tunic. However, to her, it seemed agonisingly slow as he raised the soft fabric above his head, and his arms, lithe and corded, flexed as he bent each one into the sleeves. But worse, and an instant hindrance to her ability to breathe, was when he stretched those muscled arms, and the chiseled planes of his stomach rippled and contracted.

It wasn't fair such simple movements bared more flesh, more alluring strength, than one woman should be witness to.

His chest couldn't have been bared for more than a few breaths, yet the sight was almost as stunning as his kiss.

Her stomach didn't settle back in place until he

lowered his head to wrap his belt around his tunic. Even when that was done she still felt unsteady.

And ashamed.

And angry, frustrated and incredulous. Had she hated him just moments before? Now, she hated herself.

She desired a no-good arrogant red-headed Colquhoun!

He lifted his head too soon for her to avert her eyes, so she narrowed them to hide her reaction.

He reached behind him to open the door, but his eyes didn't leave hers.

She felt like running out of the room, retreating and hiding, anything to avoid his all-too-knowing gaze. Instead, she pulled up whatever was left of her pride to confront him.

'You expect me to follow you out of that door,' she said.

He stared, but there was nothing of his thoughts in his gaze now.

'Is your silence supposed to be aye? Well, I won't be going with you.'

Caird's frown deepened.

She gestured with her arms in frustration. 'Silence again. Silence still. Barely a word out of you this morning when last night…' She didn't want to think about last night, nor his words and the way they made her feel. 'I can't care. Whatever you're thinking it isn't true; the dagger is mine and I want it back. You can keep the gem. Just give me the dagger and you won't see me again.'

He tilted his head until his eyes met hers. 'Nae.'

Her fingers curled. 'Because you Colquhouns believe we are without honour?'

He sneered. 'It doesn't matter. The result will be the same.'

'What result?'

'You'll be going where I go until this is over.'

'Why?'

He shrugged.

'You doona need me. Why are you even involving yourself?'

'You came to my room.'

'It was a mistake. As if I'd want a Colquhoun involved.'

'But I am.'

'And that's that?'

He raised an eyebrow.

Conceited. Arrogant. What evil fairy had her walking into a Colquhoun's room? 'What of these wedding games you're to attend?'

'You will be going.'

'You said this was for your sister's wedding. You're taking me to her celebration games?'

He merely blinked.

Forget the fairy. It was the devil himself that had her entering his room. 'Just where are these wedding games? The games begin tomorrow and Camron said you're late. How is that?'

He shrugged. 'Doesn't matter where. I need answers.'

The devil have him. 'You have all the answers you need! Cannot you get it through that thick head of yours? I'm not going anywhere with you!'

He smiled and stepped aside so she could pass through the door. 'Without your precious dagger?'

## Chapter Seven

She couldn't do this. She *had* to do this. What other choice did she have? It had been a fortnight since Ailbert had confessed he'd gambled again. In a fortnight, the debt became due. Neither her family nor her clan had the money he'd promised. The dagger was the only means to pay the debt. Her brother had died because of that dagger. Her family had earned the right to keep it.

Instead, she was trapped and travelling north with a Colquhoun and his cousins. None of them would believe the dagger was hers. So she had to steal it, while there was still time to return home. Still time to avoid the humiliation her brother had brought to their family.

A fissure of pain burned her heart. She couldn't think of home. She had only to think of the Colquhoun and keep her anger.

Which was easy because since they'd left the inn, the big oaf wouldn't stop touching her.

Not that he could help it, but she wasn't about to forgive him his size. Or his breadth. Or his muscles and sun-warmed skin. Not when she rode on the same horse in front of him, with his arms brushing against her sides and his legs pressing hers against the horse.

She'd already elbowed him several times, but he didn't miss a breath when she did.

Her elbows were her second-best weapon next to lying. When Ailbert teased too much, and words weren't enough, she'd hit him. If he tackled her, she could dig her elbows in until he agreed to whatever she wanted, or pretend to give her what she wanted.

He was a good brother. Ailbert.

She squeezed her eyes together, but tears sprang forth. It was too much. She was even remembering him in the past now. It was all past.

She wouldn't cry. Not here, not in daylight, not while in the arms of the man taking her further away from her brother, from his burial, from her family.

Keep her anger; get the dagger. She had no other choice. Pretending to sweep her hair to one side, she brushed her sleeved arms against her cheeks and wiped away any evidence of sorrow.

There wasn't time to grieve for Ailbert.

If only this arrogant Colquhoun would give her

the dagger. She adjusted in the seat, pulled her elbow forward. If only he'd Let. Her. Go.

'Your elbows in my ribs will not change your circumstances.'

'You're kidnapping me.'

'Not kidnapping.'

'Malcolm said the games are on Graham land. 'Tis days away! How can there be celebrations there after Dunbar? Didn't they have a loss?'

'Doesn't concern you.'

Trying in vain to distance herself, she leaned forward. Even then he was everywhere. His feel, his heat, his smell. She was all too aware of him.

Even when her mind tried to comprehend what had happened to her, her body constantly remembered last night. His presence kept her in a constant battle between her want of the dagger and... want. For a Colquhoun, who was kidnapping her, no less!

'It is too far!' She didn't want, couldn't want, to stay. 'I'm too far from home.'

Her mother and sisters might even be looking for her. Everything had happened so quickly when Ailbert was stabbed. Rage, fear and desperation had driven her to follow the thief. She hadn't rushed to Ailbert as her mother and sisters had; she hadn't told them that she was leaving. Shock had drowned out the marketplace, her mother's cries and Ailbert collapsing on the ground. Her only thought was to chase after the dagger.

Now she was further away from the dagger than she had ever been and she had been gone too long.

Her mother would be overwrought. Her family didn't deserve any more fear and worry.

'Your own actions brought you here,' he answered.

'It's not fair,' she whispered. 'Why are you even taking me?'

'A Buchanan has nae right to speak of fairness.' He leaned closer to her ear, making the hairs on the back of her neck prickle. 'Your leaning away from me defeats our ruse. Thanks to your act on the stairs, my cousins believe you're wanting to be with me.'

'As what? What am I to be to you?' She might have pretended on the stairs, but she had no experience in these matters.

She felt the satisfaction rolling off him as he answered, 'As my whore.'

She tried to turn around. 'You…'

'What else did you think? My intended? My dear?' He lowered his voice, contempt thickening his words. 'My betrothed?'

What had she thought? She had spent the night in his room and his cousins knew it; there was no other explanation. Yet it was unjust he expected her to play such a role. Regardless of her starting the ruse, this was going too far.

'I won't do it. We doona need to continue the farce.'

'You are a farce, Buchanan. Do you not like the bed you made? Do you think I like it? I can barely touch you without feeling the need to clean. But there is nae other explanation for your travelling. 'Tis safer.'

Despite her anger, his words stung. 'Since when does your clan care for the safety of mine?'

'Never,' he said. 'I'm not talking about your safety.'

Of course he wasn't. Why would he? A Colquhoun would never tolerate a Buchanan. Just as every right-minded Buchanan would never tolerate a restrictive and oppressive Colquhoun. Their families had always fought. She'd been raised with this knowledge, but Caird's hatred towards her seemed…excessive. His reaction, after their kiss, hurt.

Was he embarrassed about their kissing now he knew she was a Buchanan? Or was it only the dagger and the gem making him angry? Pulling the reins to the left, his arm brushed her chest and instantly heat coiled inside her. Her breath changed. His stopped.

He said he couldn't stand touching her, yet he left her body wanting his touch. She didn't understand her reactions since he hated her.

She didn't deserve his hatred and she couldn't be expected to endure his company for days. She refused to continue this farce for that long. She wasn't that accomplished a liar. Despite her freedom, she'd never been with a man; she didn't know how to act as a whore. Surely his cousins would realise she lied. Then what would happen?

More questions in need of answers, and she'd be even further away from returning home.

She couldn't have that. This had to be finished and soon. At least there was still a chance to escape. It wasn't nighttime. They could yet spy the thief, or at least find his trail. If so, they'd get the answers they sought and end this charade.

Then she wouldn't have to think of Ailbert or her grieving mother and sisters. She wouldn't have to think about the gambling debt still owed and the catastrophe that would occur if she couldn't obtain the money to pay it.

They'd find the thief, and this would end. Then she could do her own grieving, in her own time and away from hate-filled Colquhouns.

In the meantime, all she had to do was not think of Ailbert's death. His blood spreading across his stomach.

How it was all her fault…

To contain her helpless guilt and to still her thoughts, she smiled at Hamilton. He'd been friendly to her since they'd left the inn and she welcomed the distraction. When Hamilton slowed his horse, her smile became genuine.

Caird needed quiet. Fortunately, Hamilton kept Mairead entertained with conversation and Malcolm, used to his silences, left him alone.

. It allowed him to think and to plan.

The dagger and jewel buried in a pouch around his waist burned into his side. It was like holding a flame that could instantly torch a village, destroy lives and entire clans.

But just like that flame, as with any fire, it could do miraculous things as well. The Jewel of Kings.

He held the Jewel of Kings. He was certain of it.

Shock and doubt had washed over him when he first held it at the inn.

Recognition dawned on him at the same time as he tried to rationalise that it couldn't possibly be true. It was a legend and not supposed to be real.

But it was too exact. There could be no other jewel shaped like it, no other jewel coloured like it and it had been purposely hidden inside a dagger's hilt.

A Buchanan said it was her brother's? Impossible. He would rather believe he held the legend long before he'd ever believe that clan owned it.

But what was he to do with it? It belonged to Scotland, but Scotland barely existed now. In April, King John Balliol was defeated. Now he was held prisoner at the Tower of London. The English King continued to set up English sheriffs and English governors.

The jewel belonged to the Scotland of old, a united Scotland under one ruler. That Scotland had been lost with a child at sea…and at Dunbar.

So what to do with the jewel?

There were few choices. He had to solve the mystery of why it surfaced now and why it was wanted by a Buchanan and a thief.

Caird had no doubt the thief knew the jewel was inside the dagger, which meant he would be desperate to reclaim it. It also meant he could be nearby and danger—

Mairead laughing again.

He tensed his muscles, refusing to be as affected by the sound as he had been before.

A mistake.

It tightened her against him and the sound reverberated through him.

Was that how Mairead truly laughed or was she torturing him?

He rode closer to Hamilton to keep Mairead occupied, but now Caird wondered at his choice.

At first, he'd tried to listen to their conversation, which provided Mairead opportunity for treachery.

All he needed was for her to lie and cause the Graham clan to rise up against him, but they had only talked of trivialities, the games and village stories. Still, he had to be ready for anything. He'd never met a more impulsive female.

That first time when she laughed, he hadn't been prepared, and her laugh had struck him— like lightning.

It wasn't like him to be fanciful. But it was Mairead and her laugh. It was making him mad with need.

He held her and it didn't matter that he couldn't see all of her. The smell of heather in her hair, the angle of her shoulders and the touch of her hands on the reins teased him. The softness of her breasts and narrowness of her waist brushing his arms taunted him. Far worse, the lushness of her hips and bottom pressed against him and the horse's rolling gait was a pale mimic of what he craved from her.

Lust. Unchecked. He felt thwarted by how he held her. It was enough for him to catch glimpses of her, but not enough to ease his desire. Holding her like this only tantalised and teased his hunger for her. He wondered if she did it on purpose. Even her gown spilling over his legs mocked his need to see more of her.

So when she laughed? Lightning.

Best to think of her deceit and not his cousin keeping her company. Best to think of her lies, as he watched Hamilton enjoy their conversation. Enjoy? Hamilton was practically falling off his horse to get closer to Mairead. Caird barely stopped himself from reaching out to unseat his cousin. For what?

Laughter.

Such emotions were foolish in a time like this. He held the jewel and he should be thinking of only one thing: the person who held the jewel held the power of Scotland. After Dunbar, and after all he and his family almost lost, he needed to seize on that thought alone.

But all he wanted was to hear Mairead's laughter again.

When Camron slowed his horse to join the conversation, Caird loosened the reins. He didn't want to just hear her laughter; he wanted her to share it with him.

Eyebrows drawn, Mairead turned around. 'Why are you slowing?'

He glanced at her and that was all it took. His horse stopped. He couldn't even muster the effort to will it forward.

Mairead's hair was a wild beacon in the sunlight. Every untamed flying strand beckoned him to wrap his hands around it. It was as if she wiggled her fingers at him to come closer.

It wouldn't take much. Her lips were a mere breath away. He had stopped, but his cousins hadn't. In a few moments, he'd have the privacy needed to kiss her. To ease just a fraction of his want, to demand she give him just an ounce of the attention she gave his cousins. To take his revenge in the only way left. Pain and want spiked. Adjusting himself in the seat, he sped his horse on.

He didn't glance at Hamilton or at Camron, although he could feel his cousins' questioning gaze. He could also feel Mairead's hesitant shrug as she again engaged in conversation.

He didn't get his kiss, but he did get the satisfaction of her gaze. Her annoyance turning to understanding, turning to awareness. He had made his point. She knew why he'd slowed.

His lips curled. If he burned for a Buchanan, he wouldn't be alone in the fire.

# Chapter Eight

'She sleeps?'

Caird moved his horse to allow Malcolm to ride beside him on the narrow trail.

'Aye, for some time.' Caird adjusted Mairead in his arms. 'But she is too restless. She talks… angrily.'

'I am not getting the impression she goes willingly and our cousins are too observant.'

Caird looked behind him. 'Are they still hunting?'

'Nae, they are skinning by the stream we found over there.' Malcolm pointed off to his right. 'It will be dark in a few hours.'

Caird looked through the trees and saw no one. They would have no better privacy than now.

'We need to talk.' He slowed his horse even more. Malcolm followed suit.

'About the woman?'

Caird glanced at Mairead. She curled into his

chest and her head rested on his outstretched arm. There were dark circles under her eyes and her weight against him was heavy. She still slept.

As much as he wanted to, they couldn't talk of Mairead. They were in too much danger.

'Nae, it is the gem,' he answered.

'You do not actually believe it's hers?'

Caird shook his head. Not hers, never hers. 'It's not about Mairead. Or the dagger. It's the gem… the jewel. Doesn't it look familiar to you?'

Malcolm's smile was wolfish. 'Is it ours?'

'Nae. It belongs to everyone. It's legendary, Malcolm.'

'Legendary?' Malcolm looked behind him, his movement exaggerated. 'My brother makes colourful descriptions? You often doona speak at all.'

The trees and path showed no sign of his cousins; Mairead's weight did not shift, and her breath remained even. This conversation must not be overheard.

'The gem is not usual. Half-polished, half not. The size so large it barely fits in a man's hands. Think, Brother. There's only one *jewel* fitting the description.'

Malcolm started. 'It cannot…be,' he whispered.

Caird remained silent while Malcolm gathered his thoughts. It had taken him hours to accept the jewel's existence. As long as the conversation remained with the jewel, he would give this time to his brother.

When his brother realised they travelled with a Buchanan, his judgement would cloud.

'Do you believe this?' Malcolm continued after a while. 'It's a legend, a myth. It doesn't exist.'

'I doona believe in legends and this one was always too exact.'

'If it is that jewel—'

'Then kingdoms are at risk,' Caird interrupted.

'I cannot believe it.'

Caird lifted his hand to silence his brother. Mairead's legs and arms were moving, subtly, but he felt their insistent quiver. Whether she was experiencing dreams or nightmares, he didn't know, but her breath quickened, and her brows drew down.

They had long passed the spot Malcolm indicated where Camron and Hamilton would be skinning, but Caird kept his horse moving.

Malcolm looked questioningly at Caird, but kept his silence.

Caird hoped Mairead kept sleeping. There was still much to discuss with Malcolm. Even so, he fought the urge to wake her. Her restlessness... disturbed him somehow.

Eyes narrowing, Malcolm gazed at Mairead. Caird lowered his hand. It would not be long before his brother asked more questions about her, and he would have to tell the truth. Until then, he must use the jewel as a distraction.

'I believe we have the Jewel of Kings in our hands.' Caird turned his horse around on the path.

'It was a tale told to us as children. Something we used to play.' Malcolm adjusted his horse to follow his. 'I cannot count the fights there were over the pretend jewel.'

'Imagine the wars if the jewel was real.'

'If the legend is true, it can make kings,' Malcolm said. 'Real kings. It is too much power. Too much responsibility. Too—'

'Unbelievable it surfaces now,' Caird said, feeling the restlessness of this conversation. ''Tis nae accident.'

'What are you saying?'

If he was restless, his clan and so many others were shaking and cracking with unrest.

King Balliol rebelled against King Edward's rule and the English king's retaliation had been swift and vicious. The defeat at Dunbar in April had crushed any hope of freedom and only left unrest in its wake.

'Someone was moving it,' Caird said.

'Someone? Mairead?'

Caird held Mairead closer and brought her arms and legs into the warmth of his cloak. 'Nae, not her; not the thief either.'

'A clan?'

'Too many people. Our clans fight. It would have been put to use.'

'To create kings,' Malcolm said.

'More like to declare one true king.'

Malcolm's horse suddenly stopped and Caird steadied his own.

Caird could not doubt Malcolm's shock. Scotland no longer had the ability to make kings. The Stone of Scone now supported the rears of English kings.

He was surprised it had not cracked with grief.

Was it truly so much of a surprise that the jewel appeared now? This year had churned up too many conflicting and powerful emotions. Hope for freedom then crushing defeat as nobles, churchmen, burgesses and freeholders swore fealty to an English king. Balliol was even forced to the Tower.

Worse, their defeat was made official since King Edward recorded it on his Ragman Rolls.

Malcolm slowly turned his gaze. Fear and concern were never on his brother's face, but there was no mistaking those emotions now.

This was more than a secret. More than a costly dagger and legendary jewel. This was more than he wished to be involved with, let alone to involve his brother and clan. King Edward ruled Scotland now, and Caird held the jewel with the power to make Scottish kings.

'Aye, I'm speaking treason,' Caird whispered. 'To my brother.'

'It must stay with your brother and go nae further.'

'If this is true, it will go to all our brothers. All our family.' His clan had enough worries now. Bram, his laird and brother, hadn't participated in Dunbar and no one knew why. It had put their clan's loyalty in question.

If his enquiries into the jewel took long, his clan would be in danger. Still, if he got the answers he needed, if they could keep the jewel a secret. If they could build the momentum behind it before the English were prepared—

'You can't mean to use it?' Malcolm asked. 'It's too dangerous!'

Caird shrugged. Even as his heart swelled at the possibilities, his mind feared the consequences. With war between the two countries, whoever possessed the jewel could stop it. 'Nae more than Dunbar,' Caird said.

'Aye, a thousand times more dangerous!' Malcolm retorted.

If he could, Caird would stop the war. 'Why not use any means I have, especially when it's just been handed to me?'

'Dunbar was a mistake,' Malcolm said. 'It shouldn't have happened.'

Caird conveyed in one glance everything he felt about that fateful battle. 'Nae, it shouldn't.'

Malcolm's eyes narrowed, but he didn't look away. 'I owe you much, but I cannot allow this risk!'

Treason was the risk. But it was treason only if he wanted one side to win from the other. He had different plans.

The jewel could protect their clan. They'd have Scottish power and the English would want that jewel. It was like a doubled-edged sword, and razor-sharp. Yet, if they played it right, he could save all. He just wanted the conflict and bloodshed to end.

'I will not risk much,' Caird said.

Malcolm gaze strayed. 'I cannot accept this. Maybe it is Mairead's?'

If only that were true. She had acted sincere, but he knew what his brother did not. She was a Buchanan. None of what she had said could be true.

'Do you believe that?' Caird asked instead.

Malcolm shook his head. 'Nae, but it would be easier if this was an ordinary, albeit valuable stone.'

Caird urged his horse forward again. He heard his cousins in the woods. They would emerge soon and would wonder at their delay. 'It may be easy to find the thief.' The thief might even be trying to find them.

Malcolm caught up. 'If we cannot find him?'

'We continue celebrating and go to the games.'

They needed to act like nothing was amiss. Caird thought to flush the thief out before then, but that was just the first step.

Ultimately, he knew what they'd have to do. They needed to go to Mairead's family and her clan. She'd said the jewel was her brother's. If that was true, he needed to understand how her brother had possession of the dagger.

Tracing the true owners of the jewel would be slow and arduous, whilst all the time unknown enemies could be circling. However, he was left with little option. He had to get answers first, understand who was moving it and why. If the jewel was a double-edged sword, he had to know how to wield it. Once he had all the answers, he would go to Bram, his brother and laird, and discuss with the council the jewel's future.

Even that wouldn't be easy.

Bram was not on Colquhoun land, but far south on Fergusson land, which was close to the English borders. It was too dangerous to bring the jewel there during this time. Dangerous, but perhaps necessary.

Although he sought answers to determine the best course of action, he would not presume the fate of the jewel alone. He had to involve the clan and its laird.

In the meantime, there was camp to set, food to eat and their absence to explain to his cousins.

This was no time to tell his brother the other,

much more precarious, situation they were embroiled in. And the risk didn't come from the treasonous jewel they carried, but from the traitorous Buchanan in his arms.

# *Chapter Nine*

Mairead jerked in Caird's arms. One moment she was curled heavy with exhaustion in his arms, the next, she was leaning precariously away from him. If he had not had hold of her, she would have fallen.

'What do you do?' he demanded.

Caird tightened his arms to pull her back, but she was unmovable. This was taking stubbornness too far! He was used to being obeyed. He had become too soft with her. Her warmth and scent while she lay against him had lulled him into some sort of tolerance. No more. Now that she was awake, he would demand her co-operation.

'Come, you will—'

She turned around. Her eyes were rounder than any full moon and just as distant. But emotion was there, even if he could not name it and she wasn't quite awake.

Worried she would do something rash, he tightened his grip. Slowly, her expression cleared and he felt her body relax against his.

He exhaled, but releasing his breath did not release the uneasiness her gaze had given him. He knew, without any doubt, he had seen a vulnerability she would never have shown him otherwise.

She was looking around, taking in the denseness of the trees. She had been asleep for a long time and they had travelled far. Nothing would be recognisable now.

'You slept,' he said by way of explanation. He didn't know why he gave her consideration, but he couldn't shake the wild look he saw in her eyes.

'Are we there?' she asked.

'Nae, this is a campsite. The others are preparing food. I have waited, but this horse needs rest.'

She nodded once, but he could feel her limbs twitching as if she couldn't restrain their restlessness. What had she been dreaming of?

He needed to get her to the ground, to think and walk away his own worries. The jewel had complications; he was beginning to realise the Buchanan might prove even more complicated.

'We need to dismount,' he said gruffly.

She nodded again, then continued to nod as if answering a question. He released the breath he had been holding. At least she was cooperating now. Caird slid off the horse and raised his arms to take her waist. He was thrown off balance or the swift kick to his chest would not have thrown him to the ground.

It was over in a moment.

Not looking behind her, Mairead tugged on the reins as the large horse surged towards the road and back to her family.

She couldn't stand Caird or the deception any more. Only dreaming of Ailbert, she didn't care for the dagger, the money or the gem. She had a fortnight still to resolve the debt. She needed her family. Needed to see her brother laid to rest in the ground.

Tears whipped from her eyes, her hands slipped on the reins, her legs barely held her to the horse's heaving flanks.

Free. Free. Free.

Her feelings were echoed in the horse's hooves, and the wild cadence lifted her.

Then she heard it. Another sound, distant and in contrast to her own.

She looked behind her. Caird was on the road and gaining ground.

Too late. She'd never make it. Not like this. The horse he rode was rested, fed and bareback. She looked wildly around her. There were the trees, and she was smaller. Leaning further forward on the horse, she rode into the trees.

Caird yelled, but she didn't care; she had to get away. She needed the distance; needed to forget. Her tears flowed heavier until she couldn't see.

She fell against the horse, trusting it would feel her pain and take her away.

Caird called out again, a song, a tune and the horse suddenly slowed.

No! She pressed her body into its flanks and her hands gripped its sides. The horse reared. Hooves lashed the air as it threw its body towards a tree.

'Mairead!' Caird couldn't manoeuvre through the trees and he jumped to the ground.

Angry and weaving too close to the trees, the horse she rode was wild. With her hands still clutching the reins, Mairead's body flailed.

Caird's body jolted when she hit the first tree. Keeping little distance, and using a training tune, he tried to soothe the animal. But it was beyond wild with fear and threw itself towards the opposite tree. There was a moment of space to grab the reins. The momentum of his movement tossed Mairead into his arms, but not quickly enough.

Just in time, Caird shielded her before the horse crushed him against a tree. He felt the agonising pain before the horse gained balance and sped away.

Mairead's weight was suddenly crippling, and Caird fell to his knees.

Sides ripping, he laid her on the ground. Even as the pain eased by letting her go, he fought the urge to pull her back into his arms. She was awake, but silent. Her face was smeared with tears and blood; her breath wheezy. She no longer looked scared, or unsure. She looked angry.

He didn't care. He was furious.

'You fool! You insanely impulsive female with nae care for—'

'Doona give me your sanctimonious anger, Colquhoun.' Gasping, she sat up. 'What do you care if your horse crushed me?'

'For you, Buchanan?' His sides protesting, he sat back. 'I care *nothing* for you. That was my horse you took.'

She whipped her arm up, but he caught her hand before she could strike him. 'I wish you'd just stayed on the ground where I kicked you.'

Her hand felt cold and clammy. She was angry, but she was afraid, too. He almost hadn't made it in time. Cared nothing for her? He feared he cared too much. 'Lucky for you, I didn't. You could have died galloping into this forest.'

'I wouldn't have been in the forest if you hadn't chased me now, would I?' she scoffed.

Chased her? It had been pure desperation. Caird's anger warred with his need to protect her. She could have died. The agony in his ribs kept him in place or else his need to hold her would have won. Still her hand warmed in his and he softened his hold.

'Where do you think you were going?'

'Home, you suffocating oaf, where else?' She

wrenched her hand out of his. 'Is it a surprise? Did you think I would willingly go with you to celebration games? As if I could celebrate anything with your family, when it is my family—'

She tried to stand, stumbled and grabbed a tree.

He just stopped himself from helping her. Of course, her family. Her lying Buchanan clan.

'Without the dagger?' he mocked. He couldn't care about her stumbling. He'd be damned if he touched her again.

There were too many complications with his touching her. He must, for all their sakes, ignore any desire for her. Slowly he stood and began to attend to his horse that had returned.

Caird turned his back on her. Again. Ignoring her, he carefully felt his horse for injuries. His steady strokes calmed the animal as he checked its flanks, haunches and legs.

Guilt flickered through her belly. He did care for the horse and she had risked its life. A flick of a hoof on a branch, or hindquarter swung too hard and fast on rough bark, could maim it for life.

Her fault, her carelessness. But she hadn't been thinking. Another mistake.

Looking down, she tried to bend her ankle and gasped as pain arced through her. Caird continued his care of his horse and she suppressed her guilt.

Why did she care anyway? She shouldn't be here. She'd take responsibility for the horse, but nothing else.

'Why didn't you just let me go?' she demanded. 'You doona need me. You had the dagger and gem.'

'There's not time for this discussion.' He turned his head. 'Your lies and deceit make you necessary until I have the truth.'

'You ken the information you seek could easily be found with the thief! I've told you what you need to know.'

He stopped, his face edged with an almost cruel smile. 'What I need to know? That was never the prerequisite. It's what I want to know.' He grabbed the bridle. 'It's not as if I trust your word, Buchanan. We need to return to camp.' He gestured to the barebacked horse. 'That's your horse now.'

That horse was several feet away, where he had left it.

'I can't.'

Caird cursed. 'You push my patience too far. Obey me.'

Obey him. If she could, she'd run away again.

'This isn't about you! I think my ankle is broken.' She lifted the hem of her gown.

Caird's gaze fell on her ankle. 'Bend it.'

She braced herself against a tree, and everything in her body protested against her moving the ankle. It was already swelling, but she could move it.

'It's not broken.' Caird turned to his horse.

Could he not see the swelling? He had chased her, now he acted like he regretted catching her.

She had to imagine his arms pulling her closer to him and the comfort of his hand holding hers. Caird's ignoring her could not be plainer. To him, her ankle wasn't broken; therefore, she wouldn't receive help.

She was expected to make it to and onto the horse, but the horse hadn't come any closer. Even if she made it that far, she needed to find some sort of leverage and hoist herself up.

Dragging her foot, she limped over sticks and ferns towards the horse. It was a small victory to reach it, but an even greater one as she guided it towards a small boulder she could step upon.

Caird was watching her, but she wouldn't beg him for help. As she pulled herself up, she adjusted herself until seated.

Gratefully, the animal stood still but without a saddle or reins, she didn't know how to make it move.

Irritatingly, the increasing breeze lifted and tangled stray strands of her hair, which stung her eyes. She impatiently pushed them back and gave Caird a scathing look, but his eyes only watched her errant hair.

Exasperated, she retorted, 'Why not just leave me here?'

'Tempting,' he said, his narrow gaze returning to hers. He seemed angrier than before. 'But while

Malcolm knows what we carry, I'll not have my cousins involved.'

His cousins. All her ire left her. She had enough trouble with just the Colquhoun brothers, she didn't want the Graham clan's attention as well.

'You're not fooling them,' she said purposefully.

'It's enough.' It was for him. He couldn't give more effort to pretending to be her lover or his body might forget about the pretending.

'It needs to be more,' she argued.

Frustrating female.

He was still slack jawed from the sight of her body as she pulled herself on the horse, and she wanted more? He wanted to give her more.

He took a step before searing pain forced him to slow. His ribs needed to be bound and quickly. Even now he risked his life and all he could think about was the press of Mairead's breasts in the too-tight gown, the curve of her upturned bottom and her beckoning hair.

'I'm sorry,' Mairead said.

Not expecting an apology, he glanced at her again.

'I shouldn't have done it,' she continued. 'He's a good creature.'

The horse. She was speaking of the horse. It was the best he'd ever had and he had raised it from a foal. Still, when she had fled, it hadn't been the horse he'd been desperate to save from injury.

'You are lucky he lives,' he replied.

Flinching at his words, she said, 'I thought Colquhouns were overbearing in courtesy and propriety. Doona accept my apology, but I meant it all the same.'

She sounded sincere. Of course she did. She was Buchanan and she wanted the dagger. Therefore, her apology was for some purpose, probably to soften him towards her. Laughable.

His ribs ached and he stood in pain, but he was unable to hide his reaction to the sight of her hauling herself up on the horse. A small favour her eyes didn't flicker across his body as his eyes felt compelled to do with hers.

She was an innocent despite the way she'd moulded to his body, how every strand of her hair beckoned to be touched. She didn't even know what she looked like to him, sitting proudly and bristling with indignation.

If she wasn't an innocent, instcad of an apology to soften him towards her, she could use his desire against him. His craving for her was a weakness. If she touched him again, he couldn't be responsible for his actions. His ribs could pierce his lungs and he wouldn't care.

What would his brothers think of their reasonable, silent brother then?

He hoped it was the responsibility of the jewel making him this conflicted and forgetful of her clan. It couldn't be a Buchanan. Never a Buchanan.

Malcolm had lost his childhood love to the Buchanan clan. Malcolm and Shannon, still children, had strayed too near the Buchanan borders. Malcolm returned for help, but far too late. Malcolm insisted one of the attackers was a Buchanan, but the Buchanan laird at the time denied involvement and Shannon's family demanded no debt repaid. They never wanted to burden Malcolm with the pain of responsibility.

It would deeply wound Malcolm if he discovered his conflicting feelings for Mairead.

He had to remember only to hate her, but that would be difficult if she wanted more pretending.

'Silence Colquhoun?' she said as her horse shook its head. 'Ach, be pig-headed 'til your cousins nae longer believe us. Why not just gouge out the rubies so we can split the treasure and be done?'

He almost laughed. The dagger protecting the Jewel of Kings gouged? She couldn't know what they carried. No one could be that good at lying.

'Nae more talk,' he replied. He was hurt, angry and lustful, and there was too much at stake. Pretending to be her lover was the least of his worries.

He turned and began walking.

Automatically, Mairead's horse followed and she was forced to crouch low to keep her balance.

Caird had known what the horse would do,

had probably enjoyed her sudden loss of balance as the animal jerked forward. He was lucky she kept her seat. If she had to pull herself up on the horse again, she would not do it without some violence to him.

'I'm not at fault here,' she called out. 'If you doona pretend, then the results are on your own head!'

After his sudden start, Caird walked slowly, his gait shorter than usual.

She opened her mouth, then closed it. What did she care if he walked slowly? His ankle wasn't injured.

# Chapter Ten

The campfire outlined Malcolm poking hares hanging and crackling over the open flame. Near him, one of the twins sat skinning more.

The cousin stood when he saw them enter, the hare and knife dripping blood to his feet. 'What has happened?'

Caird guided his horse around the beddings and saddles placed in a heap. Mairead had no choice but to follow until Malcolm stopped their progress.

'The horse spooked,' Caird answered, handing the reins to Malcolm. 'I borrowed Hamilton's to give chase.'

Without glancing at her, Caird walked towards the largest boulder by the fire and slowly sat.

Looking perplexed, Camron dropped the knife and hare and walked to her.

Swinging her good leg over, she explained, 'I've hurt my ankle.' She hoped her explanation distracted Camron from Caird's odd behaviour. Running after her only to ignore her; every muscle displaying his anger, but him not voicing it.

'How bad is it?' he asked.

'She's unharmed, Camron,' Caird called out.

Glancing at Caird, his lips thinning, Camron reached for her and she put her hands on his shoulders and slid down.

Pain spiked up her leg, but she refused to cry out.

'It's not fine, is it?' Camron said softly so Caird couldn't hear.

Concern and questions filled Camron's brown eyes and his kindness tempted her to talk.

But what could she say? Her brother was dead, her family would soon be publicly shamed and Caird had abducted her. She couldn't possibly explain, nor would it do any good.

'It'll be better once I rest a bit.' She purposefully avoided his true meaning.

He offered his arm. 'Lean your weight on me and I'll help you to a soft bit of grass.'

He sat her by the fire and far from Caird. Taking a small broken log, he laid it behind her for support and draped it with a blanket for padding.

When Camron didn't leave she gave him an apologetic smile, before lifting the hem of her gown to assess her injury.

'Her ankle's swelling,' Camron said, loudly

enough for Caird to hear. 'I'll need to take care of it.'

'I can do it,' she said.

Caird looked over. 'I'll do it.' He looked paler than she'd seen him before.

Camron sighed. 'All's well and good she's yours, but you cannot do it and now her boot may have to be cut.'

'I'll do it,' she repeated, loosening the laces and pulling the boot off. She gave a small sigh of relief before the throbbing in her ankle increased.

She would have given in to the increased pain except Camron was still crouched next to her and watching her too closely.

'I doona know what happened, lass, but I have a feeling you're in trouble,' Camron whispered quietly. 'And from the looks of it, so is Caird.'

Malcolm emerged from the trees and stood before Caird. Caird was loosening his belt around his waist. As Malcolm slowly raised Caird's tunic, they talked low, but heatedly.

She didn't know how to reply to Camron. How could Caird be in trouble?

'I've got linens in my sack,' Camron said, his eyes on Malcolm.

'Any salve?' Malcolm asked.

'Hamilton's sack.' Camron gave a shake of his head as if he couldn't understand. She knew she didn't. Her gaze must have given her away because Camron explained.

'From the lack of movement in Caird's arms, I'm assuming he's broken or bruised some ribs.'

'Oh,' she murmured. Her stomach plummeted and rendered any other response impossible.

'He went to a lot of bother rescuing you from his horse, lass,' Camron continued.

Malcolm was now carefully feeling along Caird's back. Face tight, a sheen of sweat visible on his skin, Caird gave static responses.

People died of broken ribs and he hadn't said anything at all.

'I didn't know,' she said. What could she say to Camron? She had to pretend she hadn't purposefully risked the horse, herself and his cousin's life in the woods.

'You made it back, lass, that's what's important,' Camron replied. 'Unless there's more?'

He would think there was more. After all, if Caird had gone to so much trouble only to ignore her now, none of it made sense. Caird's behaviour didn't even make sense to her. He hadn't hinted that he was injured and his words to her were cruel.

Yet, she recalled how he had held her hand in the woods. It was difficult to remember when her own emotions were jumbled. At least now she knew, with his ribs hurting, Caird couldn't have raised her on to the horse.

Malcolm was rubbing the salve around Caird's sides. Glistening, his skin showed the rise and shadows of muscles wrought from training. He was hurt, she had caused it, and yet she watched with a sort of helpless fascination because his pain wasn't visible, only his strength.

'Are you worried for him?'

'For a Co—' She closed her mouth, but it wasn't quick enough and she lowered her eyes.

'For a what, lass? What is Caird to you?'

What was Caird to her? Her enemy, her nemesis, an insurmountable mountain of a man, who caused her nothing but anger and heartache. She hated him for it. Hated him.

Yet, with every harsh outtake of breath he gave as Malcolm began tightly wrapping the linens around Caird's chest, she felt concern?

That little softening of feeling, that tiny bit of guilt knowing he was in pain, made her feel something other than hatred. She knew the feeling was another mistake.

'He's nothing more than what he said he was,' she said as lightly as she could.

By Camron's expression, she knew she disappointed him.

But what else could she say? If Caird wouldn't explain his behaviour, neither would she.

As if he knew her answer to Camron, Caird suddenly looked at her. His changeable grey eyes scrutinised her as if he searched for his precious answers. Intent on finding some answers of her own, she held his gaze. They'd never decided on how to proceed. Was she to pretend to be his whore or his enemy?

Caird's eyes suddenly hardened and she saw his left thumb flex. When he had watched her undress at the inn, he had done that slight movement. He hadn't been pleased with her then and she could surmise he wasn't pleased now.

Was he warning her to stay quiet with his cousin? As if she was too simple to know better? An enemy, then.

'Never known any horse of Caird's spooking before.' Camron's voice broke through her thoughts.

Despite their joviality and gentleness, these Graham men were no fools, and she knew she would get no reprieve by asking for Camron's help.

Looking at Camron, she replied, 'I must have done something wrong, but he was able to calm it down.'

Camron's features softened as she finally said the correct thing.

Which was good because she just wanted to be left alone. For as much as her ankle throbbed, she was beginning to feel the rest of her bruised body as well.

She opened her palms and could see the blisters made from her tight grip on the leather reins. She'd ridden a horse before, but only infrequently.

'When they finish, you'll need the salve for those,' he said.

She was too much of a novice to have ridden like that. She was too much of a novice in this whole situation.

Camron stood from his crouch, but kept his voice low. 'You let me know if you need anything else. Blood on my hands or not, I'll help you. You ken?'

She gave a smile, but she feared it didn't reach her eyes. 'Thank you.'

He nodded and went to pick up the knife and hare again.

She arranged her gown as she assessed Camron's words. He would help her with her ankle or against his cousins if it came to such. She had no doubt they'd do it. Noble Grahams, their strength was without question.

Camron made quick work of the hares, before handing them to Malcolm, and disappearing into the woods.

He was quick, efficient and no doubt deadly.

But the Grahams couldn't help her. Nobody could. This was something only she could free herself from.

Her family was in danger and didn't even know it. Because not only had her brother gambled against his laird's orders, he'd done it with an English garrison. By the next full moon, they would expect payment of a chest full of silver.

It was silver she didn't have, and, after the massacre of Berwick and loss at Dunbar, an English garrison that wouldn't be forgiving.

The laird had forbidden Ailbert from gambling and the fact he did it with the English made it so much worse. Her family now faced humiliation and certain banishment. Scotland was still reeling from Berwick and Dunbar. There was nowhere safe they could go. Her mother was too frail for such an ordeal, and her sisters too vacuous. They depended on her to save them.

Her only hope was the dagger. There was simply no other way to get the money...the money!

It wasn't the dagger, it was the *money* it represented.

And hadn't she heard some of that in Caird's pouch? Where was it now? She hadn't seen it attached to Caird's belt when Malcolm tended his ribs. The pouch contained Caird's money and the dagger and gem. Caird must have removed it before he took Hamilton's horse to chase after her, which meant it was loose and—

'Do you need some as well?' Malcolm dropped the linens and salve beside her. In his other hand, he held out a speared and charred hare. She quickly took the stick and nodded towards the linens and salve. 'Thank you.'

'I'll make sure you have food, but you'll apply the salve yourself,' he said. 'I'll not anger my brother further by staying next to you.'

She glanced at Caird. 'Your brother is only angry because of his pain.'

Malcolm's eyes held a frightening light in their green depths. 'I have seen my brother in pain before. I have not seen him like this.' He returned to the fire, taking down more of the cooked hares.

Famished, Mairead took quick bites of the hare and threw the bones towards the fire.

So Malcolm was warning her, too. He might be the younger of the brothers, but he was still a Colquhoun and not to be underestimated.

If Caird was angry because she risked his horse, Malcolm was angry because she hurt his brother. She might have gained the Graham cousin as an ally, but she certainly had lost Malcolm.

Knowing she needed her ankle and hands to heal, she applied the salve and linen. Keeping her eyes low, she surveyed the camp.

The sacks and supplies were now scattered to the different rolled blankets they'd use as beds. She couldn't readily see Caird's pouch, and stealing from the others might prove to be impossible.

Resignation settled within her. Even if she could steal from the others or Caird, the money they carried couldn't be enough. Her brother had promised a chest of silver, which meant the dagger was her only hope. The same dagger that was most likely in Caird's pouch.

If Caird continued to hide or wear the pouch, then only at the wedding celebrations could she be certain of enough distractions to grab it. Yet, she'd be too far from home and might not return in time. And what of the gem?

It was probably more valuable than she could ever dream of, but there were too many complications. The way Caird looked at it. The way he had looked at her, like he was studying her.

She suspected the Colquhouns would never let her be free if she took the gem. The dagger was no chest of silver, but it should be sufficient to pay the debt. She'd just have to bide her time for now.

Camron re-emerged from the woods with Hamilton, both of them wet from a stream nearby. She wasn't surprised when Hamilton came to her, and so she asked him to help her to the woods.

Her effort not to look at Caird worked, but she didn't miss the sound he made as she tucked her arm around Hamilton's neck when he lifted her.

When Hamilton returned her, the camp was settling down for the night. Malcolm was dampening the flames and Caird, his movements hampered, was patting his horse.

He had risked his life when he pursued her into the woods. But why? He said she was necessary, but necessary for what?

She was not surprised to see his pouch tied loosely to his belt again. Anyone as overbearing as Caird wouldn't be careless with such a valuable. Yet even so, he seemed obsessive about the dagger and gem.

He was also adamant to obtain his answers. Since he didn't believe she was the dagger's owner that meant all he had to do was catch the thief.

There was no reason for him to keep her. There had to be something more here.

Weary at her curiosity, she started to lay down on the blankets they had provided for her.

'Move over.'

Startled, she looked up. Caird stood over her, his eyes unreadable.

She glanced at the others, already arranging their sacks and blankets to sleep. If they slept away from her, so could he.

'Go away,' she hissed, arranging herself more fully in the middle.

'You're on my blankets.'

They were given to her and she didn't feel like giving them up.

'Are we talking?' she whispered. 'Because I can't pretend to be your whore if you doona pretend to worry about me.'

'Done pretending.' He grunted. 'Move over.'

She was comfortable, but it was more than that. She didn't want to cede any more to him. 'Nae.'

He crouched low, his back straight. This close, she could feel the heat of him, feel the strength of his will to make her move.

'Do you want my touch?' he whispered. 'I'm a large man and those are my blankets.'

Out of stubbornness, she thought about moving, but she didn't want to sleep on the damp ground.

Her face flushed with annoyance, but she sat up and made space for him.

With a grunt, he settled beside her, but did not lie down. Instead, he propped himself against the padded log, and adjusted the pouch to his side. There was no sound of coins, and she wondered if they were removed because the weight hurt his ribs.

He moved again and stretched his legs out before him, but he did not touch her. In fact, with his arms crossed, he looked as if he made an effort not to touch her.

Bristling, she plucked at her gown. Apparently it was true when he had said he could barely touch her without feeling the need to wash. His words hadn't been forgotten. Hurting still because of the words, and chiding herself because she wondered if his ribs pained him, she vowed to do everything she could to ignore him.

Unfortunately, her vow didn't stop her ears from hearing his body shift, or the hitch to his breath. She couldn't deny it, even with his cruelty to her, his pain…affected her. She had lied to Camron when she answered that Caird was nothing more than a friend to her.

He was more than that; from that first kiss she knew he was more. It was the way, despite everything, she continued to respond to him. Even more, it was that she knew he was generous and kind. He had shown her that at the inn before they'd known their clans.

Whatever it was about him, she was beginning to feel as tightly bound to him as the linen. It shouldn't be this way. Was it her grief making her seek and want Caird? She had more than enough to worry about. She shouldn't be curious about the Colquhoun, she should only be angry at him.

'You shouldn't encourage my cousin,' he said.

Caird's eyes were closed, his manner appeared nonchalant but she felt the tension in him.

She stopped arranging her gown. 'I encourage nothing.'

He grunted.

Did he intend to humiliate her? 'I needed to relieve myself,' she added.

He adjusted his back and settled into the thicker blanket. 'If you plan to sow dissension, it will not work.'

'It shouldn't matter if Hamilton helps me. I thought we were done pretending,' she reminded him.

'Aye,' he replied after a while.

'Then how are we to proceed?' She lay down.

He didn't answer and she looked to him. His frown had deepened.

Exasperated, she adjusted herself until she was comfortable. She was done with her curiosity, done with being worried by his broken breathing, done with this confusion. She just had to wait for a distraction, steal the dagger and be free of them.

'Doesn't matter how we go on,' Caird whispered so softly, she wondered if he meant to say the words out loud. 'I will have my answers.'

When she felt Caird's eyes on her, expecting her to reply, she turned her back.

It was almost morning when Malcolm motioned Caird to follow him to the stream. Caird wanted to begin this conversation earlier, but Mairead's sleep was restless. He knew he could not leave her when there was a chance for her to wake again.

It couldn't be because in her sleep, she had turned and faced him.

Her hair spilled wildly against the blanket. He knew she was just as tempestuous, just as unpredictable.

Just as scheming. Before he'd sat next to her, he sensed she'd been planning something because she kept looking at them, and at their supplies. For a Buchanan, she wasn't good at hiding her emotions. For he also perceived her frustration.

When he sat down, he wanted to question her, but by then he was next to her, felt her ire, smelled her hair and he could only think of Hamilton carrying her to the woods, and how her arms wrapped around his neck. How he wanted it to be him instead.

Sighing, he rose to join his brother. It wasn't the lack of sleep causing his sudden tiredness or his unknown emotions about Mairead, it was the responsibility he faced right now.

Quietly, they walked away from the camp and stopped short of the stream so the ground remained firm under their feet.

'So she fled…' Malcolm started. His brother knew his horse better than Camron and Hamilton. 'Why?'

'I doona know,' Caird answered.

'She had the dagger.'

Caird lowered his voice. 'Nae.'

Malcolm remained silent.

He was glad the ground below him was firm because he knew the conversation would soon not be. 'She was escaping, but I think not with any intent.'

'I'm not following this conversation.'

Caird shifted his stance to relieve the pain in his ribs. 'She had woken, but wasn't awake. May not have even thought of why she was running.'

'Angry or scared?'

'Both.' He thought of the emotions on her face. 'But there was something more there.'

'This isn't like you. Wondering about a woman's emotions. It isn't like you to travel with anyone only to ignore them. And you are ignoring her despite sleeping next to her. Who is she?'

Caird walked further down the stream. He

knew he was supposed to make an effort at pretending to be her lover, but the farce was too heavy even for his broad shoulders.

He was the middle brother, and the responsible one. Bram was the laird, and a fair one at that, but Bram always served his own interests and pleasures first. Malcolm being the youngest would never know clan responsibility.

Caird was the dependable one. His silence was just part of that control. He carried the authority needed to rule the clan. He did not pretend anything, let alone affection.

He stopped just short of the damp earth around the stream. In this dim light, he'd likely get his boots wet. He wished he knew how to navigate the conversation. 'Mairead is who I told you she was.' he started. 'She came to my room trying to find the dagger.'

Malcolm quickened his steps until he stood in front of Caird. 'Aye, well, but who is she? What is she in all this?'

The sun was rising. Shafts of grey light were beginning to reflect off the water, but the sun's light did not reach his brother's face. Caird minded the darkness now. What he was about to say would hurt his brother. The least he could do was look him in the eye.

'Mairead,' Caird paused, 'and her clan is Buchanan.'

He did not need the light to see his brother

gutted by his words. Malcolm's startled movement was enough to know that as sharp as a sword, his words struck deep.

Malcolm took a step closer, tension in every movement, his voice tight. 'I doona believe you.'

'It's true.'

Malcolm cursed. 'If you were not weakened, you'd feel the brunt of my fist.'

'For once, I'm glad of my injury.'

'This is not humorous. I could *kill* you.'

Malcolm swivelled around and picked up a broken branch. Swinging wide, he struck it against a tree. The crack shook the leaves above and echoed across the stream. No doubt it woke the others as well. Caird hoped they would stay away.

Malcolm kept his voice low, but each word was guttural with anger. 'A damn lying Buchanan. Deceitful, untrustworthy baseborn—' He pulled himself up. 'You *bedded* her.'

'Nae.'

'She is comely. You were drunk. She was in your room all night. You're telling me you did not want her?'

Caird paused. He wanted her. Desired her as he hadn't any other woman. He had been drunk, but his vision wasn't blurred. She had been conjured from his very dreams. Her impossibly wild curly hair, the width of her hips, the feel of her thighs.

His body still wanted her, even when he knew she was a Buchanan,

Despite her lies, despite her scheming, even now his body didn't care.

The ride from the inn had been torture. Her bottom between his thighs. The curve of her stomach and breasts touching his arms with every breath she took. He was hard with the remembering.

His injury be damned. If Malcolm knew the truth of how he felt, he would feel his brother's fist.

'I did not lie with her. There was the scuffle and my head hurt afterwards.'

'Hell,' Malcolm scoffed, unbelieving. 'You and your ale. Just a few drops and your controlled silence disappears. You probably talked her to sleep.' He looked at him squarely, his tone changed. 'When did you know?'

Mairead's surprise at his hair colouring, her eyes widening with understanding that they were enemies. 'Before the jewel was discovered.'

'Still you didn't tell me. This is not a secret you should have kept,' Malcolm said. 'It would have changed everything we did since the inn.'

'I couldn't have that.'

'Couldn't have! You are my brother, but you are not my laird. You best of all know my hatred of Buchanans. All Buchanans. I can never forgive any of them for what happened.'

As if he could. Caird cursed, and his anger

rose. He had not told his brother for good reason. 'I am using my head, not my emotions.'

'Are you? Is that what you call it now?'

'Careful, Brother.'

'You have betrayed me and our clan.'

Caird changed his stance, but it was enough to stop Malcolm. He knew this would be difficult for his brother, but he would not take insults against his honour.

'The true danger is the jewel,' Caird said, 'not the Buchanan.'

Exhaling, Malcolm stepped back. 'Oh, the same Buchanan, who said the dagger was her brother's? It could not be hers. Since she lies, how is she not a danger?'

'She was surprised the jewel was inside.'

'Of course she was,' Malcolm said. 'She's lying.'

'She is, but about something other than the jewel.'

'How can you be certain?' Malcolm asked.

Caird wasn't certain at all. He couldn't base anything on his instinct. When it came to her, his instincts were hardly logical.

Malcolm snorted. 'Do you believe the dagger holding the Jewel of Kings was her brother's?'

'Nae. It isn't possible it's the Buchanans'.' Caird started walking again, slowly, not needing the distance, but the distraction this time. 'But she is a link to the jewel and it's too powerful not to have answers.'

'Is that why you didn't leave her at the inn?'

'Aye, and until we find the thief or some truths, I cannot be sure of anything.'

'You risk our cousins discovering we travel with a Buchanan. They will not be pleased.'

'Nor will they when I bring her to Graham land.'

'You intend to tell them?'

Caird shook his head.

'I would have taken the dagger and left the woman.' Malcolm picked up another stick and swung it absently. 'You have a lying Buchanan saying a costly dagger is hers. Obviously it isn't. And you have another liar, who says the dagger is his, but now we aren't so certain it isn't.'

'There is more to this than that.'

'Aye, there is. This false love interest you play?' Malcolm asked. 'At least I know why you are not convincing.'

'I'll not be pretending long,' Caird said. He knew he was unconvincing in his wooing of Mairead.

'For how long?' Malcolm asked, continuing to swing the branch. 'Because you are not doing well with it now.'

'When we find the thief, we release the Buchanan.'

'Unless we need both.'

He hoped not. He could not be with Mairead for longer than was absolutely necessary. Only last night she had been like a wanton angel in his bed, her very flesh burning into him. Despite knowing who she was and the discovery of the jewel, he could not rid himself of the way she felt.

'We do not need Mairead or the thief,' Caird replied. 'It is not the thief who controls the dagger. A man like him does not work by himself. We need another.' He might have been drunk, but there was no doubting Mairead had surprised the man in the hall. That man was a weapon, not a thinker. And a weapon always had someone wielding it. There were more people involved than Mairead and a thief.

'Could she not be in partnership with him?'

Caird paused. 'And they had a disagreement?'

'Aye.'

Caird swallowed the feeling of wrongness. Mairead a partner with the thief? He wanted to swing a branch as his brother had. Instead, he said, 'It has merit.'

'It could be why she ran. To warn him of our approach.'

Could it be true? 'I doona think so,' he replied.

His only proof was in that moment before she'd run. One moment she'd been asleep, the next agitated, but her eyes hadn't held cunning.

He hadn't expected the force or accuracy of her kick. Yet, it had been her eyes that stunned him. He understood the look now: a trapped animal. Tortured.

'How would you know?' Malcolm's words were tight. 'You can never trust a Buchanan!'

His brother was right. She was Buchanan. She called the man they had set loose a thief, but that dagger did not belong to her or her family. Just like all Buchanans, she could not be trusted. The thief could well be her lover.

'Trust will have nae play in this,' he said, trying to suppress his sudden anger. 'We still must get to the games. The thief knew we were going to Graham lands, and he could be there even now.'

Caird inhaled and felt the sharp pain in his side, but the pain was nothing compared to what he was about to do to his brother.

'She will need to ride with you to Graham lands,' Caird said bluntly.

'Never!' Malcolm exclaimed. 'She rides with us and you want me to hold her? I'm likely to snap her neck. How could you ask this of me?'

'You must. I shouldn't with my ribs and the Grahams must never know.'

'We must never know what?'

Caird looked over Malcolm's shoulder as Camron and Hamilton emerged from behind the trees.

What had they heard? He glanced at Malcolm's mutinous face before he turned to greet his cousins.

'You look surprised to see us, cousin,' Camron said. 'We know things aren't right. Spooked horse? Tear tracks on her face, and you glaring at her? Who is she to you?'

Mairead had warned his pretending was no good.

'Will you tell us?' Hamilton added. 'She is extremely comely, but a stranger none the less, and we're thinking she isn't who you say she is.'

Malcolm stayed silent, but Caird could feel the anger rolling from him. His brother was carefree, but never careless. What to tell his cousins now? Bringing them into this would make everything more complicated.

But he was no good at lying and too much was at stake. 'A Buchanan,' he ground out.

Their surprise was greater than their hatred, but only at first.

The Grahams were renowned for their loyalty. They knew what a Buchanan meant to a Colquhoun. 'Return her to the inn,' Camron ordered.

'Nae,' he answered.

'You cannot possibly,' Hamilton added, looking at Malcolm, 'you cannot possibly mean to take her to the celebrations—'

'I doona want her either,' Malcolm interrupted.

Now Camron and Hamilton looked even more confused. The Colquhouns never disagreed in front of anyone.

'We're almost to the keep. We can't call the games off. They were planned by our clans,' Hamilton said. 'Your laird couldn't hold them, and our clan deserves happiness. They should carry on.'

Camron crossed his arms. 'It's too late to call them off, but just because Colquhouns have some say in the celebrations, I'll not have them sullied by a Buchanan.'

Malcolm raised his eyebrows. 'I agree.'

'She goes or I do not.' Caird knew it was risky to give the ultimatum since he knew he must search for the thief there.

'Does she want to go?' Camron asked. 'I have not forgotten your behaviour on the staircase. There's something more happening here.'

There was more, but he'd be damned if he brought the Grahams into the danger. He risked too much dragging his clan into treason.

Hamilton placed his hand on Camron's shoulder. 'We've asked the lass. She's says she's unharmed.'

Caird didn't dare glance at his brother. He knew Malcolm wouldn't willingly agree to this. He was counting on the Grahams' natural good will to come through. He was not disappointed when Hamilton took a step back and raised his hands.

'These games are to celebrate Gaira's wedding. Caird is her brother, and if he wants Mairead, then we must honour his request.'

Camron relaxed his arms and nodded in defeat. 'Aye, she goes, but you are warned, Cousin.' Camron turned to Malcolm. 'But will you still go?'

'We all go,' Caird answered as Malcolm curtly nodded. 'But Mairead cannot ride with me.'

Camron accepted defeat and Malcolm nodded his acceptance, but that didn't mean they would volunteer.

Hamilton grinned. 'I'll happily travel with her.'

Caird squashed his irritation at Hamilton's quick agreement. This was what needed to be done.

Mairead was standing ready when the men emerged from the woods. It was the least she could do. After all, they were discussing her fate.

Quick to anger all her life, she'd never felt as uncontrolled as she did now. It was a deep, seething, swarming anger, as if a hornet's nest was inside her.

Raised voices and a crack of something breaking had woken her. Then what was being said had kept her awake.

If her ankle hadn't been hurting, she would have marched over and confronted them. And if she could have found a weapon along the way? Even better.

Instead, she was forced to listen while frustration built inside her since she'd missed some of the conversation, but thankfully not all of it.

They knew her to be Buchanan and they didn't like it. Given Caird's reaction to her, she hadn't expected their reaction to be any different.

Still, she didn't understand it. Their intense distrust of her was completely irrational. Their clans borrowed and stole. Annoyance or incredulity would have been normal, so Malcolm's vehemence made no sense.

Just as confusing was Caird's insistence on taking her to the games. Despite his family's hatred of her. Despite him not believing the dagger was hers. He wanted answers, but the joke was on him. Only the thief was left to give him answers.

Her brother was no longer able to give him any and she had never had any in the first place.

At the instant sharpness in her chest, she exhaled.

She'd never had answers because the dagger and gem had never truly been hers, only a means to pay a debt, to avoid her family's impending banishment. To escape the humiliation…

Mairead's knees began to buckle and she locked them hard to keep from falling. How had she not seen the truth before now? She wrapped the blanket more tightly around her shoulders.

She had to give it up. Everything. The dagger, the gem and what she thought they represented to her family.

Because even if she was able to pay off her brother's debts, the shame from her clan would always be with her family. She couldn't even be certain that payment of the debt would save them from banishment.

What her brother had done went far beyond losing money; he'd actually betrayed their laird to the English. There was no getting around that. No matter how many confrontations she had with murderers, and no matter how many gems she brought back.

Mairead blinked against the thin line of light now brightening the grass and trees.

Morning had returned and so had some hard truths.

The men talked of the wedding games, but she was no longer going. The wealth of the dagger would never remedy Ailbert's debt, and Caird would never let her have it.

However, there was one benefit left to her. Whoever had killed her brother had to know a Colquhoun possessed the dagger. As far as she was concerned, the Colquhouns and the murderer could just find their own answers together.

When the men finally emerged from the woods, Mairead kept her chin up and her eyes steady.

Malcolm wore his anger like a cloak, the Grahams looked surprised and sheepish as if they'd been caught doing something they shouldn't. Except she knew they weren't embarrassed by the conversation, but the fact they had befriended her. She knew this, but it still hurt.

Only Caird approached her, his eyes taking in her crossed arms.

She narrowed her eyes. 'I'm not going.'

As usual he said nothing.

'I'm not going,' she repeated, welcoming the hornets inside her now. 'It's over.'

He would never give her the dagger. She was foolish ever thinking he would. As long as he kept it on his body, she'd never be able to take it. Never. She just needed to get home and warn the laird.

'Decision's made,' he said just as she knew he would.

'You made the decision, not me.' She waved at the space between them. 'I cannot continue this kidnapping.'

'You will,' he said, the smugness of his tone irritating.

'Why? Because of the dagger and gem? I doona want them.'

'Giving up?' he said.

'Trying to goad me?' Another form of manipulation and despite him using it as a weapon, it worked, if only temporarily. But this was a game she and Ailbert shouldn't have played.

She thought about telling him her brother was dead, but it conceded too much to Caird. Ailbert was her family and a Colquhoun didn't deserve to know of her brother's death. It wasn't as if Caird would pity her, and worse it would cause only more questions for him to seek his precious answers from.

'Nae trickery, Colquhoun, nae dagger, nae gem and nae Buchanan. I'm happy to leave you to finding your answers.'

He shook his head. 'The decision was made by you, Buchanan, the moment you entered my room, the moment you fought me for that dagger and lied about its ownership. You will not leave now because I'm not returning you.'

Did he think she wanted a ride back to the inn? She'd rather crawl home before asking him for favours. 'Just leave me.'

His eyes flashed before he could hide his response. 'Nae.'

When he began to walk past her, she stopped him with her hand.

Despite the cool morning temperature, his arm was invitingly warm, and she just stopped herself from pulling him closer.

Caird's frown deepened as he stared at her hand resting on his arm. This close she felt the heat not only in her touch, but radiating from his whole body. She felt the strength, his determination and it was in direct conflict with what she wanted.

'I'll not go any further. It ends here. Just let me go. I cannot even tell anyone of this else my reputation would be ruined.'

As usual he kept his silence. But she felt the change in him.

Could he actually be giving her this favour? Hope sprang in her chest. She could return home to Ailbert, to her mother and sisters.

Removing her hand, she swiftly hugged herself to trap the heat she'd stolen from him.

Never raising his eyes, he gave a slight incline of his head before walking to the horses.

Not knowing what else to do, she let him go. All she wanted was to forfeit this game and return home. She just wanted this nightmare, which kept getting worse, over. However, with Caird's silence, she didn't know if she'd made another mistake.

## Chapter Eleven

Caird fought his frustration and lust in equal measures. Mairead had made the only request left to her and this time, he believed her. He could never physically force a woman and that's what he'd have to do if he took her to the celebrations.

Had the conversation from the woods finally broken her?

Malcolm, feeling along his horse's hoof, looked up expectantly as Caird approached him. The Grahams, fortunately, were tending the traps for more food.

'How fare the horses?' Caird asked.

'Yours will travel, I still need to see to mine.''

Soon, they could go.

'Mairead will travel nae further,' he said.

'Good,' Malcolm rose to his feet.

His brother's unreasonableness fuelled his frustration, burning the last remnants of lust he felt.

Mairead's hand on his arm had been cold, too

cold. When she had touched him, he stopped not because she wanted him to, but because he fought the impulse to take her hands between his own and warm them. His lust he could understand, but not the care.

'Not good,' he ground out. 'You know what we possess.'

'But you believe she doesn't know about the jewel?'

'She couldn't.' Mairead had relinquished everything.

'So she wanted compensation, coin instead, and a ride back to the inn.' Malcolm's disgust laced his words.

Mairead stood with no anger or guile, only resolve. It was he who had stood like a besotted innocent, wanting to warm her hands. 'She wants nothing.'

'She asked you to just leave her? It makes nae sense.' Malcolm picked up a stick, but it stayed idle in his hands.

The Grahams should have been done with their work by now, which meant they waited for his signal, for his resolution. He was, after all, the dependable one. He would fix it, but not to his liking.

'There is another plan.'

He looked around. 'Where is she?' he asked, realising he'd turned his back on Mairead. Had he been expecting obedience?

'Into the woods,' Malcolm said.

She had left already? He moved.

'The other way, Brother, for privacy I'm sure.'

Not gone, then. He frowned. Lust, anger and now…worry. He had the dagger and the Jewel of Kings. Of any man in the whole of Scotland, he was at this moment the most powerful.

He felt anything but.

And just now, he had to cede even more control of this situation. He, who demanded absolute control. 'You go with the Grahams; you look for the thief.'

Malcolm exhaled. 'You want me to go alone?'

Caird raised his brow.

'You want me to go, when I already have difficulty with Gaira's wedding celebrations.'

'You accepted our sister's happiness when she married that English knight.'

'Aye, but I doona fully ken. Then after Dunbar, how could I accept who she wed?'

'You weren't to go to Dunbar.'

'Ah, aye, I disobeyed our laird's orders. That still doesn't sit well with your rule-controlled world.'

No, it didn't. It made no rational sense for Malcolm to have gone. Bram had forbidden it.

'One of us had to go,' Malcolm replied. 'You were there. You saw. Despite your strict adherence to rules, it was the honourable act.'

Caird refused to give words to what he had

seen at Dunbar. Many a Scot had fled to Ettrick Forest but the battlefield was strewn with arrows and broken men. Malcolm was buried under another body, unconscious and unaware Caird was trying to save him.

Unerringly, Caird's eyes moved across the thin scar on Malcolm's face. He knew it cut further along his body, deeper across the chest. It would take time to heal, but would never go away.

A permanent reminder of a nightmare.

And Malcolm going to Dunbar was incomprehensible. Senseless. Malcolm had always believed in right and wrong. There was no middle ground.

For Caird, disobeying a laird's orders was wrong. So either Malcolm had found a middle ground, or they differed in what they believed was right.

Neither option sat well with him. Colquhouns always presented a united front.

'I'll go.' Malcolm exhaled, then laughed, but there was no humour in his voice. 'The jewel, and apparently you, require nothing more than my going. Silence you give me, but I'll get nae peace from you.'

Caird knew their argument over Dunbar wasn't over, might never be over, but for now he'd accept any cooperation and a distraction from his brother's wounds.

'If I find this thief?' Malcolm turned to his horse again. 'What am I to do with him?'

'Get the truth from him,' Caird replied. 'Then go to Bram. As laird, he must know the clan's involvement. I'll meet you there in a fortnight.'

'Bram has his own concerns now.'

Caird shook his head. 'He is decisive. The occurrence on Fergusson land will not take him long to resolve. There will be time to prepare the course for the jewel.'

Malcolm stopped feeling along the horse's neck. 'You still mean to use the jewel? How?'

'I'll find her brother,' he answered. He still didn't believe the Buchanans had hidden the jewel, but he had to reveal all lies to gain answers. The jewel was too powerful a weapon, and he had to be certain of how to proceed.

'Then do to her brother as I do to the thief?' Malcolm asked, his question lingering.

Caird knew what he meant. When either of them found the thief, there would be no letting him go this time. And it wouldn't necessarily be in the heat of the battle, but in cold blood.

He did not doubt his brother could do it. Malcolm had lost once and as a result had never been the same. Oh, he laughed and he enjoyed, but his grief was like an ice shard next to his heart forbidding it from ever thawing.

He masked it well, but it made him lethal. His brother could kill in cold blood. Could Caird do the same to Mairead's brother?

'I will find the truth,' he said enigmatically. He could give no better answer.

'From Buchanans?' Malcolm scoffed. 'You go to Buchanan land with the Jewel of Kings. What's to prevent them from taking it from you?'

'I will question the brother separate from the clan,' he said. 'I will keep it safe until we talk to Bram.'

'I could take it straight to Bram now,' Malcolm replied.

'The jewel is too powerful; we need answers to know how to proceed before we address him.'

'Why not separate the dagger from the jewel? You take one, I the other.'

'I cannot know if the dagger is somehow tied to the jewel. I may need both to discover the truth.'

'Answers. Which is why you won't let Mairead go,' Malcolm said, not a question but a fact. 'It never occurred to you to give it to me, did it?'

Caird remained silent. He couldn't give it to his brother without knowing more about the jewel. He'd never knowingly risk his brother like that again.

Malcolm grunted at Caird's silence. 'I won't give my blessing with this, but I'll do what you ask. If only to give you time to come to your senses.' He turned back to his horse to feel along its sides. 'I'm assuming you want this done without the Grahams' knowledge.'

'It is necessary.'

'What if the thief is not at the games?'

Caird relished the thought of seeing the thief again. 'It makes nae sense he'd be elsewhere.' The thief had been at the inn where they'd started celebrating; he had to know where they were headed.

He heard the sound of sticks breaking as Mairead entered the campsite. Her hair was loose, untamed, and a leaf stuck to one tendril.

Mairead was just as wild. Just as impulsive. He wondered how she'd respond when she discovered she'd only be travelling with him.

Want coiled too easily in his loins at the thought. He hoped for her sake he found the thief. There was too much responsibility, too much lust and he had nothing but a Buchanan, with hair and curves that taunted him.

He forced his eyes to return to his brother. 'A fortnight,' he ground out. 'Nae more.'

# *Chapter Twelve*

Worse and worse and more and more mistakes. The hornets buried in her body swarmed as Mairead rode with Caird. She'd given him everything he wanted, the truth or at least what he needed to know, the gem, everything. She negotiated, begged, for him to release her. Exactly want he wanted since he couldn't stand touching her.

But that's exactly what he did as he rode with her, alone, heading towards her clan. Touching, forever touching. A loose lock of his hair against her cheek, his breath against her neck. Even his clean scent seemed to touch her. It was so intoxicating, she wanted to lean against him and inhale it.

Still they rode over the rough terrain. The tall summer grasses hid the dips and crevices Caird tried to avoid. Hours they travelled. So when his broad legs tightened and swayed, she felt him controlling the great horse as if she was the very beast. When his hands tugged the reins, she felt his arms' movements as if he was guiding her home as well.

Home to a clan that would ransom a Colquhoun without question. All to get answers that didn't exist.

Because of that, she knew Caird wouldn't leave her alone. The hornets swarming made her nauseous and she was no closer to a resolution.

It had been a mistake to believe he'd let her go.

She should have trusted her instinct when he'd left to talk to Malcolm. If she had, she'd have gone into the woods and not returned.

Yet, like a baby deer, she had skipped back to the campsite, only to be caught in Caird's trap.

He wasn't going to the games; he was taking her home.

She didn't understand. He had insisted on going to the games. Of course, at that time, he had believed she would be going with him. No, that was being too generous with him. He had made plans and he had changed them. Ultimately, she had no argument against him taking her home. Nothing.

So Caird took her home. Home to a brother who was no longer there. With his continual arrogance and superiority, she knew Caird didn't deserve to know of her brother's death. A part of her thrilled at the fact the journey would be wasted for him. That she now used him to get her safely and quickly to her family.

But that still didn't change the fact something else was going on.

'I want to get off this horse,' she said. Her limbs were beginning to numb.

He ignored her just as he had dismissed her requests before. She could do nothing. So as not to backtrack, they were travelling towards Buchanan lands, not near the inn, but directly south.

Travelling this way meant crossing the streams and river that riddled this entire length of land. There had been much rain this summer making the river full and causing dangerous flood plains.

'I can see from here that the stream up ahead is full,' she said instead. 'How are we to cross?'

Silence as wide as the loch separating their clans.

Anger stung her eyes. She hated to feel helpless. She hated to be trapped and not understand why.

For his abduction wasn't about arrogance, or pride or any Colquhoun trait she could fight against. The brothers held a secret. An important secret. That was why the Colquhouns had separated. They might not know everything about the dagger and gem, but they knew more than she did.

All she knew was the dagger was dangerous. Her brother had died trying to sell it and Caird had kidnapped her because she said it was her brother's.

'It's the gem and dagger, isn't it? It's why you won't let me go,' she said.

She felt him become alert, but he did not respond. 'Since you've kidnapped me, you should tell me what is happening.'

She knew she was but a mere pawn in whatever game was being played. Her only regret was that her brother had found out too late. 'You think the dagger doesn't belong to me, but you think you know who it does belong to.'

Nothing from the silent Colquhoun and it frustrated her that she couldn't see his reaction. But she heard the light tapping of his teeth as if he wanted to say something, yet kept his jaw tight to prevent any sound.

'Even if you won't tell me, I know the gem is costly, that men fight over it, that it has some great importance.'

'We'll need shelter after the streams,' he answered.

The hornets began to sting. 'You talk of weather?' she said, barely understanding her own words through her clenched teeth.

'There are dark clouds on our left,' he replied.

'I want to get off this horse. Now. Or I'll jump.'

He flexed his left thumb, letting her know exactly how he felt, but he slowed the horse. It wasn't fast enough for her.

Frustration like she'd never known flashed through her at the delay and at the tiny movements he made until they fully stopped. Anger flared when he waited for her to dismount first. A reminder of when she'd kicked him and run free.

She loathed his control, his arrogance, his secrets, and she hated her body for not caring. Her desiring him made her angrier still.

Untangling herself, she jumped to the ground and waited.

When he dismounted, she reared back and hit him for all she was worth.

# Chapter Thirteen

Caird grabbed her fist, realising she aimed much lower than his stomach. But by securing her fist, he put his face directly in the aim of her second swing. The blow to his jaw was swift, with just enough force to make him angry.

Very angry.

Holding both her fists in his hands, he pinned them to his side to stop her struggling. He was quick with his leg, wrapping it around her own just as she tried to kick.

She pulled against his two holds, her body precariously bowed. If he let go, she'd fall to the ground. With the sharp rocks and sodden ground at their feet, he was tempted.

'Let me go!' Her dark eyes glared at him with a malevolence that only mimicked his own anger.

'Elbows, now fists?' he scorned. 'Did you think that through, or were you just improvising again?'

She pulled at her legs, trying to free them from

his own. 'Ach, I thought much worse, Colquhoun.' Suddenly pivoting towards him, she rammed her elbow into his stomach.

The reverberations in his ribs seared through him.

'Impulsive female!' Tightening and adjusting his hold, he straightened to his full height. She fell against him with a sound. 'Doona you know how to think first?'

He wrapped her fully in his embrace. She moved still, but she couldn't gain any purchase. When she stopped struggling, he just checked his smile at her defeat. Some of his anger dimmed. Some, but not all.

His ribs ached with her against him. They were already paining him because the horse seemed keen on finding every bit of uneven ground. Her elbow's jab had almost forced him to release her.

'Let me go!' she demanded.

When he didn't reply, Mairead looked at him. Her dark eyes were wild, but there was something else there now. It was swift, fleeting, but he saw her fear. Good. She should fear him. Something flitted through his chest, but he ignored it.

'You cannot keep me here for ever,' she said.

He quirked one eyebrow. True, but he could do it just long enough until she realised the error of her actions.

'Ach!' She tried to pull away, but he only wrapped his arms tighter around her, and forced her even closer. 'You are the most stubborn, arrogant, overbearing man I've ever met.'

'Aye.'

'Aye?' she said. 'That's all you can say?'

He shrugged. Out of all his brothers, he was the most in control. His need for answers and adherence to rules almost an obsession. As a result, he was respected and he intended to keep it that way.

Mairead exhaled. It was a breath too full of wrath and frustration to be one of defeat, but that slight release relaxed her more fully against him. Her head now rested against his torso, her cheek on his sore ribs.

He knew this wasn't a reprieve; there would be no reprieve. Neither from her, nor from his body.

He held her again and his need for her was torture.

She was small and yet generous of frame. His hold prevented her from doing him any more damage, but it also pressed her to him just as she had been at the inn. He was fully, painfully, aware that he wasn't drunk now and there would be no stumbling to break their hold.

He could hold her firm now. He *burned* to hold her firm.

Especially since the soft strands of her taunting hair wrapped so sweetly around his arms and hands, her full breasts flattened against his torso and her lithe legs were pinned against his own. But he was acutely aware of holding her hands at his hip. He could so easily move them lower and just stopped himself from doing so.

They fought, she was a traitorous liar and he was almost shaking with need. He shifted just enough to avoid her obvious effect on him.

He had the Jewel of Kings and was committing treason. Yet this one woman pressed against him was enough that he forgot all else.

This woman, this *Buchanan* upended everything. He couldn't allow it while the jewel was exposed.

There had to be a reason it surfaced now and he meant to find that reason. Whether he could believe her brother or not, he was yet another link to this mystery. As long as they travelled, they could still find the thief.

But he was aching and wanting. Mairead leaned against him and he longed to pull her to him until his ribs killed him.

'Why are you taking me home?' she asked, her voice almost tentative.

Instantly suspicious of her soft voice, he replied, 'You didn't want to go to the games.'

'That's not the reason you're taking me home.'

'To talk to your brother.'

'But that's not the reason you're taking me to my family,' she repeated.

'It's the reason,' he growled, his tone indicating it was the end of the conversation.

Ignoring this, she turned her head to look up

at him. 'Maybe, but not the reason you gave up on the celebrations. Not the reason you sent Malcolm there instead.'

'The thief is free. It isn't safe.'

'You care not for my safety. It's the dagger and gem.'

'Doesn't matter what you think. It's not yours,' he said.

'Because I'm Buchanan?' she said. It was a statement rather than a question.

'Aye, because you're Buchanan.' He couldn't carry on holding her like this. She could swing all she wanted, but he had to let her go. Releasing her hands and legs, he stepped away. He would be prepared for her now. 'Because your kind lies. You're nothing but deceit and dishonour.'

She stumbled in her gown before straightening to her full height.

'Ach, and it's because you've met every one of us? Or maybe you doona need to because you're an all-knowing Colquhoun!'

'History and meeting you have been enough to know your kind.'

'Meeting me?' She stepped away from him, her foot landing in a puddle, her body vibrating with annoyance. 'How have I shown dishonour? When did I deceive?'

'What haven't you done?' He felt like roaring; his mind tried and failed to keep rational. To keep quiet as he had always done to maintain control.

'Stealing into my room like a thief, lying about the reason, lying about ownership. Deceiving my cousins the next morning.'

If she looked confused before, she looked dumbfounded at his confession.

'Deceiving?' Her free hand clenched in a fist.

He eyed her fist, but knew it was the second swing he'd have to watch more closely.

'What has been wrong with my deceit? You used my deceit when it was convenient for you. So I would say it's *our* deceit.'

'Nae mine,' he replied, wanting this conversation done.

'Ach! So that's how all Colquhouns are. Pious in their belief they are above a few tall tales.'

'We are above tales,' he said. 'Unlike Buchanans.'

'What have I ever done to you?'

'Nothing,' he repeated. 'And I'll not give you a chance to.'

She waved her arm in front of her. 'I doona ken any of this…this…madness,' she said, her voice rising. 'Our clans fight, aye, but why this hatred?' She pointed at him. 'You're not going to explain, are you?' She spun around. 'Not. Going. To. Even. React!'

Something began to seethe within him. He'd trained himself to not express emotions, he'd become skilled in listening and not speaking, but this? This was rage and every hair on his body bristled with it. Not react? He was about to explode.

Facing him, Mairead stood almost on her toes. If he felt rage, barely checked, her emotion was right there along with his.

With fingers taut, she pointed to him. 'You continued to use my deceit on the stairs, which I fully admit I created, to distract our audience from—'

'The dagger,' he interrupted, the words just tumbling out of him. His rage wouldn't let him hold the words back. 'Which you also lied about and continue to lie about. You cannot be trusted.'

'Who's deceitful now?' she replied. 'When words flow out of your mouth with ease. I doona think you're the quiet one, but the cunning one.'

'Enough,' he growled, when he realised she was right. He was saying too much. To a Buchanan. Now, when lust assailed and anger lashed him with every breath he took. He needed control and was relinquishing it all to her.

'Enough!' She smiled as if he'd just given her a bow and arrow to point at him. 'Enough! What a convenient word for you, but not for me. A Buchanan, who begged to be done with this. You have nae right to enough, when it was you who continued it. Now you're stuck with this, as you are with me.'

'I return you and we end this.'

She pulled herself up, her eyes narrowing, her anger reining in and becoming more powerful. He could see it. Feel it. 'This won't end when we reach my home. I doona believe you. I, a duplicitous Buchanan, can tell an arrogant Colquhoun lie. Again! You believe yourself so high and mighty, but you know what you have? False honour!'

His rage flared and he stepped towards her. 'I could kill you for those words,' he said low, steady, so she would understand every word.

She smirked. 'Nae, you wouldn't. Not when you need your precious answers.' She shook her head. 'I doona ken you. We travel a great distance, soon we will risk our lives to cross turbulent waters, all to find answers.' She raised her hand to stop him from interrupting. 'If you're so wise, so bent on obtaining knowledge, why haven't you asked for facts from me? What could I say to make you believe me?'

'Nothing.'

'Then set me free.'

'Not until I see your brother.'

Her eyes widened again. Her mouth opened, then shut. Trembling, she spun around so he couldn't see her face. When she turned around, he was unprepared for the look on her face, unprepared for the emotions in her eyes. He recognised that tortured look.

He looked away. His lust he could barely control, but he didn't want to feel other emotions for her as well. He took the few steps to his wandering horse and grabbed its bridle.

'Understand me, Buchanan,' he said, looking at her again and seeing nothing in her dark eyes. 'I will have answers whether you, your brother or the devil give them to me. We'll cross these waters and until then, I'll talk nae more about this.'

She pointed to the wide stream before them. It was breaking its banks and now flowing almost to their feet. 'How are we to cross?'

'Straight through,' he replied through gritted teeth. This journey couldn't end soon enough.

## Chapter Fourteen

'You sit too close to the fire,' Caird said. Mairead jumped, her hand fluttering closer to the flames before she pulled it back, but she didn't scramble to a safer distance.

'Not close enough,' she retorted, her teeth chattering. 'And the sun is going down.'

'Aye,' he said, walking to the fire to balance their food there. The few hares he'd found were meagre, but it was better than nothing. He was starving and he knew she must be as well.

It had taken longer than expected to cross the swollen streams. Fortunately, they had not been deep, barely reaching the horse's knees, but the splashing water had soaked her gown.

He had remained mostly dry and searched for food. Now he could see he shouldn't have left her here.

'You need to be out of that gown,' he said.

She snorted, thrusting her hands towards the flames again.

Her movements pressed her breasts even more tightly against the strained fabric.

Suddenly fumbling with the hares, he forced his hands to steady the rope over the flames. So easily she affected him. He had been long without a woman, but this went beyond anything in his experience. He felt like an untried lad.

Especially now. Whilst he'd been gone, she had loosely plaited the front of her hair, enough to take its length out of her face, but it framed her, like an unruly halo. He could so easily gaze at the arch of her eyebrows, or the way her lashes cast shadows over her cheeks.

But it was her skin glowing warmly that captivated him. Her pale skin beckoned to be touched. Like the finest of cloth, just as soft, just as smooth.

Flexing his thumb that felt suddenly taut, he knew he couldn't stand here any more. One more moment and he'd be spouting poetry to her beauty. He forced his hands to work faster until he was free to leave the meat cooking.

'I'll need to wash,' he said after he was done.

She looked beyond him, at the streams they had just crossed. 'Wasn't it wet enough?'

'I didn't get wet,' he said.

She frowned, no doubt irritated by his smug comment. 'And the horse?'

The animal had seemed out of sorts. Since

there was no harm he could see, it was probably suffering from something it had eaten. It might be serious and he had to keep watch on it.

'I'll see to it,' he replied.

'Like you do everything else?'

He crossed his arms. She was angry. Still. 'I'm returning you home,' he replied.

'That's not all you're doing, Colquhoun.'

She sat before him, her lips trembling from the cold, but her eyes glittered. Their depths flashed a fire more bright than the flames she sat next to. He didn't feel like an untried lad before her now. His desire for her changed and became more dangerous.

At his continued silence, her frown deepened as her ire increased. It was almost his undoing. Lust's talons that had been whispering across his skin sunk deep. He was instantly hard and wanting.

Turning abruptly, he hoped the water was as cold as Mairead said it was.

Caird hadn't returned. It wasn't dark yet, not at this time of year, but the fading light cast everything around them in orange and yellow. It was getting late.

Mairead had eventually undressed and hung her gown nearby. The spare blanket covered her enough, even though it pained her hand to clasp it to her.

Hours had elapsed since she'd struck Caird and

her left hand still hurt. She had never hit another person; there never had been a need to. At the time, it had felt...necessary.

Of course, she hadn't thought of the consequences, or how he would retaliate.

Holding her against him until she couldn't move. She had struck him, he was an enemy and yet he had only captured her hands.

It hadn't made sense. Not when she thought of his words, which so clearly revealed his revulsion of her.

And then there had been a moment, when she had stopped struggling...she could swear... She shook her head. There were too many questions already; she didn't need to add imaginings to this forced journey, but she couldn't still her errant thoughts. They compelled her to try to understand.

A laugh or something closer to desperation bubbled inside her. Maybe she and Caird had more in common than she thought. Now it was she who wanted answers.

She'd never needed answers before; when she had felt, she acted. If there were consequences, she dealt with them afterwards. She'd always just...done.

But Caird wouldn't let her be, wouldn't give her freedom. He forced her to be reflective, forced her to sit here, wet, ragged, when all she wanted was to end this torment.

Her nightmare. What would happen when she returned to her mother and sisters? Even if they were relieved to see her, it wouldn't be for long. They'd have too many questions and she'd have to answer all of them. Truthfully. The laird would demand it when the English came for the silver. She'd have to prepare her family. Tell them about Ailbert's debt, the dagger and how she'd begged him to sell it.

Her nightmare, her grief and it was unavoidable. She clutched the blanket tighter and looked around, desperate for some diversion from her thoughts. If she had only listened to Ailbert's caution, if only she had *waited*. He'd be alive.

She took in a ragged breath, and another. She felt cowardly for looking for a distraction. She didn't deserve one.

Waiting, she remained trapped with her thoughts.

The sun was dimming when Caird approached the hill. His movements were rhythmic, and full of a warrior's grace.

She blinked once, and again. He was naked from the waist up and wasn't wearing his braies, leggings, tunic or bandages which were all wrapped loosely around one arm. He wore... breeches. Wet, sheer breeches.

They barely covered the mass of muscle which moved fluidly as he took the slight incline towards her. The hill flexed his thigh muscles, the movement rippling up his torso. Every masculine indentation of him was outlined, and the lack of spare flesh flaunted his strength and power.

Strength and power which he had used to hold her. Mairead released a shaky breath and pushed a lock of hair out of her face. So easily her body warmed to his. It reminded her she needed to be free, to stop questioning things she couldn't control.

She would be home soon. Relief tried to rest inside her, but she was in too much turmoil to let it settle. The closer she got to home, the less she could avoid her brother's death. Her brother would never return home. Grief's claws that had been gripping inside her began to pierce.

Caird continued towards her.

Her eyes absorbed the rivulets of water running down his chest and arms. The glistening of droplets which highlighted the thin trail of hair that ran straight down his stomach.

The breeches surprised her. Even from here, she could see they were different than the braies he'd worn previously. These were held up by a cord that swung as he walked. They were made not of wool, but of the finest linen. There was no doubt they were English remnants and yet, on him, they changed. He'd distressed them. Stretched the fabric until it merely outlined his body.

He continued up the hill and stopped. Corded muscles rippled across his torso and she noted the flexing of his arms and arcing of his back as he thrust his heavy garments above his head to hang them from a tree.

He was a strong and lethal warrior. Scars from old wounds were healed into the landscape of his skin. But it was these dangerous patches her rebellious side wanted to touch the most.

She yearned to touch him. A Colquhoun, who didn't believe her.

It bothered her that he didn't believe her and it bothered her more because he was right. She was lying to him still. Her brother was dead. The journey they took was useless for him. It got her where she wanted to be without having to risk her ankle. After the kidnapping, she thought she deserved that much.

She tugged the blanket's corner that suddenly seemed constricting. She did deserve it. She repeatedly told him to leave her alone. It was his folly he took her on this pointless journey.

She clutched at her anger, tried to wrap herself in it as Caird bent to retrieve the small blade from his boots. His still-damp hair fluttered across his naked shoulders like a caress, like her hands wanted to do. But she didn't want to touch as gently as his fallen hair. She wanted to press her palms and sink her fingers into his skin.

How could she feel this way? Overflowing with bewildering and conflicting emotions. Why did *he* make her feel this way? She welcomed the hornets awakening inside her again.

He straightened and looked over his shoulder. She didn't look away soon enough.

So she watched every aching change in him. The surprise darkening his eyes, the sudden tightening of his body. The look of a great beast before a kill. Elemental.

He uncoiled and slowly faced her. His movements were precise and predatory. His chest expanded as if he, too, held his breath.

Blushing, she held still, her body responding to whatever question lingered in his. He released his breath, and his blade fell to his feet as he took the few steps to stand before her.

His presence relieved and escalated the tension in her body. All at once, her nipples hardened. Between her legs she felt a liquid heaviness she'd only ever felt with him.

Even as she fought it, her body readied for him, but he did not bend to touch her.

He stood. Yet she felt the heat of his body, the humming vibrations of his want and need. Her lips parted, her normal breathing no longer possible and she felt her hands loosening on her covering.

His cycs caressed her face, followed the exposed, delicate skin of her neck and shoulders. Then he paused as if bracing himself, before his eyes heatedly traced up her bare arms to the loosening blanket that revealed more to his eyes.

'You sit too close to the fire, Buchanan.'

He was warning her. He had caught her staring

at him and he stood close. So close she felt the desire from him. She hadn't been wrong. When she had hit him, when he held her, desire had been there, but also anger. Just as now. It rolled off of him. He desired her, but didn't want to.

Shame enveloped her. Only a fool would continue this. She was so close to home and it was almost over.

But she didn't care; she couldn't take this any more. Her body craved, when she needed to be *grieving*. Grief's claws no longer pierced, they slashed her from the inside. She needed to be holding her mother and sisters. Not feeling this madness.

She was raw from holding back and she refused to cry in front of him. Grief. Lust. One of the emotions had to go. The hornets swarmed, stung, insisted.

She stood.

If possible, his eyes narrowed even more and his breathing changed at his surprise. 'You stood?' he said, taking a step closer to her.

'Aye,' she replied, waiting for him to take another step, but he didn't.

So she did. The smallest step, feeling his heat, his breath, but no further.

She had never done this before, and, as bold as she'd been with him, there was much she didn't know. Knowledge that he might expect from her.

She had kissed him like a wanton, stood before him like a wanton. But she knew nothing.

'You're angry still,' he said, his voice rough.

'Aye.' She was angry. Angry at his arrogance, at his assumption that no matter what he wanted, she would just follow. Angry at herself because so far she *had* just followed. Even when she tried to defy him, he changed everything and made her powerless. She didn't like it.

'But you still stand,' he answered.

She stood because the hornets inside her demanded she have some power over him.

His wet hair framed his jaw and curled around his shoulders. His eyes, rimmed with black, swirled grey and green. Despite the emotions he could not hide in his eyes, he held almost unnaturally still. Why didn't he entice and kiss her like he did at the inn?

She might have been able to forget the kiss they had shared and the urgency of his hands. But not when she rode with him. Not when he'd chased after her. Not when he was constantly touching her.

Grief. Want. She was going to break; she didn't *want* to break.

'Reckless Buchanan,' he growled. His body looked as taut as hers felt, but his hands remained at his sides.

Was he waiting for her acceptance of him?

She would never accept him. She just wanted this over with.

'The arrogant Colquhoun won't just take?' she mocked, her voice husky and sounding strange to her.

His body coiled, as if ready to spring. Still he did not move to touch her.

Then his left thumb flexed. She knew that movement and she was pleased he wasn't as in control as he appeared.

She stepped closer, their bodies now touching with every breath, her trembling thighs flickering against his more steady ones.

'Why won't you just take!' she said, her frustration mounting. 'That's all you've been doing! You've kidnapped me, kept me from my home, wouldn't return the dagger though I begged—'

'Impulsive woman!' he interrupted. His actions were so quick that she didn't see his hands thrust into her hair. All she felt was the sudden restrained cradling of her head, his fingers tangling in her hair, his thumbs moving and making her feel fragile against his strength.

'You want me to take?' His fingers tightened, and she felt his anger and desire. In his warrior's hands, he cradled her head. So easy to kiss, so easy to kill. And his words had a bite.

'Aye,' she answered, because there was no other answer.

When he lowered his head, she raised hers, craving his kiss, the pressure, the heat.

Instead, his fingers grew gentle as he tilted her head, his lips lingered at her temple and along her jaw.

Heat from his desire and fear at his anger brushed her skin. Turmoil kept her still when his breath whispered across her waiting lips.

But he didn't touch them. Instead, he angled her cheek in his palm, exposing her chin, her neck, as his fingers caressed, his breath fanned, his lips hovered.

He did not ease his touch. She felt the power there, the intent, but his hold wasn't enough to release her anger or her grief. The hornets inside her buzzed. She wasn't standing for gentleness. She was going to break with his soft caresses weakening her anger.

'Aye,' she repeated more firmly, sure that he hadn't heard her, that he teased not out of cruelty, but out of misunderstanding.

For a moment, he held his breath, and then with uncoordinated fingers he removed his hands from her hair. But he didn't release his eyes from the dishevelled strands; it was as if he, too, was dumbfounded he relinquished them.

By letting go, he made the longing more intense. She growled in frustration. 'You doona want me,' she said, her voice no longer hers.

His eyes, grey swirling with green, locked with

hers. She couldn't read his thoughts and he did not answer.

'You resent me,' she offered him instead.

She tried to comprehend his resentment, but couldn't. Because what she felt was so much more. Anger at his kidnapping, at him keeping her away from her family and the only financial means they had to at least ease the humiliation they would incur.

'You do not know what you ask,' he said.

His words were meant to rebuff her, but he stood so close the words touched her. The conflicting acts sent shivers across her skin.

He released a breath; the swirling of his eyes stilled. His expression was resigned.

'I kissed you at the inn, Mairead,' he said. 'Felt the softness of your lips, your response to my tongue, my intent. Your skin heated beneath my hands, your heart fluttered. You lit up against me with every caress I gave you and I burned. When you fled me, I *followed*.'

His words, the remembrance of his urgent hands, flared heat inside her.

'You responded,' he said accusingly. 'And my body will not let me forget.' He stepped back, almost shuddering on his exhale. 'But I will not take.'

## Chapter Fifteen

The ride the next morning was quiet.

For the first time, Caird hated the silence. It punished him, just as the woman in his arms did. Mairead kept her silence when they woke, kept it as they prepared the horse and started again on this cursed journey. But her silence wasn't full of defiance like before. Now she sat stiffly away from him, her back straight not from ire or frustration, but out of sheer need not to touch him.

Confusing, contrary, maddening woman.

He'd gone to the streams to bathe in the cold water. His clothes had got wet and he'd pulled on the linen breeches to sleep because he required their restriction. Only when he had thought he could control his need for her did he return.

Then like some dream she was there, watching him. The fire behind her highlighting and brightening her dark curling locks until they looked part of the fire.

She had been wrapped in a blanket, but her shoulders were bared to him. Uncovered, the fire accentuated every creamy curve of her skin.

Then despite the wait, the icy water and the breeches, he knew he hadn't gained control. It was neither her uncovered shoulders nor the bared tops of her breasts that made him realise it. What caused his breath to catch and his blood to pool was what she revealed in her eyes: her need for him.

Instantly, he had fought his reaction, but still he walked closer to her. Sure that at any moment she'd turn her back and avert her eyes.

But she didn't and he wanted more and fought more. Because what she needed could not happen.

He couldn't allow the distraction, he couldn't allow the trust, couldn't allow any weakness. Because if she was treacherous and only wanted the jewel, then he was a lustful fool and all of Scotland would weep at Clan Colquhoun.

When she stood, she was just as glorious as all his imaginings and more. Then she demanded that he take.

A Colquhoun from a Buchanan.

No, it wasn't the clans' differences that had stopped him last night. Even he could admit to that. It was the jewel. A good reason.

But his body gave naught for reason.

So he resented her and wanted her and they

rode in silence. He felt like a man heading to the gallows.

The horse gave a shudder and he welcomed the interruption to his thoughts.

'We have to alight,' he said.

She waited until he dismounted so she could, too. Then they moved quickly away from the animal.

This wasn't the first time they'd stopped since they had woken and he doubted it would be the last. The horse had definitely eaten something it shouldn't.

With another shudder, it cleared its bowels again. Given that it hadn't eaten, Caird was surprised how much came out of it.

'We can't ride it again,' she said. It wasn't a question.

'Nae,' he answered. 'Your ankle?'

She flexed her foot. 'It doesn't hurt.' She pointed to the horse. 'Is there something we could give it?'

'Mint.' But Caird hadn't seen any. 'We'll need to walk.'

This journey would take days. It hadn't rained last night, but he knew it would and soon. The clouds that had started darkening yesterday now hung heavy over them. They were wet just from the mist alone, but that wasn't what worried him.

There had been too much rain over the last sennight and ahead there was a river surrounded by plains. He could only hope the river hadn't broken its banks.

The plains were worse than he imagined. He'd known they were getting close to the river as dense trees turned to open meadows and rockier soil.

He'd thought they would travel a bit more, but even from here he could see the river had broken its banks and flooded the plains. It raged with every wild emotion he wanted to express himself. Shrubs and trees were half-drowned beneath the rapidly flowing water that curved and carved its own way forwards.

This was Scotland. And it reminded him that along with its beauty, the land demanded freedom with force and persistence.

The horse still hadn't eaten, but had been settling to their pace and looked no worse. He hoped it would have the strength to make it. He and Mairead would need their strength as well.

The water was nigh impassable, but the jewel pressed heavily against him as it, too, demanded its freedom. If they travelled further east, as he and Malcolm had done to reach the inn, he knew it would be a safer crossing. However, they'd lose another day, maybe two. There was also no telling what further danger they would come across.

No, it wasn't an enemy making him reckless and taking away his control.

He glanced over at Mairead, relieved she wasn't looking at him.

Since they started walking, she'd stolen furtive, frequent glances to assess him. He practically felt her questions and the conclusions she came to. The closer they got to her home, he could see her emotions change. Anger, resolve, her dogged persistence and determination.

In those moments before she turned her face away, before she hid her emotions from him, he saw something wild, exposed. That same tortured look she'd given him before she'd kicked him in the stomach and taken his horse.

He raced after her then. Now, when he saw that expression again, he could barely stop his feet from taking him closer to her. To hold her, to comfort her. But he was no fool. Even he knew it wouldn't end there.

He couldn't go through another night like the last. Hard, aching, letting her sleep, while he stole away, the restriction of his breeches no deterrent to what he needed to do. But it hadn't been enough.

If she demanded again for him to take her, he wouldn't be able to stop himself.

So he was foolish. Rushing the journey and risking their lives. He knew there would be shallower sections of the flood. Unfortunately, the water covered most of the landmarks, and Caird could only guess this section would provide a safer passage. His guessing was only another risk.

'There's too much water here,' Mairead said.

'Didn't you come across some when you came to the inn?'

'Nothing like this and there was a bridge of sorts. This water here's too high.'

'We won't go around it,' he answered.

'Do you mean to do this?' she asked, a tension in her voice. He had never heard such a tone before. She was more than worried. She was terrified.

'Aye.'

'There's a dead deer over there!'

The dark clouds overhead had left the deer in shadows. Still, she had seen it, bloated, its head buried in the turgid water.

'Wouldn't happen to us.' There was no hope for her fear.

He pulled the reins to the left and the horse shied before Caird had him going forward again.

Crossing here would work. In truth, the river was better with broken banks. The water slowed as it spread shallowly over the land. It would give the horse time to become used to the water.

'It's nae more than five men's length of swimming,' he added, to quell her fear. He knew it was a paltry comfort. Five men's length of swimming, aye, but he had a sick horse, Mairead with a hurt ankle and he with sore ribs he'd hastily re-wrapped. 'You can ride the horse.'

She stopped walking, forcing him to look at her. He'd avoided looking directly at her since they'd woken.

'Can it carry me?' she asked.

He nodded. Another guess, but there was no choice. With Mairead on the horse, she would make it across. If they started to go down, if the water got too deep, he would simply let go. The only loss would be him.

And the jewel. But maybe that wouldn't be such a loss. It could go back to being a legend, become a beacon of hope again. Better a legend than to be captured by the English. To be used—

No. He wasn't thinking rationally. He needed the journey to end, the mystery of the jewel to be solved.

When they had got as close as they could, he halted the horse near a boulder for Mairead to use to mount. The boulder was wet and slick with lichen. He would have to help her.

She quietly approached him and he chanced a look at her. It wasn't her fear keeping her quiet. There was a light in her eyes.

'You're looking forward to this?' he said, unable to hold the words back.

She shrugged and took his hand. 'What if I am? I'm almost home.'

'Can you swim?' He lifted her until she was

mounted. Only when she'd settled, did he let go of her hand.

Her mouth curved, not out of embarrassment, but out of daring. 'You care for my safety?'

He ignored her and tied his cloak and the pouch carrying the dagger and jewel to the horse. She watched him, but he did not raise his eyes to her. At least now, if he did drown, the jewel would not be lost.

Adjusting the damp hem of her gown, she asked, 'I know you would not go to all this trouble to be rid of me here.'

He frowned, unable to answer her. She confused him. She was scared, couldn't swim and she now teased him? What questions and conclusions had she reached while they walked?

Certainly different conclusions than his own, which had seized on only one emotion since yesterday: desire. Even now, when they could drown, he wanted her. He craved to just touch her hand again.

Refusing to answer her, he looked the horse in the eye. Gently, but steadily he brought it to the water's edge. He was in control now.

'Would you, Colquhoun?' she demanded of him.

He glanced heavenward for patience. The cloud cover made it darker than usual for late afternoon. It would rain and soon. The water would only get deeper.

'Brace yourself,' he ordered, leaning forward. The water was cold, unforgiving, stronger than he was expecting, but no deterrent. He kept moving steadily forward. The horse trusted him and did not shy.

'What for?' she called out.

Exasperating female.

When he felt the sharp incline, he widened his stance as water rushed over his chest. Despite her bold words, he saw her tighten her grip on the saddle.

Wrapping the reins tighter around his wrist, he pushed away and stroked hard to get the horse off the bank. Immediately, water battered them, hard, fast. He lost direction more than once, but he kept his focus on the far bank. The horse jerked, pulling him under, but he couldn't look back; his entire being was focused on getting them to the other side.

They were close.

He felt a sharp pain as his shin smacked against a boulder; he tugged to the left to get the horse around it. He pulled again, the leather biting into his hand and wrist just as the horse found purchase. Trying to avoid getting trampled, he loosened the reins to increase the space between them. They were safe.

And then Mairead disappeared.

Just as he turned around, he saw a slender foot as she upended into the water. Never taking his eyes from her, he tugged at the reins wrapped around his wrist, but the wet leather wouldn't give.

She slipped further away, the weight of her gown pulling her under. Furiously he fought the reins that cut deep into his bleeding wrist until he was free. Slapping the horse to the shore, he dived.

Nothing.

Coming up for air, he saw her head bobbing up. She was sputtering, fighting the water and already out of his reach. The fierce current would keep them apart. He'd never catch her this way because there was no log or branch to find purchase and bridge the gap.

His heart lurched as she went under again.

Swimming to the shore, he ran along the broken bank. The water slowed him, but he began to gain ground, overtaking her until he pushed into the deep water again.

Closer!

He stretched his strokes towards her. Her hands reached for his, the erratic current twisting them away until he caught her and pulled her closer to him.

'Kick!' he ordered as he dragged her to shore.

Finally, land beneath his feet, water becoming shallow. When he could, he let go of her and fell on his back. She flopped down next to him.

Searing pain in his side restricted his breathing. His ribs weren't broken, or he'd be dead. He was very much alive and his body made certain he knew it.

He felt throbbing in his leg from the boulder and hundreds of abrasions stinging across his skin. Roaring in his ears; lungs desperately filling loudly with air. His heart not quite comprehending, thundering in his chest. Alive.

The water had been like ice shards battering him. His push off the bank, his faltering, knowing too late he entered deep waters. His ribs, loosely re-bandaged, restricting movement. The strong water sweeping his bandages away.

Then making it to the bank, the flutter of relief, only to turn and see Mairead disappear. Swallowed by the same water that had tried to seize his life.

But he had reached her, pulled her here. They were alive.

His heart comprehended, eased and then he heard it. Laughter. Sputtering, choking gasps. Great bursts of unbridled sound.

Mairead in shock.

His tunic twisted as he rolled on to his side. Mairead lay next to him with clenched eyes, and skin mottled from cold and lack of air. Her sodden hair clung to her cheeks and forehead.

When she opened her eyes, he saw that recklessness, excitement and laughter all danced inside her.

'Oh, you almost killed me!' she gasped between her lost breaths.

He knew other emotions tainted her laughter: hysteria, fear, the same incomprehension he felt that they were alive. But she laughed and it was lightning to him. Alive.

He raised himself up and placed his head on his bent arm.

Her tight yellow gown, now sodden and torn, threatened to burst. The bright fabric outlined her body's peaks and shadows, and exposed every facet of her ample yet petite frame.

Her right arm was carelessly thrown above her head, her left lay by her side and near his. He didn't need his hands to know where her breasts swelled, her stomach curved or her legs dipped. He hungrily saw it all.

A question entered her eyes. 'You had the dagger.'

The dagger, inside the pouch and strapped to the horse along with his cloak, was now further up the shore. Not here, poised on a cliff as he knew he was.

'Are you hurt?' he asked, peering into the chasm of her eyes. He felt suspended as if his feet had already stepped off the edge and his mind hadn't caught up.

She stopped laughing, her dancing eyes watching him.

'Have you come to harm?' he asked, anticipation lacing his words.

Tangled in her gown, her legs were unknowingly open, bent by a resting knee. He knew exactly where her right ankle was, how he could wrap his hand around the slender bone to gently lift and place it across his hip.

Her eyes darted aside, running an internal inventory as she stretched her legs, her arms, unconsciously bowing and arching her body.

'Aye or nae, Mairead.' His voice was urgent. He was going to jump off the cliff and it was imperative he take her with him.

She shook her head, the wet tendrils sliding across her now pale cheeks. Her skin was no longer mottled, but warming with the air she breathed. Very much alive.

'I doona think so,' she answered.

Moving closer, he hovered over her left hand resting beside him, and eased himself until he was acutely, agonisingly, aware of where it touched. As she curled her fingers into the earth, his mind went blank as he imagined her palm raised up instead of down.

'What are you doing?' she asked, her eyes darkening with comprehension despite her words.

'I'm taking.'

# Chapter Sixteen

Caird's eyelashes, spiked from water, framed eyes swirling grey, then green. Eyes darkening with conflicting emotions far more dangerous than the flood. Then Mairead saw nothing as his mouth took hers.

Before, his kisses had coaxed and teased, delighted in the feel of her being with him. Even as his hands firmly caressed with need, he had only given a gentle pressure of his mouth, a faint touch of his tongue.

Now Caird's mouth was pitiless against hers. Taking only, seizing her lips without asking for any response from her. Kisses punishing every word and deed since that night at the inn.

Her sodden gown chafed and abraded. Soil and pebbles prickled against her skin bared from rents in her clothes. Freezing rivulets of water pained as they flowed across her cheeks, her neck and cut down her body. She was cold to her very bones.

Yet she also felt the saturating heat of Caird's body, the warmth of his breath and his hands tracing along her cheeks. Heated flurries from his calloused fingers roamed up and over her ears, down the sides of her neck and back again.

Furious kisses, tender touches.

His lips, wet from the water, slanted over hers and conquered with every touch. Kisses tasting of water, salt, sand. Tasting of *him*.

Her body did the only thing it could: respond.

Her gown, shrunken tight across her back, bound her arms. She could only caress along his shoulders, to the tops of his arms, but her hands flowed along every indent and cord she could reach, every sinew of muscle and bared skin.

Under the weight of her heavy gown and the press of his legs locked rigid with control, she restlessly moved her hips.

But she wanted more and could find no purchase. She was confined and restricted by her gown, and that hurt more than his kisses.

A sound emitted from deep inside his chest, a conflicting growl of anger and approval.

He raised his head and her eyes opened to find him watching her. A flare in those grey-green eyes framed by black. More heat. More cold, as his long darkened hair dripped icy water to her chest. Brow furrowed, breath deepening from need, he whispered, 'Ah, Mairead, your *response*.'

'Now, Colquhoun?' she asked. 'Now will you—?'

'Do you want me still?' he whispered and his lips hovered across her cheeks, and along the delicate shell of her ears.

She gave the only answer she wanted. 'Aye.'

'Then your clothes,' he murmured as his fingers trailed along her bared left arm, the sleeve claimed by the flood, 'they need to be removed.'

His fingers continued, further up, gentle caresses seeking and finding the slash across her chest, moving with such surety until her covered nipples ached.

His mouth returned to hers, his tongue tracing, tiny bites beginning and ending along her lower lip. She gasped at the sharpness felt there and instantly between her legs.

His hands moved across her body, gripping the fabric and trying to move it. His lips and tongue demanding her response, secure in the knowledge he would receive it.

She wanted to give, tried to reach more of him, barely registering the sound of tearing fabric before she could reach no more. He pulled away, even as her fingers sunk deep to keep him close.

'Your clothes!' he cursed. Releasing her hands, he kneeled. His frown was fierce as he fisted her heavy gown, lifting and dropping the fabric pinning her body down. The mist surrounded him, surrounded her like a cold heavy blanket. The air was becoming difficult to breathe with the storm waiting above.

She rose to lean back on her hands.

His eyes searched hers then searched her clothing, looking for an opening through the too-heavy fabric. His white tunic was transparent and stretched; his breeches ripped from the crossing. But his countenance was just as stretched, just as ragged as his clothing, when he gazed at the apex of her thighs. Her gown left no detail unveiled, and her legs were opened causing a sharp dip of fabric.

She ached as he looked, and as his eyes burned heat, she ached more.

Against her bared skin, drops of rain fell from above, tiny pinpoints, warmer than the river, hotter than her icy gown.

Caird cursed; his eyes were wild and unwavering.

More drops of rain, and Caird hurriedly pushed the hem of her gown above her legs to her waist and pulled her on to his lap. The fabric surrounded them, but bared her underneath, where neither of them could see, but she could feel.

Ah, how she felt as Caird's thighs parted her own, and pressed against her. As his hands, supporting her waist, pulled her closer. As she felt what he couldn't hide pressed within the stretch of his breeches. She leaned further into him and gasped.

At her sound his head lowered, his fingers kneaded, his eyes locked between their bodies, as if he coveted to see what she could feel.

Only knowing she needed more, she grabbed his shoulders and pulled closer. 'Oh!'

His head jerked up to watch her response. 'Mairead?' His eyes were swirling chips of need.

Rain fell, stinging her eyes, blurring her vision, making her colder still. She didn't care. She couldn't keep her breath; her body urged her to move again and she did.

His cheekbones sharpened as he pulsed against her. Taking in her every response, he seemed relieved, seemed agonised. 'Not alone on the cliff,' she thought he murmured.

Her breasts pressed against him, her arms stretched above his head. Shifting his thighs beneath her, he clenched her gown, her hips, her bottom, supported her as he now purposely moved her body against his.

His eyes watched hers. Again and again he rocked her and pressure built. Not enough.

'Your arms,' he urged. 'Raise your arms. Clutch my shoulders, pull yourself up. That's it.'

When she tilted forward, his fingers flexed as he pushed her down against him. 'What is—?' she gasped.

Pelting rain drowning out their sounds, their breaths. Smatterings of Caird's words. Cruel rain falling harder, trying to separate them. Caird holding ever tighter to her gown at her hips, keeping her pinned to him, refusing to let the rain win. She could feel his shudders, his need, flexing against her, her own clenching response.

'Mairead, let go,' he pleaded as his eyes demanded.

He lifted her again, tilted, pressed her over him. She shuddered, feeling it, knowing she was almost where he wanted her to go. Her grip on his shoulders loosening, her arms and legs floating, as everything within her tightened. Rain now lashing against her back. His hot grip flexing, again, pressing, again, closer, again. There.

'Caird!' she said, using his name, as she released against him. Over and over, as the rain drove down.

He pulled away to release his breeches, to end his need.

Then the flood that had almost drowned them fell from the sky.

Caird clutched her against him, and kissed her unremittingly. But the rain insisted. Frustration built, as need was denied. She couldn't breathe, couldn't see. Caird yelling at her, but she couldn't understand, her hearing and her body no longer her own.

More words from Caird. One word breaking through: *shelter.*

Caird grabbed her hand and gathered the horse. Her gown impeded every step; she couldn't find her balance. She was hot from his touch, cold from the rain.

Pulling her closer, he protected her from the worst of the wind. She tried to match his steady pace, knowing he wouldn't be looking at her, that his determination was moving them forward until there was a solution. But she struggled with her clothes, with her hair, with the droplets sliding off her nose.

His long strides were defiant against the nature trying to break him. The elements battered against him, but like a mountain, he came to no harm.

For her, the assaulting rain taunted and reminded her. He was Colquhoun. Arrogant. She hated him. Must hate him. But he held her hand, radiating his warmth and strength. The contact was enough to keep her body tethered to him, and her errant thoughts were swept easily away with the rising wind.

The horizon changed, and darkened into hills. Walking faster, tugging the reins of the horse, until it bucked, Caird didn't miss a step. He held a tension that was palatable even in the little visibility offered her. He knew where he was going. When he released her hand to pick up branches, and she wiped the hair from her face, she saw it: a cave.

When they reached it, he tossed the wood on the floor of the cave. It was dark, but dry and he pulled the horse in.

'I need to care for the horse,' he said, his eyes searching hers. He'd care for the horse, then come for her.

She understood, nodding at the inevitability and giving her acceptance before she turned away.

The cave was large, but too small for what had occurred to her. She had to move and the only direction was further into the cave. It was darker, but the entrance was wide enough to see a little, until she turned a curve and blackness engulfed her.

She made a sound and listened to the faint echo. Her body trembled from cold and Caird's touch. If she didn't find dry wood here, there would be no fire. It was still day, but unless the rain let up—

Her left foot hit a boulder and she fell. The jolt stunned her until she felt the slight pain of scrapes on her hands and knees.

The cave floor was wet, slimy and she wiped her hands against her gown, but they soaked up the cave floor and she felt the smear spread with the dirt.

It was wet here, but the entrance of the cave was dry. Suddenly embarrassed that she'd slipped in animal leavings, she groaned. At least she smelled no dung or urine, just an earthy smell. Since the rain still fell, she could walk outside and clean herself.

She used the boulder to push herself up and screamed.

## Chapter Seventeen

Caird dropped the bridle. Never in his life had he heard such a sound. Petrified anguish. Sharp, quick and then nothing. It took not even two full breaths to reach her.

Utter silence amplified the dark. He shouldn't have known where she was, but she was sitting and flinging her hands like she was throwing debris. Her movements, like a wild animal with its leg in a trap, were noticeable even in the dim light. Her gown bloomed voluminously around her, and it was heavy when he picked her up.

Something was wrong. It was then he saw it. A man lying on his side. Mairead was still flinging—blood—from her hands. Swiftly, he carried her outside.

Rain fell, but the wind no longer lashed it down. So he saw the blood saturating her gown, running in rivulets across her arms, hands, legs, her *face*.

'Look at me!' he ordered.

Her hands still shaking, she didn't acknowledge him.

'Mairead!'

Pain ripped at his chest, but his arms refused to let her go and the blood ran over him as well. Her trembles turned violent before her eyes locked with his. The anguished fear of her scream was nothing compared to what he saw in her eyes.

He tightened his hold and talked low, soothing, trying to reach her. He knew what he said didn't make sense, his mind on the blood still wet, the kill recent, the murderer nearby.

When her eyes lost their confusion, he reluctantly let her go. He stepped back to prevent himself from brushing her hair out of her face, and sweeping the remaining blood from her arms.

Her eyes focused, her trembles lessening, but he didn't want to leave her.

Yet, he had to. He needed to confirm who lay in the cave. The danger to them both was near. Something of his hesitation registered with her.

'Go,' she said and her voice was stronger than the paleness of her face and the tremors in her hands.

It was enough. Caird ran to the darkness of the cave. Soon, he would have answers.

Mairead continued to walk from the cave, not far, just enough. Most of the blood had washed away except for that on her gown, but there wasn't anything to be done about that.

She felt too raw, too open. Layers of trembles coursed through her.

The first trembles were those from Caird, the wanting and the denial.

Then when she fell, her body a jumble. More trembles so that it took longer to realise what had happened to her; what she sat in…what she touched.

Her scream had been wrenched from her before her mind had come to its own conclusions. Her shuddering body determined to go in one direction, while her mind, just as determined, to go the other.

But now her trembles eased, just like the rain. Until she fully comprehended what had happened in the cave and to her and her family. While the diminishing rain washed the rest of blood from her, she knew that it could not wipe away the torment she had lived through these past few days. Her nightmare needed to be over.

Unfortunately, she also knew when Caird saw who was in the cave, her nightmare would be worse.

Blood on his hands and sleeves, Caird emerged from the cave, strode to his horse, and pulled on the pouch carrying the dagger and gem still strapped to the saddle.

Wrapping the belt and pouch around his waist,

he roiled with anger and disgust at himself. It was then Mairead turned to face him. Even from this distance, he could tell she was different. Her hands were clenched at her sides, her chin lifted. Her sodden clothes and hair looked ominous against the brightening skies and rays of light now shafting through the still-dark clouds.

It hadn't taken him long to realise who was in the cave. It hadn't taken him long to remember his true duty.

How could he be so foolish? How could he have forgotten why he was here?

With the thief dead, Mairead and her brother were the only two people who could give him answers. Two *Buchanans*.

He'd done exactly what Malcolm had feared. He'd become too involved with a woman, had forgotten the importance of the jewel. Forgotten she was a Buchanan. A lying, no-good, deceiving—

No, he hadn't forgotten. He just thought she might be different.

But even if Mairead was different from her clan, she could be lying to protect someone else. He knew she kept a secret and the jewel was too valuable for any secrets.

His anger eased enough for him to think clearly.

Too much had happened between them since he'd left Malcolm and his cousins. He needed to understand, to get more answers.

But to do that he had to plan and, as he walked

nearer to her, he did. He wanted to take advantage of Mairead's vulnerability, but he saw none of that now and he quickly changed his strategy. Directness was needed and he felt relief with that. He had no stomach for subterfuge and he would not be the foolish Colquhoun.

'Your friend is dead,' he said calmly, never letting his gaze drift from her. To press his advantage, he needed to catch her every reaction. Buchanans were liars and this one might be the most deceitful.

'So it was the thief.' Her lips pressed tightly together. 'He wasn't a friend,' she said, 'but you already knew that.'

'I know nothing.'

'You'd know a great deal if you'd only believe the truth.'

'From a Buchanan?'

'Are we back to clan names, Colquhoun?' She stepped nearer to him, a certain boldness in her stance and eyes. 'Even after—' she pointed '—the river?'

He hadn't felt shame in years and he forced himself not to feel any now. He had spent too much time with her. Had got too close, had wanted her too much. The more fool he. 'The river changes nothing.'

Something flashed in her eyes, anger, hurt, he didn't know. But he felt it all the same. Had she felt something as he had or had seduction been

one of her ploys? He couldn't know. He carried
perhaps the most valuable weapon in the war
they waged. He could make no assumptions. The
stakes were too high.

'Who is that man in the cave?' he demanded.
'Why was he here and not heading to the wedding?'

'Why would I know any of that?' she retorted.

He was a fool. The thief shouldn't have been
in the cave. Back at the inn, the only plan was
to head north to the Graham clan. To follow the
jewel, the thief should have been headed there.
It made no sense the thief travelled towards Buchanan land. Unless...unless Buchanans were involved.

Had Mairead been partnered with the thief?

'You know more than you say,' he answered.
'I demand the truth from you.'

Mairead had darkened after the rain, but there
was something more. Something burning dark
inside her.

Did she mean to fight him in truth? Laughable.
Entire countries would war over this. No woman
could stop what was happening all around them.
The truth must be revealed and actions justified.

'If you will not believe what I say, there's nae
point answering,' she said with derision.

He felt a sudden urge to intimidate her. Images
of Dunbar, of Malcolm fallen, his wound open,

the birds already circling. Already picking at the men who could not rise. His brother, among them.

If he had to frighten a mere slip of a woman, to make her think he'd harm her, he would. He'd use anything to his advantage, leave nothing to chance.

She merely lifted her chin, keeping her eyes on him. Unafraid.

'Who was the dagger going to?' he demanded.

She quirked her eyebrow. 'Another direct question? And you're using multiple sentences. These answers must mean something to you.'

'Nae stalling. Nae games.'

'I agree,' she said, easing her stance. 'But then I haven't been playing at anything.' She turned from him, making a complete circle, showing the curves of her body through the soaked and torn gown. Was that intentional? He didn't think so, but he noticed anyway and his damned body reacted.

'You play,' he said, his voice hoarse with anger too long restrained. 'Too much has happened since you arrived,' he said.

She laughed, harsh and quick. 'Why, because that man's dead?'

He didn't answer her. The wind was drying her hair and the tendrils lifted. He took another step closer, barely restraining himself as her hair waved towards him. It threatened to ensnare him.

'You couldn't believe I had a hand in it,' she

whispered. 'Do you think… Do you believe…this was all some clever plan?'

'You said the dagger was yours. That thief was near Buchanan land.'

'You think I'm capable of murder.' Her voice tightened, momentarily displaying her emotion.

He had hurt her. Good. He needed her vulnerability. He needed to break her down before she did him. He held tight to his silence, which came at a cost for him now.

Mairead stared incredulously at Caird. What was wrong with this man? Huge, indomitable. A mountain she must remove! Her family were only a day away and a dead man in a cave was keeping her from them.

A dead man. Like her brother. Dead, and his presence was crushing her. She had no doubt the man who had killed her brother had also killed the thief.

Caird thought she lied to him and she did. Why not? He didn't deserve the truth and it shouldn't matter to him that her brother was dead.

But because she concealed her most private pain, Caird thought her capable of murder?

Avoiding his accusation and the hurt, she looked around him. The now shining sun gave no comfort when she was more embroiled in this nightmare.

The thief had been recently killed and the murderer could be nearby. But perhaps the company of a murderer was more agreeable than that of a Colquhoun. She squashed the hysterical laugh bubbling inside her. She needed this *done*.

'You know what the irony is?' she asked. 'I'm actually telling the truth.' She took a step towards him and poked his chest. The slight deepening of his frown gave her great pleasure. 'Whereas you, I'm sure, are not.'

His eyes roamed to her tangled hair. She pushed it impatiently away and he pulled his gaze to hers. 'Colquhouns doona lie.'

'Now that was evasive,' she replied, her frustration only increasing. Because she knew. Absolutely knew he was not telling her the complete truth. 'And it was a lie.'

She poked his chest again. 'You lie with your quiet, your silence, your steadfast arrogance in thinking everything will go your way.'

'It must,' he ground out.

She waved her hands in frustration. '*Why?* Because you say so. Ach, I'll tell you right now that a compromise must happen.'

'Nae.'

'Aye!' she almost shouted. 'Aye, again. For what else are you to do? Drag me around Scotland, and for what reason? I gave you what you want. Yet you reveal nothing!'

Stony silence.

Tears threatened and still he loomed over her. What if the murderer wasn't here? What if he

knew she had been with her brother that day and
he was waiting for her at home? Her family might
already be dead, their blood spilling out along
the ground.

Grief and anger were overwhelming her. 'Why
does this matter to you? Just let me out of—' she
indicated the space between them '—this madness!'

Silence again, while she choked on her emotions. She wanted him gone. 'The dagger and gem
are all yours,' she bit out through her teeth. 'I
know nothing more about them!'

'But your brother might—'

She screamed. One long agonised and frustrated scream that ended in hysterical laughter.
She didn't even try to hold back the welcome release.

'You jest,' she declared. 'Because my brother
is dead.'

The ground suddenly left his feet. Caird stood
free-falling as his veins turned to ice, then to fire
and back again. The woman before him was mad.

'What did you say?'

## Chapter Eighteen

'She said her brother is dead.' A man emerged from behind a tree. 'And now, so are you.'

Caird freed his sword, but it didn't take the noise of the others emerging from the trees to know they were outnumbered and trapped.

It only took the tiny sound from Mairead, her pressing close to him and taking the small blade from his boot.

He turned around. Seven men, including the one in front of him. He was small and grey streaked his pale hair. There was something shrivelled about him, despite his fleshy jowls and the feverish look in his protuberant vengeful eyes.

'You can try, Englishman,' Caird scoffed.

Seven men. He'd done it before. Not all at once, though, and not with a woman to protect.

The Englishman smirked. 'I will do more than try, Caird of Clan Colquhoun. I will succeed. As I always do.'

'Not today.'

The man stepped forward. 'You are a mere delay.'

Caird felt Mairead shift her feet as if readying to fight. Whatever lack of trust between them, Mairead's brave response indicated she wasn't in partnership with these men.

Which was no comfort now. It only meant she needed to be hidden and somewhere they couldn't find her. She needed to be anywhere but here.

Mairead recognised the Englishman. Too late, far too late, but she remembered now. Intent on Ailbert selling the dagger, she'd been barely aware of the people in the market around him.

Walking to the stall, even her brother hadn't noticed the two men approach him. Then there had been a flash of steel, an arm thrusting forward, her brother collapsing to the ground. The other man, the thief, was slow to react, eventually grabbing the jewelled dagger and putting it under his cloak.

Why hadn't she remembered there had been two of them? Or the thief's hesitation? There was only one reason for the hesitation. The killer, this Englishman, had deviated from a plan.

Which meant there was a plot, and this was not a random taking of a valuable.

As if she could doubt that now, surrounded as they were. She had been so afraid of her family being trapped she had never considered herself.

Maybe it was because she wasn't like her giggling sisters. This man had killed her brother and she wasn't backing down. Her only regret now was that Caird faced the man, while she faced his accompanying soldiers, but for once she'd have patience.

'A delay from what?' Caird demanded.

The man gave a disapproving tut. 'You wouldn't disappoint me now, would you? Pretending you don't know anything. Such a shame as you've been clever so far.'

The men shifted. Were they following silent orders? She kept her eyes on them.

The man's voice cajoled. 'Come, you found my man, acquired the woman, but started towards your cousins' lands as if you were to continue to the games? Brilliant. Truly, I admired you for the deceit.'

'I doona ken your meaning, Englishman,' Caird answered.

'Your sword's drawn. You understand enough.'

Caird was silent.

'Or maybe not, eh?' The man laughed. 'Come, then, hand it over and I'll make your deaths quick.'

'Nae.'

'No?' Movement to Mairead's left alerted her to the Englishman shifting. She could just see him out of the corner of her eye. Caird did not move. Was he allowing her to see or was it a tactic?

'You disappointed me when you separated from

your cousins and brother,' the Englishman said, shaking his head. 'I almost wished you'd left it with one of them, but I knew you wouldn't.'

The man's lips curved. 'I can see your surprise. Even you must know there's too much at stake.'

The man circled around until he stood in front of Mairead. She felt Caird tense as the men around them circled as well.

'The Buchanan looks confused and incensed. An interesting combination for such an arresting face. Perhaps she doesn't know?' He reached to touch her but she raised the blade. Lowering his hand, he laughed, but it didn't reach his eyes. 'She doesn't know, does she?'

'What do you think I doona know?' she demanded. She hated giving him the satisfaction of being right.

'Truly, dear, it's for the best you don't know.' He gave another disapproving sound and a wag of his finger. 'Might even be convenient today. Your—brother?—maybe he, too, didn't know. But he was going to that market stall and that wasn't a chance I could take.'

A quick dash and the man was in front of Caird again. 'Then you delayed me, but no more. I know you have it. It's why you head this way and not to your laird.' She felt Caird's subtle adjustment. What was his plan?

'You feign surprise?' the Englishman derided. 'Of course, people are so tiring in their predictability. I thought you were clever, Colquhoun. Clever enough to recognise what was in the dagger, to keep things silent, to cover your tracks, to think about the consequences of such a treasure. But then you headed this way. Predictable.'

Mairead fought fear and rage. There was something the Englishman said that sent ice through her blood, something that made her realise— No, no more thought.

She was sick of the Englishman's condescending voice and all-knowing manner. She was sick of everyone's arrogance. Tightening her hold on the dagger, she whirled to face him. 'Why?'

'Explanations are tedious.' The man gave an exaggerated sigh. She wanted to imbed the blade in his heart. 'I knew everything that would happen because a Buchanan would never trust a Colquhoun and vice versa. You were probably not entirely truthful, and he...' he gestured to Caird '...probably didn't believe you. Truly, dear, don't move again.'

Facing Caird, he raised his sword. 'Now give it to me.'

Caird moved, shielding her from the killer. 'Nae.'

'So be it.'

It happened fast. Faster than she had anticipated even though she knew it was coming. She tightened her hold, ready to fight, and then Caird's foot swiped under hers and she was flat on the ground.

'The horse!' he yelled. She looked around her. The men were ignoring her. In this position, she could only cut their feet, while they could slice her between breaths.

Caird had ensured her safety and vulnerability. Scrambling, avoiding swipes of swords, feeling the cuts even so, the sting and heat of blood, she shut out everything but her survival. She saw the horse now standing near to theirs. A sign that she and Caird weren't meant to survive.

Once she was far enough away, she half crouched, half ran, not looking behind her, knowing Caird was near. Another flash, the Englishman suddenly in front of her, grabbing a horse, his look darker than murder as their eyes met. Would he cut her down?

He swung up, giving a nod in her direction as if in greeting before he urged the horse to flee.

Suddenly a man fell beside her as Caird just stopped the downward swipe of his sword.

She blinked. Men were falling now, their vacant eyes before her. Caird was with her, but the last soldier was, too. She forced herself forward. Survive! Move!

By some miracle, they reached their horse. Caird swung up before her, his sword sweeping again, the high ground giving him the advantage as he grabbed her hand and pulled her behind him. There were no more soldiers and no sign of the Englishman.

She wrapped her arms around him as they raced through the woods.

Her eyes focused only on Caird, on his breath, on his strength, on the blood. There were no sounds of pursuit and her eyes and mind finally comprehended. Too much blood.

Was that his?

## Chapter Nineteen

'Oh, wake up, wake up, wake up!' Mairead cried again. How long had they remained here? A few minutes? Hours? A lifetime?

For ever. It was nighttime and the slightest noise or movement around her made her jump. Her heart would not stop a frantic beating and it beat even harder now.

Ever since the horse had slowed and Caird—

Caird *crumpled*. Slid off the horse and slumped into a puddle. Mud smeared with sweat gleamed off his body and there was blood from the wounds, from the scratches, from the *slices* of his skin. Blood beaded and ran in rivulets off his arms, legs, from his face. Blood that mocked her feeble attempts to care for him.

And the worst. The worst had her kneeling, praying and pressing against him. On his left side, above his hip, a small cut—a deep cut.

Holding a torn fragment from his tunic against

it, she watched as the blood continually seeped around the fabric and her fingers.

If only he'd wake up to demand she do something. To mock her as he gave her instruction.

She expected the Englishman to arrive at any moment. To take the dagger and gem, and slit their throats.

Caird's sword, swathed in blood and mud, lay by his side but it was useless to her. Even if she had some skill, she couldn't lift it. They were vulnerable, exposed and defenceless.

Did Caird seem paler? His lips had parted; his breathing becoming more jagged than before. He couldn't just go. Not here. Not like this.

She pressed harder on the wound.

He groaned.

'Ach!' She released her hands and watched every flutter of his eyes. They didn't open. He was quiet again, his breathing just as shallow.

She had to rouse him, not only because a mortal enemy was searching for them, but also because she didn't know what to do about the wound.

'You'll hate me more for this.' Watching his face, wincing even before she did it, she pressed hard into his side.

He groaned again, but this time it sounded angry.

Inhaling, preparing to scream, she leaned over his face. 'Wake up, you lazy, arrogant Colquhoun!'

He opened his eyes.

Hope flipped and fluttered inside her.

'Paining me,' he whispered.

Her heart sunk as she heard the admission and the agony in his voice.

This wasn't the Caird she knew. The mountain of a man, who used his size to intimidate, and his sword to back up his pride.

Seven men. He had taken on seven men, with her as helpless as a butterfly.

He had kept her safe.

'You fell off the horse, you nae-good Scotsman. What kind of man falls off a horse?'

His brow furrowed. 'Safe?'

At his voice, her heart began to beat normally. She doubted it would stay that way. 'Nae, we're not.'

He turned his head, his body tensing, as if he meant to rise.

She pressed on his chest. 'Not like that. There's nae one but us. The wound in your side won't stop bleeding.'

'Stitches,' he growled.

Maybe. 'Do you have any thread?'

He shook his head, his eyes closing again.

Futility swept over her. 'Nae! You're going to die.'

He whispered, 'Fire.'

'I doona care if it hurts like fire, I need help.'

He growled again. 'Seal it.'

Mairead recoiled at his suggestion. Heat a blade, burn his skin, but close the wound.

Why hadn't she realised it before? Her panic had blinded her. She released her hands and moved his tunic. The wound was small and clean enough to use Caird's boot blade. In her panic, she'd forgotten she had seen this done before.

Pressing his hand on top of the makeshift dressing, she hurried to make a fire.

Everything was wet, so she looked to the trees and was rewarded with an empty nest inside a crevice. The small fire didn't take her long. Thrusting the blade into the flames, she waited.

Caird's eyes remained closed. His skin was greying and sweat dripped from his brow.

No one had pursued them and she began to fear they were in no rush because they knew he was injured. That he was a dead man and they just needed to wait.

Pain! Yelping, she dropped the blade into the fire.

Cursing, she scrambled to get the blade out with a stick, until her knuckles on her good hand got burned. That did it.

'Why?' she vented. 'Why are we doing this?' Blowing on her hand, working the blade out of the flame, she continued, 'What could possibly be worth any of this?'

Hand throbbing, her fingers not wanting to bend, she felt the blade. It was cooler.

'No one wants the dagger. Why? It's beautiful, the jewels sparkling and set in with decorated silver, but, nae, I'm thinking this is all about a big ugly rock.'

Wrapping her hand this time, she thrust the blade back into the fire. She glanced at Caird. His eyes were closed and she couldn't tell if the blackness had claimed him again.

Her anger and frowns were wasted on him. 'That rock had better be important and when you wake, you best tell me why.'

Even through her wrapping, she felt the blade's heat. It had to be enough. Trying not to think what she was about to do, she removed his hand covering the wound. As she bent over, Caird's eyes flew open.

His gaze was distant and she knew he wasn't truly awake, wasn't truly looking at her. But this close, his eyes were clear and mesmerising. She didn't, couldn't, break her gaze. She was lost in the vastness of grey.

'Beautiful,' he whispered. 'You're so beautiful.'

Startled, hands jerking, Mairead burned his flesh.

Even after blackness claimed Caird again, Mairead's hands trembled, making cleaning the wound with the spare water difficult. Too fearful to leave his side, too terrified to find an enemy, she didn't dare go to the streams for more.

She laughed a harsh release. There was so much blood and mud, and she couldn't move him. Couldn't even make him comfortable except to prop his head up with his rolled cloak, so he didn't drown in the puddle he had fallen in.

For him to have fallen, the wound had to be worse than it looked, and even though she had sealed it, he could still die.

Fierceness and desperation sliced through her. This huge indomitable man was now helpless and dependant on her. She wouldn't let him die.

She recognised that now would be her best chance to take the dagger and gem and escape. A quick ride and she'd be safe, could find food and maybe reach her home.

But she stayed.

All her life, when there was trouble, she'd always just done whatever needed to be done. No thinking. Thinking and consequences she avoided. Sitting here, she couldn't help but think and there were many, many consequences to her thinking.

Soon there would be no sun, no warmth; the ground was sodden and her gown was soaked in blood and mud. She was cold, hungry, uncomfortable and at any moment the Englishman could come and kill her.

But she stayed, and his words kept whispering to her.

*Beautiful.*

Had she done enough to save him? His skin

was red, bruised, blackened and blistered from the burn, but no more blood seeped out.

Still, she worried. Worried that she hadn't sealed it right, had, in fact, made it worse. She didn't want to make it worse, she wanted him better. Better because...because she needed to repay him.

He had kidnapped her, risked her life and yet she realised she was alive with barely a scratch from their danger. He had protected her all along.

*When you fled me, I followed you.*

When she'd confronted the thief in the hallway, when she'd fled on the horse, when the flood had swept her away, when the rain and wind had whipped against her, he had protected her.

And her kneeling next to him, gently wiping away the worst of the mud caking to him, tending his injuries, was her response to all he had done for her.

Something in her chest tightened and her hands stopped trembling as she breathed in deep.

This vigilant, protective feeling washing over her was beyond what he made her feel with his words and touch. She had no doubt about it now. A part of her...cared for him.

He was unkind to her, called her cruel names and had opposed her at every opportunity. It was a mistake to care for him. A mistake. She refused to care for him. It had to be worry and desperation and hunger making her feel this way. Making her—

The sound of twigs snapping underfoot. The horse was in the woods. Probably trying to find food to make it feel well. Another worry.

Sighing, she chastised herself for her contemplations. They wouldn't help her predicament.

Caird had collapsed, but the horse, who she thought was getting better, had only got worse. She'd have to find mint or else it wouldn't be capable of carrying them.

For now, she wouldn't leave Caird. Not when his face was pinched with pain and his skin was slick with sweat. She gave in to her worry, and when she looked up it was too late.

'Thank you for building a fire for me, my dear.' The Englishman emerged from the woods. 'I was beginning to doubt my finding you.'

## Chapter Twenty

The pain in Caird's head was excruciating. His side burned, stinging pinpricks needled him along his arms and legs letting him know he suffered from many wounds. He knew they could be ignored. But he couldn't ignore the tight grip on his arm, or Mairead shouting at him.

He forced his eyes open. Her face was close. He could feel the fan of her breath, see the frantic worry in her eyes.

'Danger?' he whispered. 'Where?'

His eyes searched and could see nothing but her.

He moved to sit up. Searing pain pulled at his skin. Mairead pushed him down; she was telling him something, her words fast.

Blood rushed to his ears as he tried to roll to his side. He stopped, unsure if he'd black out or be sick. When he could control both, he opened his eyes again.

Mairead had moved with him. He tried to focus on her words.

Horse, something about a horse. He had fallen from it. Safe.

Pulling up his tunic, he could see his flesh cut, red, burnt...crooked. He prodded it with his fingers. Sore, but no blood. The wound was sealed.

They were safe, alive, but she was gesturing as if they were not. He focused.

'—Horse!' she said, her breath coming in pants, but there was a look of pride in her eyes.

He dropped his shaking arm to his side. 'My head...hurts.'

'Have you heard anything I've said?' she asked, her tone strident.

Looking around, he didn't see their horse. 'Where's the horse?' he said.

'Sick!' she said. 'Oh, I'm so relieved. I thought you'd be angry. But now you understand?'

Not a word. Why would she be this proud over a sick horse? They rode it hard, maybe it was worse. He rolled on to his back and almost blacked out. 'How?'

'Enough to slow him down, which is why—'

He raised his hand to stop her. He needed facts now. 'How long have I been asleep?'

'Are you following what I'm saying?' she asked pointedly.

She was frustrated with him and desperate. He didn't understand or like her desperation.

He needed an explanation. Just now, he didn't want to jump to assumptions, didn't want to think he'd been asleep for days and left her alone and vulnerable. 'Need to know.'

She raised her arms in frustration. 'Ach! You've been asleep all night. It's the middle of the day now. I've been trying to tell you, but you're not listening. You blacked out. I couldn't do anything to wake you. We were left out in the open and there was that fire.'

Mairead looked at him, as if waiting for a response. He rubbed his forehead, trying to alleviate the pain, but it didn't help. In this condition, he couldn't travel on foot.

'Where's the horse?' he asked.

She waved to her right.

He peered into the trees. 'That's not my horse.'

Exhaling, she said, 'That's what I've been telling you. We have to hurry.'

He closed his eyes, became dizzy and opened them again. His vision did not clear. It was not his horse. What had happened to his horse? He'd been asleep and it was day again. He feared the answer. 'Where did that horse come from?'

She crossed her arms, but her teeth drew in her lips. She was irritated and unsure. 'You've been asleep. He came. There was nothing else I could do. You doona look well.'

*He came.* 'The Englishman?' Rage, and something akin to fear, swept through his weakened body.

'Of course the Englishman! It's not as if you'd killed them all before we fled.'

He only had the strength to clench the mud beneath him, when all he wanted to do was shake her. 'Are you hurt?'

She released her arms and leaned over him. 'Nae, nae, I'm unharmed. But you're awake now, and we need to make haste if we are to catch up with him.'

Incredulousness caused a slight slackening to his jaw, but did nothing to stop the foreboding building within him. Then the stark realisation of her meaning slid down his spine like ice water, fast, cold, shocking. Everything was lost.

While he had lain defenceless, the Englishman had come and relieved them of the jewel and all the promise it represented. Devastation and dizziness almost overpowered him and he struggled to stay awake.

'The gem,' he said. 'He has the gem.'

'Aye, he has the gem,' Mairead said, impatience lacing every word. 'You look pale. You're too poorly. I doona think we can go after him.'

'Are you saying—?' Black spots were before his eyes. 'Are you saying,' he repeated, 'that the jewel is gone?'

She lifted her chin a bit more. 'I did the best

I could under the circumstances. I thought you'd understand by now.'

He didn't even have the strength of a babe and the weight of the loss was crushing him further into the mud. 'I need to eat,' he demanded.

'I have nae food; I didn't know if—' She shook her head. 'I'll go and look for something.'

Caird was grateful when Mairead left for the woods. He didn't know what she would find there, but it didn't matter. Anything was better than nothing.

His horse had supplies. Had she bargained for those as she must have done for her life and his?

The risks she took; how she must have feared.

And the jewel. Gone. He tried to concentrate on it. But all he could see was him lying on the ground, Mairead over him. Her bargaining with a monster.

He had deserted her, and she had faced the Englishman alone.

After everything they had been through together, he'd lost the Jewel of Kings to an Englishman. As if Scotland, as if he, could take another loss after Dunbar. For a moment, he had held Scotland's hope—his brother's salvation—and now it was gone. The Clan of Colquhoun would weep at his folly.

Mairead foraged for water and berries. The Englishman had given her a bare handful of food from Caird's plentiful supplies. A handful. Enough for her since he hadn't expected Caird to live. But she was grateful for that handful now. Berries were scant and her hands shook so she dropped more than she could hold. Caird was alive, but he didn't appreciate what had happened. She had to make him understand.

When she returned, Caird looked little better than he had before. But he had moved himself out of the puddle and was half sitting, the cloak stuffed behind him. He watched the fire she had built up after the Englishman left.

'You moved?' She knelt beside him to inspect the wound. 'You could have undone everything.' There was no damage, but it didn't stop her irritation. She pooled the berries on leaves next to him and threw the water skein and oatcakes in his lap.

Caird frowned and picked at the bounty before him.

'This is all I could find. I never learned to build traps.' She waved towards the woods. 'But there's water nearby. I already had my fill. This is for you.'

He took the skein, but didn't drink. Instead he sloshed the remainder from side to side. His movements were slow, methodical and she knew he was weighing his words as he weighed the water. 'Was he alone?'

Not the question she expected. 'Aye, at least, I didn't see anyone else.' She sat beside him.

'What happened?' he asked.

Caird's expression was grim. She could see a burning frustration there, but also a heaviness that burdened his broad shoulders. The gem. Always that ugly rock. But she'd take his arrogance over this Caird. This one she didn't understand.

'I need to tell you—'

Caird glanced at her, but it was enough to stop her words. She was frustrated, but his silence was tumultuous, and it stormed against her. Shaking her head against it, she rallied. She had to tell him. 'He took the gem, but I gave him the horse. I hope it'll be enough to—'

'Nae,' Caird interrupted, his voice low, but not soft. 'After you put the blade to me. After I *abandoned* you, when did that monster appear?'

She didn't understand his questions, but she thought she understood his anger. She'd lost the gem.

Maybe she could have done more to save it. Maybe, if she could have thought, but when faced with the Englishman, she could barely comprehend anything above her fear. Now the gem was gone, and Caird needed facts and answers. She must tell him from the beginning.

Tucking her legs underneath her, she grabbed some berries. She'd eaten enough for a belly ache, but they gave her something to do with her hands.

'It was the fire,' she said. 'He found us because of the fire.'

Caird's hands showed white on the skein before
he released them.

'Then he laughed,' she said. Ice-cold fear had
flushed through her at the sound. She knew then
that, despite Caird killing those men and their
race to escape, it had all been for naught. They
were going to die and Caird would never wake
to realise it.

But she had been awake and for a frozen moment she'd felt the cowardly desire to close her
eyes as well.

'He laughed,' she said again. 'He seemed very
pleased and I was surprised when he sheathed
his sword.'

She had stood then, refusing to kneel before the
Englishman. He had been gleeful at her defiance,
while Caird lay wounded at her feet.

'He spoke of my ignorance about the gem and
your imminent death.'

She breathed in, held it. 'He didn't think you'd
survive.' She exhaled, getting the worst of the
story out. 'I didn't either. You were very pale and
there was so much blood.'

She tried to give him a little smile, some en-
couragement since he was, indeed, alive and well,
but Caird didn't look at her and his expression remained unreadable.

Not knowing what else to do, she nibbled a
berry. It wasn't sweet. 'He said he had won as
though it was some game. Your fate made nae dif-

ference to him. He had taken a great prize from you, so he'd won the game. I didn't contradict him; I didn't dare stop his speech. I thought as long as he kept talking, he wasn't killing me.'

Caird made some sound deep in his chest, but he did not look at her. The colour in his cheeks had improved. He would live. He would live and things would be better now.

She took in a shaking breath. It had taken all her strength to stay upright before the Englishman. She'd been petrified; the trembling in her body weakening her knees to the point she thought she'd collapse.

'I didn't care if he won; I knew I'd lost. I'd lost everything.' Her mouth was dry, so she ate another berry. It was sweet, juicy and she had trouble swallowing it.

'Then…he smiled again. He smiled and I didn't ken the words he was saying because his pale eyes went black.'

Caird looked at her then. 'He hurt you.'

Her hand fluttered, but trembled too much for her to gesture properly. 'Nae, he didn't touch me, didn't even threaten me.'

'You expected his sword.'

'Aye,' she whispered. She looked around her, trying to shake her thoughts. 'But he was telling me I'd live. All I had to do was hand over the dagger and gem as well as your sword and he would let me keep some food.' She lifted her chin, meeting his eyes. 'So I did. I gave them to him.'

He searched her eyes. 'You expect me to be angry with you?'

She did. For days they'd been fighting over the gem and dagger. He was angry now. She *felt* his rage.

'How could I be disappointed in you?' he asked.

She didn't understand his surprise and she didn't understand the way he was looking at her now. As if he was searching her soul.

Avoiding his eyes, she looked at the fire instead. 'Then he just left,' she said, ignoring his question. 'Not believing he'd keep his word, I watched him go.' Talking of the Englishman was easier than answering Caird's questions. Even if she wasn't telling him all.

The Englishman hadn't just gone. When she'd handed him the pouch his face had held such triumphant evil. He'd closed his eyes as if he relished tying the pouch to his belt. For all his killing, that one moment of watching his pure pleasure had frightened her the most.

Shaking herself again, she looked at Caird. 'And then I knew,' she said.

'You knew what?' he asked, when she didn't finish.

'It's more than just costly; the gem means something.'

Caird blinked, surprise flashing in his eyes.

'Aye, it means a great deal,' she said. For days she'd been guessing the importance of the gem, but the look on the Englishman's face and Caird's surprise confirmed it.

'It's gone now.' Caird shrugged, his voice grim.

Since the Englishman had arrived, she'd been through every emotion that had ever existed. But only this Colquhoun could bring her frustration to the forefront with such speed.

'You haven't heard a word I've spoken!'

Caird was angry and disappointed at the loss of the gem, but she had done her best to safeguard it, and he hadn't listened to a word she'd said.

'I know you're frustrated, but you have to hear me now!' She stood and brushed the dirt from her torn gown. 'I knew then that the gem meant more than its price, so I gave him your horse.'

Caird's body stilled. 'You bargained away my horse?'

'Greedy devil that he was, aye. Yours was obviously trained and had supplies.'

'You gave him the jewel and offered the better horse?'

Mairead waited for him to laugh, or at least grin at her cleverness. She hadn't much to save them, hadn't a chance of surviving if she attacked the Englishman, but she had used her Buchanan guile and wit to save their necks.

But Caird didn't laugh; he didn't grin. There was nothing but obstinate disbelief and anger in his expression. She was tempted to just let him rot with his confusion because she was tiring of explaining herself.

'Aye, your best horse!' She capitulated. 'The one that's so faithful, all you have to do is whistle and it halts for you? The one that is sick and can't go very far?' She crossed her arms again. 'You know...*that* horse.'

Jaw slackening, Caird's eyebrows rose. Oh, she was glad she hadn't let him rot without telling him. Because this time, she knew a Buchanan had bested a Colquhoun.

The anger and hopelessness drained from Caird so suddenly, he was glad he sat else he'd have fallen. He was certainly dizzy as he comprehended Mairead's declaration.

She'd *lied*, fabricated some story and that monster had believed her. He took a horse that couldn't possibly travel far. It would slow him down, maybe even stop him. A Buchanan had saved them.

His chest swelled, ached. His breath kept expanding until he couldn't hold it in any more.

Caird let out a strangled, choking sound. When concern filled Mairead's eyes, it tipped the balance of his control.

Caird laughed. Great rolling waves of laughter. He couldn't stop it, didn't want to. Never before in his life had he laughed like this, with freedom, with shock, with absolutely no control.

For this laugh required true emotion, surprise and a freedom he'd never experienced. Rightly so, for how could he be this free or this surprised when he hadn't known Mairead before? Mairead, who had stayed and saved them.

Grabbing an oatcake, he asked, 'Which way did he go?'

It might be too late and he was weak. By the time they would be able to travel, the jewel might have changed hands, but they had a chance. She had given them the chance.

'You laughed,' she blurted out.

He took a bite. 'Aye.'

He felt like doing it again. To watch the wonderment continue on her face. He couldn't stop smiling.

'I didn't know Colquhouns did that.'

His brothers and sister laughed all the time. He didn't know he could do it. She had given that laughter to him.

It was a wondrous thing. The jewel might not be lost and they were alive. This impulsive, never-think-things-through woman was responsible. A *Buchanan* was responsible.

It was as if he suddenly arrived at a different place in the world.

He watched as her astonishment was quickly

replaced by ire again. Taking another bite of oat-cake, he waited to be surprised, to be intrigued.

Mairead crossed her arms. 'I'm not telling you which way he went until you tell me about the gem.'

'I cannot.'

'Then we go nowhere,' she said.

Intriguing, and stubborn. 'He let you live be-cause you didn't know.' He broke the last oatcake and offered her half.

She shook her head. 'You need to eat all the oatcakes. You still doona look well. If he finds you alive, do you think he'd let me go again?'

He took a bite. It had been a miracle they'd lived at all. Only a madman would have let them go when they were absolutely defenceless, but posed a threat. A man crazy or one supremely confident Caird would die.

Yet even in the face of such an adversary, Mairead had kept her lying tongue and her wits to save them. He would have bled out and died without her.

Now she was demanding he trust her, when he had too many questions. 'Why did you do it?' he asked. 'Why did you stay?'

She looked away, and shrugged. 'What else was I supposed to do? You're an irritating, arrogant, kidnapping Colquhoun. But a dead one?' Shaking her head, she continued, 'With your family miss-ing you, you'd even be more trouble.'

Caird frowned and brushed away the crumbs. What she said was true. If he didn't return, his family, with swords drawn, would pursue the entire Buchanan clan. But her reasonable reply didn't sit well with him.

Wanting more, he started to ask another question, just as the sun broke through the clouds. No longer hidden in pale light, he could see dark shadows under Mairead's reddened eyes and her skin was more ashen than pale. Her hair that had once taunted him with wildness lay limply around her; leaves, caked mud and blood weighed it down. Part of it looked burnt. She was exhausted, and he shouldn't press for more.

Yet she intrigued him. She had stayed and protected him. She'd given them a chance.

In the face of everything, when he had already vowed he'd do anything to stop this war, to stop his brother getting hurt again, did that mean also trusting a Buchanan?

Mairead began to pace. Her face and hands were smudged with dirt and soot. Her clothes were torn from the flood.

No, it was more than a rational choice to tell her. He *owed* her an explanation. But this had to be done right and he needed to sort his words carefully.

'It is the Jewel of Kings,' he said with all the reverence he could give it. He waited for there to be wonder and surprise or even regret on her face.

She did turn, but he saw none of the expressions he expected.

'I doona ken what that is,' she replied.

How could it be? As children, he and his brothers had played the game. Hadn't she or her brother? Her brother.

'Your brother's dead,' he said, remembering all.

She closed her eyes briefly. 'Killed,' she corrected.

'The Englishman?'

She nodded her head.

There were too many questions. 'How?'

A myriad of emotions flooded her face. He recognised them now. Pain, desperation, guilt.

He didn't understand the guilt. 'How?' he insisted. 'If your brother owned the dagger, how did he die?'

She jerked and crossed her arms. He had startled her with his question. Was this her lie?

'I'll not tell you now,' she answered. 'Now we talk about the gem.'

'Your brother had to know about the jewel.' He owed her much, but this was no time for secrets.

She loosened her arms and clenched her fists to her sides. Her eyes looked pointedly at him. 'If he did, he didn't have time to tell me.'

'What do you mean, didn't have time to tell you?'

Mairead's expression turned mulish.

This was her secret. He felt a million times the fool to be part of this lie. 'But—'

She shook her head. 'I'll tell you nothing now. That Englishman threatened me, threatened you. I need to know why my brother died. I need to understand this gem.'

She had called him stubborn, had called him arrogant. Now, just now, she was those things and more.

He knew what was at stake here. His country falling; Malcolm's near death. But what did it mean to her? From the tilt of her chin, he knew he wouldn't get an answer from her now and she was right, she did need to understand. He'd have to compromise.

He'd never given a description of the jewel before. He didn't know where to start. With the legend? It had been forged before mankind by the very elements around them. Then it was given as a symbol of peace to the warring clans. But, like all powers, it had been ill-used over the centuries by greedy lairds. There were different meanings for the jewel as well. It was a legend and stories changed as to its true power.

Too many words were needed to describe it and even then she might not understand. He barely understood himself and he had been raised with the legend. But only one of the legends, one of its powers, held his interest. He had to keep to the present.

'You know the Stone of Scone?' he asked.

'It's used for the king's ceremonies.'

He nodded. 'To give future kings their *crown*,' he continued. 'The Jewel of Kings isn't a tradition for ceremony. That gem, that jewel, *makes* kings.'

She became still.

'Whoever holds it holds the heart of Scotland,' he said. 'All clans will bow to that power. Nae matter *who* holds it.'

'So if a Scottish clan has it…' Mairead's eyes glinted, her brow furrowed. 'After Dunbar, I didn't think Scotland had any chance,' she said.

'None of us did,' he said.

'I didn't think such a jewel existed,' she whispered.

'None of us did,' he repeated.

Mairead couldn't stay still. She had known the gem was important, but she couldn't comprehend, even now, just how important. No wonder the Englishman had murdered for it. She shuddered.

Everything made sense now. Caird's incredulousness, his relentless need to know why she claimed it was hers and not believing her. So he'd kidnapped her because she claimed it was her brother's.

She glanced over her shoulder. Caird was waiting, keeping his silence, as she knew he would be. It was her turn to speak and it would not be easy.

'My brother didn't know the jewel existed either,' she said. The ground underneath them was drier. It was the middle of the day, the sun shone, but their clothes needed to dry and they would need more fire by evening.

'My brother gambled,' she said. 'The laird forbade it, but Ailbert didn't stop.' She reached into a bramble bush for loose branches. 'He kept losing, but he didn't stop, not even when he promised the English soldiers a chest of money at the next full moon.'

She pulled her hand out and ignored the scratches. She needed small kindling and there wasn't much close by. 'There wasn't any such chest.'

She turned to look at him. Caird was tiring. He'd eaten all she could provide and slouched heavily against the mud-saturated cloak. She crouched before the fire and threw in a few branches.

'We went to market. The thief from the cave was there and the dagger fell from his pouch. It happened just in front of us. The fair was busy and the thief didn't stop walking away. Not knowing its value, Ailbert grabbed it and we quickly went in the opposite direction.'

Mairead stared into the fire. How did she talk of the rest? Of the fear, but the gleefulness when they saw the silver workmanship and the glinting rubies. Stealing was a sin, but the dagger had just landed at their feet. As if God had given it to them. The dagger was valuable. Maybe not a chest of silver, but enough.

Then she— She wasn't ready to tell him everything, but Caird would have too many questions. 'My brother had me hide in the shadows when he went to sell the dagger. It was quick. I now realise there were two of them.'

Standing again, she shrugged, letting him know she couldn't tell him anything else.

'When?' he asked.

Typical Colquhoun, demanding more answers. Never assuming, never jumping to conclusions as she would have. Rubbing her eyes, she answered, 'The day I met you.'

A tilt to his head, a sudden inhale. Caird stretched his left thumb as if to flex it, but didn't. He didn't like what she told him. He'd have more questions.

She also had questions about that night. Such as how could she have run, grieving for her brother's death, and then recklessly kiss a stranger at an inn? How could she have thrown herself into Caird's arms like she did? Responded like she did? She still didn't understand it and feared it was another impulsive mistake.

'Where?' he asked, looking away.

'The market was on Buchanan land. I spent all day and most of the night following the thief. I kept thinking he'd stop and—'

'Nae, where were you at the market?'

Caird sounded angry but his face was turned away from her, so she didn't understand.

'You said your brother went to sell the dagger.' He enunciated every word, his eyes focused on his hands, his thumb now flexing repeatedly. 'Had he reached a stall? Had he exposed the dagger?'

'He—' She didn't know why Caird wanted to talk about this. His concern was the jewel. She had purposefully rushed the ending, not wanting to relive it. 'It happened as he crossed the crowd. The stalls were on the other side.'

'Are you not getting me?' he demanded, turning his grey eyes on her.

Shaking her head, she felt exposed to the tumultuous rage in his eyes. She was talking about that day, about her brother's death and how she'd been too far away to stop it from happening.

'Since they killed him before he reached the stalls, they knew your brother had the dagger,' he said. 'They were watching for him, and knew you were with him.'

Mairead locked her suddenly weak knees. They had murdered her brother before he took the dagger out of his cape. As though they were waiting for him to be in a crowd, or maybe they were stopping him from exposing the Jewel of Kings.

She knew what Caird was truly trying to tell her. That if she had not suddenly hid, that if she hadn't accidentally gone to Caird's room, she'd be dead. She knew it, because before they had

fled the fight at the cave that's what the Englishman had been telling her. And Caird seemed...
angry...about that.

She didn't care how he felt.

Her brother had been stabbed, had experienced
agony. Caird's observation confirmed her worst
imaginings: it *was* her fault he was dead. If she
hadn't made Ailbert sell the dagger he'd be alive.
Alive.

Her teeth started chattering and she rubbed her
arms. Suddenly needing to do something, she told
him, 'I know how to fish and I need to get clean.'

She knew she didn't make sense. Caird had told
her she should be dead and now she was off to
fish. But she ignored him and his watchful eyes.

'Wait,' he asked, seeming to war with himself.

His expression contained more questions than
answers, but she couldn't confess any more. She
was going to break. The things she did remember, she wanted to forget. He made her think too
much and now, she just needed to act.

'Nae more answers, Colquhoun,' she said and
walked swiftly away.

Caird woke to the smell of fish frying.

Mairead was just removing a flat stone from
the fire. A fish with burnt fins lay on top.

'I slept?' he asked.

Turning suddenly, Mairead fumbled the stone.
'Do you hurt?'

'Nae.' He felt stiff, but the pain in his side had lessened enough so he could sit. His wound's sharp tugging now made the pain in his ribs feel dull. A small comfort.

Mairead had bathed. Her hair flowed gently in the breeze and she wore her now much wrinkled and half-torn gown from the inn. He remembered her insisting on keeping that gown and his suggestion to burn it.

'Did you burn the one I got you?' he asked.

She shot him a questioning look before she pointed above his head and he saw the yellow gown hanging to dry. It was more holes than fabric, but he knew she meant to keep it.

'Are you hungry?' she asked.

'Aye, but I need to—' He nodded his head to the trees and quickly held up his hand when she moved to help him.

'You could undo it still,' she protested.

He could lose his dignity, but he did that anyway as dizziness almost overcame him when he stood. He had lost too much blood. When he returned, there were three fish upon a stone placed near a boulder padded with his cloak.

'Smells good,' he said, easing himself down and leaning back against the rock.

'It's been a day since you last woke.' She delicately pulled away a fin to get to the meat of her fish. 'And days before when we ate sufficiently.'

He shoved the hot fish in his mouth, knowing

he needed to be cleaned as well. He could feel the mud caked to the back of his neck. 'Another day lost?' he said.

She nodded. 'I returned from the stream and you were asleep. Stayed that way through the night. I ate without you.' She indicated the fish cooking on the stones. 'This is today's.'

He had slept, when there was much to discuss and to plan. Shame hovered over him. He did not question where it came from.

It was because of her.

He kept failing her. The Englishman had come when he'd been unconscious and unable to help her. Yesterday, she had been frightened, had practically run away from him when she realised she could have been killed that day at the market. Instead of providing her with assurances, he'd fallen asleep. She had faced these trials on her own.

He had fought her this entire journey and she'd only wanted the dagger to save her family. Now she offered him food.

He was wrong about her.

Buchanans were a lying deceitful clan, and she too lied effortlessly. Yet, he was beginning to realise that when she lied, she did it with a purpose.

She was from his family's most hated clan and yet, without any doubt, she was different.

'Can you travel?' Mairead asked.

She was as anxious as he. Maybe more so given

her impulsive nature, but if she wanted to go, he couldn't.

He had to lean against a tree to relieve himself. He could travel, but wouldn't be able to protect Mairead if they caught up with the Englishman.

He had to wait, but he was alive and there was a chance to get the jewel. He welcomed the feeling of satisfaction coursing through him. 'I'll need another day and more food.'

'This was all I could—'

'Nae, Mairead, this was most welcome.' He licked his fingers knowing he needed food more than manners. 'I could not be more grateful. Or beholden.'

'Do you have a fever?' She put down her piece of fish.

He knew what she meant. He had given her a kind word. But she had surprised him, made him laugh and saved his life. A kind word was a paltry act in comparison. 'We're different,' he explained.

'My telling of my brother and we're nae longer enemies?'

She made it sound insignificant, but the telling of her brother's death had pained her. She'd shown vulnerability.

He had...craved...to take the pain from her. She was impulsive. Stubborn. *Brave*, his mind whispered. Brave and had more care for others than was good for her.

Never in his life had he met such a female. To

face a killer on her own. To face him, knowing the odds were against her. *Buchanan*, his mind reminded him. But what did he know of Buchanans?

One horrific and tragic act, when he and his brothers had been young, had shaped his opinions of Buchanans. One act that never was spoken of again. So long ago that Gaira had little knowledge of it or didn't remember. Shannon's death had changed Malcolm, but marked him and Bram as well. Painful. Tragic. But should Shannon's death mark Mairead as well?

Caird rubbed his forehead.

Since the beginning, he had been fighting his knowledge of Clan Buchanan with the reality of Mairead. All her true feelings had always been there for him to understand. He had just been refusing to see them for what they were.

She railed at him, fled from him, struck him and lied to him. Every duplicitous action done not because of greed or deceit, but out of her helplessness. For what other options had he given her?

None.

If he'd faced the same odds, if all his options had been closed to him, would he have done everything in his power to help his family as she had tried to do? Aye, he would have.

He had been blind when it came to her. She had never been the enemy.

'We're different now,' he repeated. 'Why would there not be some accord between us?'

'Accord? Beholden?' She set down the rock. 'I'm going to believe this talk is blood loss.' Her movements were wide, exaggerated. 'How am I to believe you? How am I to believe we're different, when there's been nae evidence that's different? I'll always be from Clan Buchanan. And you've been cruel, kidnapping me and saying my very touch is vile.'

Everything she said was true. But then it was him with the misconception of her. With her actions, she had taken his prejudices just as the flood had taken his bandages. Quickly, harshly. With his prejudices gone he actually was in a different place in the world. But it was the same place she had been the entire time.

It was a world he knew little about. He needed more answers to his questions. But this time, the question was Mairead and he was beginning to realise he wanted the answers to her, very, very much.

'Why did you tell me of your brother?' he asked.

She gave him an enigmatic look. 'You told me of the jewel.'

'But you didn't need to tell me all.'

Mairead turned, but not before he saw her face flush.

This was something he needed to know. He'd told her a tale that most of Scotland knew. She told him a tale that was private and full of woe.

With her flush, he realised she'd told him more than she intended. But he didn't understand why.

'Mairead?' he prompted.

She looked over her shoulder and shrugged.

It had been personal, and very painful. He owed her. 'I've wronged you,' he said.

'Wronged?' There was a moment of surprise and softness to her voice before she turned towards him. 'These confessions are pity at the most. You know my clan will most likely banish my family for going against the laird's orders, for getting in debt to the English. Worse, my brother's dead. Dead. This is pity and I doona want it. Especially from an arrogant all-knowing Colquhoun, who is, nae doubt, wanting to lecture me on all my mistakes.'

'Mistakes? You have made nae mistakes. You're nothing like your clan.'

'My clan? What have my mistakes to do with my clan?'

He'd said too much.

She took a step closer to him. 'You are too certain of your opinion. This goes further than Colquhoun arrogance. What do you know of my clan?'

'You're different. You're not like them.'

'Tell me.'

He couldn't. In spite of everything, he couldn't.

'Secrets, Colquhoun?' She almost laughed, but the sound was full of derision. 'Secrets coming from you, when I told you all?' She turned away again. 'We are not different.'

He showed her trust. 'I explained about the jewel.'

'That I gave away!' She spun around. 'You should be even angrier with me. Not beholden!'

He frowned. 'You saved us. You saved me.'

'Is that it?' Something flashed across her eyes. 'Because I saved you? I explained that was for my own self-preservation. It would be worse for me if you'd died.'

'Is that why you did it?' he asked. Her reactions were unexpected. There were secrets still, he knew, but they were beginning to trust each other. Why was she not realising it for the miracle it was?

She scraped her fish remains into the fire and dropped the stone next to the flames to burn off. She was ignoring him and he should let her.

Yet, now that he understood at least a part of her, he wanted more. Desire? It was there and could not be ignored. Even now, he wanted her. He wanted to wrap her within his arms, breathe her in. Protect her.

The want, with the knowledge she had saved his life, that he had risked his life for hers, was overwhelming. He could no longer deny the trust beginning to spring between them. Yet, she was denying it…no, she was lying about it.

'You know we're different together now,' he

said, his mind just now understanding. 'You noticed it first.'

'I have nae idea what you talk of, Colquhoun.'

'I had the dagger,' he said. He'd had the dagger at the river. When she was drowning, and he had been at shore, the dagger had been strapped to the horse. He'd had everything he thought he needed and he had still gone back for her.

He pointed to her. 'I had the dagger. At the river. You noticed it.' His mind had been too full of need; he hadn't given a thought to the dagger, just her.

She moved impatiently away. 'I was half drowned; I said many things.'

She wasn't looking at him now and he couldn't see her thoughts. Which meant she was hiding something again and she only lied for a purpose. He just didn't understand the purpose now. Complicated Buchanan. He was too weak and too hungry to reason with her.

'Aye, you said much at the river. Little doubt why I remember it wrongly.' He stood slowly, carefully. 'After I clean, we'll need to make traps.'

She looked as if she wondered if he lied to her.

He kept his face impassive. He was lying to her, but he did it with purpose, as she had, and he was a quick learner.

'I did it.' Mairead lifted the snare for Caird's inspection. It was crooked and her fingers were bleeding and stinging from tying the nettle stalks together, but it somewhat resembled the other snares finished around his feet. The three snares he'd completed to her one.

'Aye,' he said. 'And it's a fine one.'

The day's light showed the green of his grey eyes as he seemed suddenly riveted by her accomplishment and what she knew was a ridiculous grin.

Embarrassed, she tucked a stray curl behind her ear and his eyes darkened as he followed her hand.

He had been looking at her too closely all morning. Since he'd left her to get clean and find the supplies to make snares, he had stopped his talk that they were different.

But his gaze remained disconcerting. Even if she didn't believe they were different, he certainly did. His encouraging and teasing her, while they made snares, was doing riotous things to her insides. So much so, she continually failed to concentrate and, when handling nettles, she needed to concentrate.

'Why are your hands not hurting?' she asked more irritably than she meant. The nettles were old and they had dipped the remaining leaves in the fire, but it didn't remove all the needles and there was no dock to be found.

'They do,' he said. Caird stopped picking nettle leaves from a stem. 'You'll need to tie the stalk to a twig like this.' He wrapped his stalk around a small stick. 'Then tie it to a larger one.'

He'd already explained the procedure, so his voice lulled her into just looking at him again. If his gaze was unsettling, looking at him rattled her. No matter how many times she looked, she was struck again by how comely he was. When she had seen him in the inn at night, she had thought him mesmerising. During the day, Caird was staggering.

He had emerged from the water with his clothes wet as if he'd walked into the stream to wash himself and his clothes together. He wore his breeches, but his tunic and cloak were hanging in the trees next to them.

His chest was bare. With no bandages, she saw the bruising around his ribcage, the blackened burn from the sword thrust, the numerous scrapes and scratches she hadn't tended.

He'd earned them all in his fierce pursuit of the jewel. Now when he no longer had the jewel, he patiently taught her to make snares.

She couldn't stop staring at him. She seemed uncontrollably fascinated by the width of his shoulders, the broadness of his chest and his earned injuries, both past and present. But those weren't what held her eyes, or made her toes curl. It was remembering how his body had felt against hers at the river and what happened afterwards... what would have happened—

'I thought you'd be different,' she said, trying to mask her erratic feelings.

He raised an eyebrow.

She kicked herself on her choice of words. 'We're sitting when the jewel's out there. I thought you'd be more impatient.'

'I'd thought that, too,' he said. But he didn't elaborate. Instead, his eyes were doing that searching thing again. The look he gave when he thought more than he said.

'Tell me of your family,' he said.

'My family?' she asked, surprised at the subject when there had never been anything but animosity between their families. 'Why, when you're soon to meet them? We should think about how we'll capture the jewel.'

He shrugged.

She sighed exaggeratedly. 'This journey has only been about the jewel. I do not ken why we talk of something else. It's sudden.'

'I'm curious.'

It was her turn to lift a brow.

Tension thrummed through him and she could feel him waiting for her to talk, but he hadn't answered her last question.

'The jewel is important...' he began, looking at her with dissatisfaction for making him talk. 'But other things are as well.'

She waited, but he didn't tell her what other

things were important and she knew he'd keep his silence.

Sighing in defeat, she said, 'I live with two sisters and my mother.'

'And Ailbert?' he asked, his voice rougher than usual.

'He was the eldest,' she said. 'I was born just after him.'

'Twins.'

She looked startled. 'I'm a girl.'

'It can happen. Like the Grahams. Did you look alike?'

It hurt to think of her brother. Her brother, with the dark eyes and curly hair. 'Aye,' she said. 'We did, although he could eat without it doing him any harm.'

Caird huffed.

It sounded like he was disagreeing, but she couldn't guess with what. 'My father died when we were young. Losing him was hard on Ailbert and my mother never quite recovered.'

He tilted his head, his eyes telling her he was waiting for something.

More answers, no doubt, but she didn't know what to say about her family.

'Who taught you to use your elbows and fists?' he asked.

'Ailbert.' She felt lightened by that question. Her fighting was a happy memory of her brother.

'I didn't want him to be the only one to protect our family.'

He frowned. 'He didn't teach your sisters?'

She shook her head. 'My sisters were too young when Father died.' She could barely remember her father, but she remembered the grief. Her mother's collapse. Ailbert's increasing recklessness.

How quickly this conversation turned to pain and how much she wanted to avoid it. Too many times, Ailbert gambled, took risks and harmed the family. Yet, with the last risk Ailbert had taken it was she who had irreparably broken the family.

Her heart clenched, suddenly, violently. Grief reminding her of its presence. It was dangerous talking of her family and she didn't know why she told Caird anything. No doubt his silences encouraged people to talk.

Swallowing the lump in her throat, she asked, 'Who do you have beside Malcolm?'

He opened his mouth, closed it and gave a slight shake of his head.

'Secrets?' she said.

'You will not like it.' Holding up the snares, he said, 'We need to set them.'

They rose together, his protection of his injuries putting them in too-close proximity. One step and she'd be against him.

From the look in his eyes, he'd noticed their closeness. The gown she wore covered her, but it was still torn at the top and only held together by her hasty tucking.

'I have an older brother.' His eyes travelled from her cheekbones, down her neck to the fine bones across her shoulders. It was indecent that they were bared to him, but even if covered, she knew she would have felt his gaze. She couldn't remember a time when she hadn't felt this way around him. He was altogether too much *there*.

Taking a step back, Mairead tried to remember the conversation. Families.

She thought of Malcolm as she had first seen him. Emerging from the room with a wide smile and jests. 'What is this other brother like?'

Looking for animal trails, Caird walked towards the trees. When he found one, he stopped. He carried the snares, but she'd have to set them. He risked injury just by walking, but he refused to rest.

Bending a sapling over, he tied a part of the snare to it. 'You'll need to anchor this to the ground with a stick.'

She took the snare, bent the sapling even further and secured it.

When she was done, Caird, with uneven gait, walked further down the trail. She followed until he found another spot and stopped. 'My other brother,' he said, 'his name is Bram.'

She'd asked what the brother was like, not his name. It wouldn't matter what his name was unless—

'Bram?' she asked, kneeling down, feeling a cold dread in her stomach. There was no sapling this time, so she pounded a thick branch into the earth and covered the base with leaves before holding out her hand for a snare. 'That name's significant.'

'Aye,' he replied, his movements slow as he handed her another trap.

He was hurting, but from his confident tone she knew he was also smirking. She was afraid she knew the reason why. 'Is it the same Bram?' she asked, tying the snare to the branch. It wasn't easy because, trembling, she suddenly felt caught in a trap.

'He's laird, Mairead. My brother is laird.'

They were the ruling Colquhouns. She should have known, should have guessed. She had heard of the Colquhoun laird. Bram was rumoured to be diplomatic, but absolutely ruthless. And the man had two brothers...

How could she have missed it when every arrogant, autocratic order Caird gave indicated exactly who he was.

'You are surprised?' he asked.

Standing, she gave a quick shake of her head. She didn't feel surprised. She felt foolish. She had been so blind in all of this. Trying to sell the dagger and entering the wrong room at the inn. How many mistakes did she have to make?

'I had two sisters.' He continued walking, turning right to find different trails. 'The youngest died in April.'

Mairead almost stumbled. Still following him, she couldn't see his face, but she heard the pain in his voice. Caird adding to the conversation was unexpected. But what was more unexpected was that he mentioned something that obviously hurt him. There was now a slight stiffening to Caird's shoulders. She didn't know if it was regret that he'd told her or if it was grief.

Mairead now had questions. If his sister had died in April, it could have something to do with the English. But as much as she despised the English, she understood grief and pain more.

'The sister, who is having these wedding celebrations, is she fierce?

He hesitated slightly before he answered, 'Very.'

What else could she be? 'With red hair?'

'Like a poppy with freckles.'

Mairead could see the tension ease from Caird's shoulders; she also heard the surprise in his voice. Suspicion instantly laced her stomach as she realised Caird was watching her again. Had Caird shared something of his family because he'd read her feelings of unease so clearly?

'What about your sisters?' he asked, heading around some grouse. She looked at the yellow of the flowers and was reminded of the colour of the other gown. She doubted she had looked any better in it than the straggling shrub.

He wanted to talk of her sisters. It was a familiar conversation. On Buchanan land, her sisters were famous and not for making mistakes. In appearance and temper, they were as opposite from her as possible.

'They are my sisters. They giggle.'

'Descriptive,' he murmured, his hand drifting to his injury before he lowered it.

'You're hurting,' she said. 'We should return, you need to rest. What if you collapse on me?'

'I need food,' he replied, pointing to another spot. 'And you're changing the subject of your sisters.'

She didn't feel like describing her sisters to him. They could flirt and fit in gowns properly. 'I doona think you should be complaining of my conversational skills.'

'I'm not,' he replied, but his look implied he wanted to hear more.

Of course, her lack of description intrigued him. As if they needed any extra endowment. She grabbed another snare and set to work.

'Their hair's lighter than mine and straighter,' she said grudgingly. She couldn't lie to him; he'd soon see for himself, but that didn't mean she was telling him everything.

'That's not what I'm curious about,' he said.

He wanted more than their hair colour? She'd heard her sisters described often enough. Entire poems were dedicated to them. 'Their golden hair cascades down their back like sunshine,' she mimicked, pounding a stake into the ground with a rock. 'Their eyes are like cloudless summer skies and their lips? The ripest of berries.'

'Hmmm,' he answered. 'What of their manners?'

She fumbled with the snare, almost tearing the stalk. 'Dainty and refined.'

'Their laughter?'

She concentrated on connecting the stalk to the stake. 'Like heavenly bells.'

'Are their feet like flower petals?' he added.

'As a matter of fact—' She quickly stepped away from the trap, so as not to make it completely useless. 'I'll not describe them any more to the likes of you.'

'But I'm still a wee bit curious,' he said.

Caird knew he was more than curious. This was a Mairead he hadn't seen before. Her chin jutted out just so; her cheeks were flushed from the walk and from her annoyance. She was ireful and all too tempting.

He knew what she felt like, what her lips tasted like and he wanted more. Much more. He took a step closer to her. 'Aren't you asking whom I'm curious about?'

'Nae,' she answered primly.

Caird chuckled, which earned a scathing look from her.

She was jealous of her sisters' beauty, though he felt no interest in them at all.

Not when Mairead showed honour and bravery. Not when he wanted to laugh and kiss her. Not when he was ensnared by her hair, and the scathing look in her dark eyes. If it wasn't for the danger they were in and Malcolm's grief, he'd be on his knees before her, begging her, he'd—

He shook his head. Fanciful thoughts. Changing thoughts. He'd said they were different together, but until that moment, he hadn't realised how different.

She stood before him with her hands on her hips and he didn't care how much conflict was still between them. He wanted her.

Mairead couldn't move. Not when Caird stepped closer. Not when her annoyance and anger kept her stubbornly still, and certainly not the moment Caird touched her cheek.

Then Caird crooked his finger under her jaw and lifted her lips to his. His kiss was nothing more than the feel and heat of his body against hers. It was slow and gentle, though she could feel his desire for more. She wanted more. Wanted to press against him, to wind her hands around his neck and pull him tighter against her.

But Caird never moved his fingers from her chin, never increased his kiss. Instead, he pulled away and tucked a stray hair behind her ear.

'Ah, Mairead,' he whispered, his eyes warm.

The kiss wasn't just a need to bed her. Caird kissed her as if he *cared*.

The anger and annoyance that had kept her feet firm to the ground flared and propelled her away from him. The feeling increased until her hands fisted at her sides and she stood almost on her toes.

She didn't want gentleness. Didn't deserve caring. She wanted this nightmare over.

'*Never* do that again, Colquhoun.' She spun on her heel to return to the fire.

## Chapter Twenty-One

Caird strained his eyes to look further into the darkening sky. They rode steadily and had travelled all day, but manoeuvring the horse was difficult since the Englishman had taken the bridle. Now night was upon them and they still had not found a village or the Englishman. They moved too slowly and it was taking too long.

Mairead's lies had bought them time. But he wasn't even sure they went in the right direction, and he could find no tracks to follow.

As if to make the horse go faster or maybe because she was still angered, Mairead leaned forward.

Yesterday, describing her sisters had hurt her. He couldn't help but kiss her, to let her know her beauty far surpassed anything she described.

Her response hadn't been what he expected. He'd still been reeling from her anger when she stormed off. So he didn't return to camp, but went in the opposite direction and waited until the traps worked. Catching and skinning the hares had given him something to do with his hands, but eventually he'd returned to the fire.

By then hours had passed and she was still angry with him.

When he put the hares on the fire, she had only wanted to talk of the jewel. No family, no sisters, no confessions. Just anger. Just the jewel. It had to be her anger that faulted her mind. For when she'd told him her irrational plan to recapture the jewel, he'd become angry.

'We'll have to stop or risk this horse,' he said. With the hills and the light, it was getting foolish for them to keep travelling.

'Can we walk?' She turned, her hands gripping his thigh. From the look in her eye, he knew she focused only on gaining the ground they'd lost. She didn't know what her body did to him, or where she gripped his thigh. But he did.

'Aye.' He stopped the horse. With the moon full, they could make another mile or so. It wasn't time for them to stop. He wasn't hungry…at least not for food.

She accepted his assistance and, with his hands on her waist, he was rewarded with a brief feel of her body.

It did nothing to relieve his wanting.

'With our noise. We'll nae catch him like this, you ken?' he said.

'I'll take the horse to keep your hands free in case we do.'

Caird grunted, but he moved away from the horse. His gait was the only indication his injury pained him.

'How is your side?' She lightly gripped the horse's mane.

Caird shrugged.

She was getting used to his silences. Knowing the way to understand him in any conversation was to look at him.

The dimming light created shadows which covered and revealed the rugged planes of his face. She remembered that first night at the inn. Then, the dim light could not hide his comeliness, but now—

Now, she knew what colour his eyes were, how they stormed and swirled from grey to green when he looked at her. She knew what his lips felt like against hers. How his kisses could punish or coax.

She should be thinking of catching her brother's killer, or of her family on the cusp of banishment.

But the end of the day was too still, she could see nothing of her brother's murderer and Caird was walking by her side, silent, strong and purposeful. Ignoring him was like trying to avoid a mountain that needed crossing. He was just *there*.

'Have you thought of another plan for the jewel?' she asked.

''Tis nae plan,' he answered, his voice tight. 'A plan needs facts and strategy. Your notion has none of those.'

Caird hadn't liked her idea and still didn't like it. But she didn't expect an overbearing rule-orientated Colquhoun to agree with a Buchanan.

'If you cannot think of another way to capture the jewel, we'll have to use mine.'

He remained silent.

'It'll work. He knows our clans argue, so he wouldn't expect us to co-operate. He thinks you're dead, so he won't expect you to sneak up on him.'

'We doona know how we'll find him.'

'The plan will work in any situation. A field, a village street, an…an inn.'

'And leave you exposed in front of a madman before I come up from behind?'

She shrugged, feigning nonchalance.

'Never,' he said. The same word he had used the last time she'd suggested this.

She understood his reluctance; she had the same unease. If Caird couldn't get to her in time, or if he died, she'd be standing before the Englishman, whose only thought would be to kill her.

No, she wouldn't be in the Englishman's thoughts. Now that she'd met him, she knew killing her would be of little consequence to him.

How different her regard of her brother's murderer from just a few days ago. Before when she'd crept into the inn to retrieve the dagger, she hadn't been thinking. Grief and anger had fuelled her, but now she knew what she faced: the Englishman's empty eyes, his lustful pleasure at acquiring the jewel. Now, he terrified her.

'Stop,' Caird whispered and pointed to the trees ahead.

Mairead tightened her hand on the horse as Caird walked towards the trees. She saw nothing, heard nothing, but she didn't know what to listen for. A sword removed from a sheath? Soft footsteps sneaking about in the dark?

Caird waved her forward, but did not change his position from the trees. Walking ahead, she stumbled sharply and the horse butted her with its side. Quickly sidestepping its hooves, she got behind Caird as they walked through the shallow line of trees. They quickly reached the clearing on the other side and she breathed a sigh of relief.

The clearing revealed a slight valley. Within a short walk from them were several homes, fences and the distinct smell of animals.

It was cold with the oncoming night, but while they travelled, there could be no more fires. The sight of the homes had her envisioning warmth, food and shelter. Safety, but only if....

'Could he be here?' Impatience and cold made her ask a question there could be no answer to.

'Are we stopping here?' she asked when Caird kept his silence.

She knew he wasn't ignoring her, but assessing the risk of what lay ahead of them.

'You stop here,' he finally replied. 'I need answers.'

When Caird returned it was fully dark. He was carrying a bundle, and all alone. As he approached, his strides slowed. Only then did she stand and emerge from the tree cover.

'Over here,' she called.

He took the remaining steps and threw the bundle on the ground. She smelled the bread before he handed it to her.

'It's still warm,' he said. 'There's venison as well.'

His body was only a shadow. Her hands fumbled to find the offered bread. Touching his hands seemed oddly intimate in the dark. 'Bread making at night?'

'The wife was heavy with child. The daughter was making bread.' He took a bite.

Caird must have frightened the family when he knocked on their door. A large unknown man and a wife and daughter in need of protection. Caird might have been in more danger in that home than if he'd run into the Englishman.

'You were there for a while.' She took a bite of venison, and offered him their supply of water.

He shook his head. 'There were chores.'

Chores. A domestic hearth and a family together.

Their journey had been full of lies, revenge, legends and murder. They were so removed from hearth and home, she'd almost forgotten it existed.

'They saw the Englishman,' he said.

She almost choked.

'He was walking next to an ill horse.'

She swallowed and didn't hide her smile. Her plan to slow him had worked. But Caird's voice didn't project the same satisfaction.

'There's a village just beyond the next hill,' Caird continued. 'We'd see it now, but it's dark. He's there, Mairead.'

So close. She took another bite. The venison was delicious, but its taste was dimmed by the fear and relief giving her gooseflesh. The nightmare would get worse before it was over.

'He's *returned* here.' Caird's emphasis held a warning. 'You ken?'

She nodded even if he couldn't see. That he'd returned meant the Englishman had come this way before. This could even be his home, his seat of power. By the cave, they'd been surrounded by men. Caird had killed them, but that didn't mean there weren't more.

'You think he has accomplices?'

'Soldiers are here.' His words were clipped. 'Trained men and only God knows how many.'

He was angry, very angry. When she offered him the water, he took it.

There were dangers besides the Englishman. 'He's here though. He's here and we can still get the jewel.'

'We've nae time, nae defence, nae men,' he said.

'Are you saying we cannot get the dagger and jewel?'

Even in the dark she saw him flinch.

After all his arrogance, his forcefulness, his determination to get them here. After she had risked her life, he was giving up?

'That's your plan?' she said. 'Wishing for things we doona have? Is that a trait of all Colquhouns? Because us Buchanans are not that fortunate. The odds are never in our favour, Colquhoun. But my idea will still work.'

'Nae!' Water sloshed in the skein as he tightened his grip. 'I make nae *wishes*. I plan, I get answers and I learn all the faults of my enemy. When I am through, I make conquests. Your idea is nothing but impulsiveness. You risk too much.'

'But the jewel is right there,' she said, exasperated. 'We'll make adjustments.'

It was dark, the moon cast only a faint glow, so she couldn't see, but she felt his glower. So she glowered right back. 'You'll just need to go into the village before me and take care of these soldiers.'

He made a sound, which sounded stupefied and pleased at the same time. 'By myself?' he said.

'Odds not in my favour are familiar to me. Are you saying a Colquhoun cannot do it?'

'Are you questioning my bravery?' he said, his voice unamused.

Since that was what she was doing, she stayed quiet.

'It's dangerous and will get us killed,' he said. 'I will go this night and see what the village entails. Find the soldiers and count them.'

'Thus getting spotted by the Englishman because I'm not there to distract him.'

He cursed.

'We have nae other choice,' she argued. 'Tomorrow, you'll go to the village before I do. The horse is sick, it cannot be held in a barn. When I get there, I'll pretend to steal it. You ken I'm good at lying.'

He remained silent, not liking this part of the argument.

Perhaps reminding him of their differences wasn't the way to sway him. 'I'll distract him while you keep his soldiers busy,' she continued as if she didn't sense his disapproval. 'Then you can come behind him.'

'What if it's a soldier who finds you before the Englishman?'

'I'll make certain I'm recognised.' She had to

believe she was enough of a concern that the Englishman would want to kill her himself.

'You have to know what you risk,' he said. 'Why do you want to risk this?'

Didn't he realise this was almost over? She wanted it to be over. For years, she had been sheltering her family from her brother's recklessness. This nightmare was just more agony. Caird acted as though he didn't want her to risk herself. She didn't want to think this was more caring from him.

'Why do you ask a question that has already been answered?' she replied. 'Nothing has changed in this. You've mentioned the importance of the jewel. You can keep it, but I want the dagger.' Although the dagger may not repair all the damage her brother had done, she still needed the money.

He shifted, not away or towards her, but almost as if what she said shocked him. She was glad the cover of darkness hid her expressions from him, but she needed to see his reaction to understand what he was thinking.

'You do this for gain, Buchanan?' he said.

Good. They were back to their clan names. There would be no more caring from him, she could stop her errant fascination and this could be over.

'Why did you tell me of your brother?' he demanded.

She jumped, but should have expected his question. He kept asking even though she refused to answer him. In truth, she didn't fully understand why she'd told him. Now, if she confessed to more, if she trusted him with the whole nightmare, then she feared it would mean she cared for him. She knew any feelings for him would be a mistake.

However, he wasn't giving up this relentless need to ask her. So she'd tell him some. Some. But not everything. Not the reason, for that guilt was hers alone. The fact was, by her impulsive mistake, she'd killed her brother. And that shame must stay buried deep in her, like a knife.

'Maybe I need to make this right,' she said. 'Ailbert died. Maybe I need it to mean something.'

Caird moved towards her. 'Who are you?' he said. He was close enough to see now. 'Everything I've ever known—'

A brief gust of wind blew a tendril of her hair. Caird captured the loose curl. While his fingers stroked the strand, he watched the spring coil and uncoil.

He was so reflective she wasn't sure he knew what he did. Her hair tangled easily, and if she pulled away it would hurt. That was the only reason she stood still while he brushed his fingers through her hair. It couldn't be because she felt his eyes gazing as if he was in awe.

'Your hair, Mairead,' he whispered. 'I could follow this hair anywhere.'

He smiled, a brief glimpse of white in the dark. 'I *have* followed this hair everywhere.'

When he found a tangle, his other hand reverently undid the knot. 'Even before I knew who you were or what meeting you would mean, your hair beckoned me to follow you.'

There were many knots. She waited for the pain, but it never came. For a man who wielded and killed with a sword, he gently freed each lock.

'But I cannot follow blindly on this.'

Shaking his head, Caird released his touch. 'This is nae plan. We doona know how many soldiers there are; you won't know how much time to give me. I could be killed and you may not know.'

All true, but she'd seen him fight. If he could surprise the soldiers as well, she believed he had a chance.

'This plan will work,' she insisted, her hair still tingling from his touch.

The plan had to work. Her goal was the same: find the dagger. But now she felt fear. Now, she knew the consequences even with Caird there to protect her. Maybe her fear was because of Caird. Knowing, if she made a mistake, as she always did, she would put his life at risk.

'You cannot even stay safely here until I tell you they're dead.'

She couldn't. She had to go into the village soon after he left. The Englishman couldn't know

Caird had killed his soldiers. To ensure that, she had to distract him.

It was frightening. Before, she had impulsively chased after her brother's murderer. Now, she knew how deadly the Englishman was, and still intended to confront him. She didn't want to reflect on how many soldiers there'd be or where they would be hidden.

She was scared. But it still had to be done.

'I cannot allow this,' he said firmly. 'Not while I have breath left in my body.'

'Worried for my safety?' she taunted.

'Aye,' he replied.

Trying to gain distraction from his words, she took the last bite of bread.

'We've run out of time.' She swallowed. 'If we wait, he could go where we can't find him. We can surprise him.'

His hand swept over her chin to cradle her face and bring her eyes up to his. It was too dark to see what was in his gaze, but she felt it all the same.

'How could you trust me in this?' he said, too evenly.

There was something he wanted her to understand. She didn't want to understand. It would be over soon. He didn't know everything and soon they'd return to their different clans.

'Does trust have something to do with this?' she argued. 'I saw you fight.'

'But I've failed you, Mairead, more times than

I've protected you. I abandoned you to that madman. He could have taken so much more!'

'Abandoned me?' Even unconscious and slumped into a puddle, Caird had provided her with comfort and strength. If it had been just her, she didn't know if she'd have even raised her eyes to the Englishman. 'You almost died. How could you think that was abandonment?'

He was silent, but she knew he was weighing her words. He wanted to tell her something.

So she waited. She waited while he cradled her cheek, while his other hand skimmed down her arm and back up again.

His eyes roamed where his hand went, but she didn't think he saw what he was doing. She couldn't see either, but she felt every bit of it.

'Clever Buchanan, haven't you guessed?' he asked.

She didn't understand and something inside her didn't want the answer to his question. 'You almost died,' she repeated. 'I never felt abandoned.'

His hands stilled, then he drew her to his chest. She felt and heard his sigh. 'This isn't the time to tell you...' he started. 'Nae, I must think and we must try to sleep. We have blankets now.'

Stepping away, he snapped open the blankets and lay down.

When she lay down, she didn't protest as Caird adjusted his body around hers and pulled her tighter into his embrace. In the cold of the night, she welcomed his heat.

Warm, fed, protected, she fell asleep.

'It's time,' Caird whispered.

Mairead opened her eyes. It was still dark, but she knew morning approached. He had to leave before the sun.

If he was leaving.

Caird shifted beneath her and, releasing his tunic, she reluctantly disentangled her legs. Yet, greedy for his warmth, she remained on top of him when their eyes met.

Grey, fathomless eyes met hers. Her Colquhoun had been searching for his answers all night.

Warm, rested, she didn't question why she was on top of him. Pushing on his chest, she adjusted her position to look more fully at him. 'Have you decided?' she asked.

A brief nod. 'It is—'

'Impulsive,' she offered.

'But the surprise could win us this.'

Grateful she hadn't moved, Caird held Mairead. He needed to hold her more. He couldn't believe he'd agreed to it, a Buchanan plan, an impulsive plan.

There were answers he needed and too many variables. They talked of the soldiers, but there were villagers, too. Enemies or friends, he didn't know. If he could take down the soldiers, maybe they would rise against the Englishman or maybe they would kill them.

It was madness. But because of the madness, because of her, it might work.

Anything else was unacceptable. The Englishman could not have the Jewel of Kings and Mairead insisted on having her dagger. If they waited any longer, they could lose both. Surprise tipped the odds in their favour.

He stood and pulled her up with him.

'You've agreed?' she whispered.

Caird felt Mairead's hesitation and could almost touch her fear. It was her idea, but it was risky. How could he be a man and send her into the village alone? It would only take a moment for the Englishman to kill her and the plan meant he would be too far away to prevent it. He couldn't ask it of her.

'All night, I have thought of this plan and how to change it,' he answered. 'It's madness when we doona even know what we face.'

She shook her head. 'We must do this. I must do this. You'll be protecting me, Colquhoun. You're not saying someone else is better at swordplay?'

She teased, but her eyes held fear. Her fear almost undid him, almost made him stop this whole madness. But the only way to stop it, to end her pain and fear, was to capture the dagger and kill the Englishman.

'Mairead, my hesitation has never been for me,'

he said. 'I know what I face. With one soldier down, I will have a sword. Even wounded, I've the strength of many men. But I can't keep you safe because you must distract the Englishman. You risk too much.'

Mairead blinked tears away before he could see them. Caird was displaying more care. And something in her was answering him. She was beginning to believe they were different, but everything in her knew they couldn't be. She'd made too many mistakes.

It would be over soon. He'd have the jewel; she'd have the dagger. They would part. But she had been held throughout the night. He had feared he abandoned her, when she'd felt only comfort from him. Now he risked his life, but was only worried about hers.

After years of battling with her brother's gambling, her sisters' empty giggling and her mother's frailty, she found, despite everything else, comfort in Caird's silences, his need to plan, his need for answers.

There was a part of her that wondered if she wanted to keep some of this nightmare. At least the part with Caird.

'Nae, I doona risk anything at all,' she finally answered, knowing what she was about to say would surprise him. But she liked the idea of surprising him. Especially now. So even though it was a mistake to tell him anything of her feelings for him, she couldn't help it. 'We're different to-gether now,' she said.

Caird held absolutely, unerringly still. Waiting.

She wouldn't make him wait long. They didn't have long and she wanted to see his expression.

'I knew we were different,' she continued, 'that day at the river. When you had the horse and the dagger, and I was being drowned by the water. You came back for me.'

'I thought,' he whispered, 'you didn't remember. You said you didn't remember. Why do you mention this, Mairead?'

'Today, I know there's nae risk,' she answered. 'Because, like then, I know you'll come for me.'

Caird didn't blink and though he held still, it wasn't because he was waiting.

It was because a Buchanan had bested a Colquhoun. Again.

She grinned.

Then she couldn't any more as he hauled her into his arms and pressed his lips to hers.

His hands, his arms, his mountain of a body wrapped around her. She was instantly, whole-heartedly surrounded by overpowering male de-sire, and it wasn't for domination over her, or for taking, but for giving, and giving more.

When his mouth eased, when his tongue be-guiled her, she did the only thing she could: she gave back.

Then when his hands lifted her up and against

him, she clung to him. There wasn't anything else she wanted to do.

He ended the kiss before he ended his tight hold on her. Deep shudders shook his body and he held her until they stilled. She couldn't stop her own trembling. So it was he who disentangled her hands and slowly, and very reluctantly, let her down.

'You will wait; you will give me time,' he said vehemently. He peered straight into her eyes. The grey depths demanded she understand and obey exactly what he ordered. 'Promise me this.'

She didn't have a voice. Not after that kiss. She didn't even know how to nod, but he seemed satisfied with whatever response she gave him because he was quickly gone.

She waited. She had to. Even though everything in her screamed to rush forward, to end the nightmare. To protect Caird.

She couldn't care for that man. But the impulse was there, inside her, just as insidious as her want for him. She couldn't allow it. It had to be this trouble they were in that made her feel this way. When it was over, she wouldn't feel anything for him. Nothing at all. It just needed to be *over*.

So she waited and she paced. When the sun's light reached her feet and she didn't have to wait any longer, she moved from the shadows. It was time to show the Englishman what it truly meant to be Buchanan.

## Chapter Twenty-Two

The sun was just covering the morning in light as Mairead stood in the village centre. She was early enough for her to appear scheming, and she was late enough to be caught. She had to remember she needed to be caught.

'That horse is no use, my dear,' the Englishman said behind her. 'But then you know that.'

Nerves frayed, Mairead exhaled shakily. She stopped pretending to unravel Caird's horse from the post. When she managed to untie the reins in truth, she slowly turned around.

The Englishman was fully dressed; his cape was courtly fine. His stance was casual, but his hand caressed the hilt of his sword and his light blue eyes glanced around.

She raised her chin. He was intimidating, but she couldn't let him see that. If she was to be brave or stupid enough to steal from him, she was brave enough to stand her ground.

'A true Buchanan slowing me down with an ill horse,' he said. 'Will you assuage my curiosity about why you'd take such a risk?'

'I doona think I got the better end of our bargaining.'

His mouth curved as if he was amused. 'Such discourtesy when I had so gallantly let you live.'

'But you killed my brother.'

'For stealing from me. As you are about to do.' He looked around him again. 'And you are alone? You were with another when I last saw you.'

She feigned surprise. 'That Colquhoun lump? He never woke. Just rattled away until the end.'

'All by yourself?' he said, his hands wandering away from the hilt of his sword, to a dagger in his belt.

Of course, he would think she wasn't worthy of a sword fight, not when a sharp blade would end her life just like her brother's.

Her hands and legs shook from the torrent of emotions. She felt her eyes narrow to pinpoints focused only on the Englishman. Her shaking limbs wanted her to move. But she couldn't follow that impulse; she had to remain still for Caird.

'Nae, not alone,' she answered, glad to see a moment of hesitancy in her brother's murderer. 'With this horse, I'll have two.' She held up the reins.

'So you hide the more worthy mount.' His

amused smile disappeared. 'I am losing my patience with you.'

'I never had any with you, so I will be on my way.' She stepped forward even though there was nowhere to go except through him.

He didn't move.

Mairead saw a movement across the road from her. It could be a villager, it could be Caird or it could be a soldier. But whoever it was, they gave her the courage to continue. 'You think to kill me here, in front of all these witnesses?'

She hoped the movement was Caird.

He tilted his head, his eyes never leaving hers. 'You think there are witnesses? This is almost… fun,' he said.

It wasn't what he said, but the way he said it, that made her falter. When he smiled, she stopped pretending to move.

'You still do not know and I know everything,' he said. 'It is like a game, is it not?' He fingered his dagger. 'And I know all the rules, because I made them.'

This was no game she wanted to play. They were close enough, he could throw the blade, but she didn't dare move. It was imperative she kept the Englishman looking at her.

'Tell me your rules then, and maybe I'll play,' Mairead said.

Before she blinked, Caird appeared, a blade drawn at the Englishman's throat.

Not registering surprise, the Englishman's mouth quirked at the corners. Then slowly, hypnotically, his protuberant pale eyes grew cold.

Looking into his blank stare, Mairead felt more chilled than when she'd stood alone.

'Where is it?' Caird demanded.

'Under my cape. I could hardly keep it anywhere else.' The man raised his hands, but Caird did not let him go.

'Lift your cape,' he ordered.

Waiting for any sudden movement, Mairead didn't take her eyes off the Englishman until he lifted his cape above his waist. Only then did she see Caird's pouch.

With a glance to Caird, who nodded, she stepped forward and untied the pouch. Moving quickly away, she felt the contents. There was no mistaking what it held.

Clutching the pouch, she asked, 'What do you do with this?'

'Nothing now.'

'Ach, what did you mean to do with it?'

'The same as any man with that much power, I intended to use it.'

She'd get no straight answers from him.

His posture threatening and deadly, Caird kept his blade steady at the Englishman's neck. But the killer remained nonchalant, and no villagers emerged.

Caird argued that there were too many questions to this plan and she was beginning to agree.

'Who are you?' she asked.

He cocked an eyebrow. 'This is hardly a time for introductions now, is it?'

Caird gave a growl in his throat that raised hairs on the back of her neck. 'I'd like to know whom I kill.'

'Then if I answer, you'll kill me? It makes not answering ever so easy.'

The hornets woke inside Mairead. She wished she could release them so they could attack her brother's murderer. She had always thought the Colquhouns arrogant. And they were. Caird stood as proud as any king, his strength and swiftness a testament to hundreds of hours of training.

But this man's arrogance was dark, sinister, like poison.

The Englishman's hands never lowered; his eyes never left hers. He looked as innocent as he could and just as vulnerable. Which didn't sit right. Something was terribly wrong.

'You'll answer him,' she demanded.

'Oh, I don't think so.' The Englishman circled his right arm in the air.

Nothing moved.

Brows drawn, he circled his arm again and looked down the road of the village. It remained empty.

A grin breaking on his face, the Englishman

slowly turned his head to Caird. 'Oh, I may have underestimated you, Colquhoun.'

Caird's stance eased. 'Aye.'

The man's grin didn't drop as he turned to Mairead. 'You posed such a pretty distraction and they were simply dispatched.' Looking only slightly inconvenienced, he chuckled. 'I trained some of them, too. Pity.'

'You'll give answers now.' Caird's voice was as deadly certain as she'd ever heard it. 'Why was your accomplice returning to Buchanan land?'

The Englishman shrugged and winced as the blade cut into his neck. Caird did not ease his hold.

Not losing his pomposity, the Englishman swallowed. 'I like the direction of these questions, so I'll answer you this—where else would he go except to find me?'

'Why are you here? Why was the jewel on Buchanan land?'

'A *Colquhoun* asks that question?' The Englishman did not hide his smile, a macabre contrast to the blood trailing down his throat. 'Oh, truly, I am enjoying the direction of these questions.'

'Enjoy nae more,' Caird growled, pushing the Englishman away. 'We draw swords.'

Pulling the horse, Mairead swiftly moved to the side. They'd gained no answers with their questioning. Now Caird planned to fight the Englishman after he'd fought the soldiers? She didn't know how many he had killed. But it was more than a few and he had to be exhausted.

Sweat and dirt peppered his body. There were more bloodied scrapes along his arms and legs, but it was his side that caused her to gasp. He had reopened the wound and it bled.

He couldn't remain standing, let alone fight their enemy.

The Englishman, ever confident, didn't stumble as he gained equal distance from Caird and her.

'But you killed all my men, Colquhoun. You obviously have the better sword arm.' The Englishman reached slowly to his waist. His intent was clear to reach his dagger, but he threw it to the ground.

Caird threw his blade to the ground as well.

The Englishman simply nodded and reached for his sword.

Caird's sword was out and ready. Mairead tightened her hold on the horse. Caird was too injured for this fight. If she had to, she'd make a distraction until they could escape. One way or another she would help end this.

But then the Englishman simply threw his sword to the ground as well.

Caird did not change his stance, but his frown increased.

The Englishman did not do what was expected. She glanced around, and glimpsed people in windows and partially opened doorways.

'Pick up your sword,' Caird demanded.

'Oh, I don't think so, Colquhoun.'

'Pick up your sword or I'll cleave you in two.'

'No, you won't,' the Englishman replied. 'Your sense of honour would never allow you to kill a defenceless man. So predictable.'

He turned to Mairead. 'Frustrated, Buchanan? I killed your brother so easily. I cut into his stomach like I was cutting butter for my bread and with as little thought. This cannot sit easy with one such as you. You'd kill me, wouldn't you?'

The hornets swarmed in answer. Ignoring the madman and the insistent feeling inside, she glanced around; some of the villagers had moved forward. Were they friends or enemies?

Caird's tunic was saturated with blood. He'd soon weaken. She wanted to ram a thrown blade into the Englishman's stomach and be done. But that choice would get them killed if the villagers were enemies.

'So many decisions.' The Englishman smirked. 'But you cannot fight me and survive, Buchanan.'

He clasped his hands in front of him. 'So it appears we are at an impasse.'

Caird's stance changed. 'Nae, there will be justice.'

'Me, be your prisoner?' He laughed. 'I believe you now underestimate me, Colquhoun.'

The Englishman clapped. Loudly. The echo rang throughout the village.

Which was suddenly no longer empty. Doors opened and men stepped out of their homes. Their arms were full of weaponry: swords, daggers, farming tools. Steel and iron in different shapes.

There was too many of them and they were surrounded.

# Chapter Twenty-Three

Caird did not glance at the doors suddenly opening. He'd tried counting the homes as he killed the soldiers. With his wounds, and Mairead's vulnerability, he couldn't fight them.

Every ounce of honour demanded he fight and kill this man. To end this. But he could never risk Mairead. Caird glanced at Mairead; her eyes were wide with fear and confusion. It was a look he never wanted to see.

'You don't appear to be puzzled, Colquhoun. You probably guessed my power was more. I am everywhere and where you'd least expect me. You are wise enough to guess my power goes beyond this tiny village. Taking me as a prisoner would never be an option. But I'm sure you're relieved we are no longer at an impasse.'

Caird didn't reply.

The Englishman gave an almost imperceptible shrug. 'I know I am,' he continued almost glibly.

'Truly, if you knew how much trouble I have gone to in order to secure the dagger with its treasure again, you'd appreciate my deserving them both.'

He held out his palm to Mairead. 'Now, I will have that jewel and let them kill you both.'

Dread held Caird still even as every instinct in him roared to slash the Englishman into pieces. 'These are not men to fight for you.' Caird did not lower his sword, or his gaze, which took in the village. 'These are not soldiers.'

The Englishman's brow lifted. 'Yet they will kill you if you kill me.'

Caird had no doubt. They were bribed Scots. His heart broke for them, for every Scotsmen, who had lost hope. Hundreds of villages like this covered his precious homeland. He had no doubt this man, or his soldiers, had infected every one of them.

For the first time, he felt some of that hopelessness possess him, too. Then he saw Mairead take a step closer, saw her pull the horse closer as well. She was planning their escape and he felt awe.

The Englishman might have an entire village at his command but he had Mairead. As long as there was breath in his body, he would get them out of here.

Mairead, the Englishman and Caird stood in some nightmare triangle. She held the horse's reins, but knew it was useless to run. They might have escaped if it had been just the Englishman, but they were surrounded by villagers.

She looked at every single person. They weren't foes or friends. They were afraid, and so was she. But she was also very, very angry. This madman would never let them go. She welcomed the hornets' stings inside her.

'Help us!' she cried, her voice echoing as if the village was empty. 'We're like you. On the other side of his sword! Like. You!'

The Englishman didn't thrust a blade now, and her brother wasn't collapsing to the ground, but she felt just as helpless, just as powerless.

Her nightmare. Not over and so much worse.

Desperation tore through Mairead, a longing so deep and jagged, it ripped free. It should have hurt, but the hornets made her too crazed to feel.

Pacing, ignoring Caird's wariness and the Englishman's amusement, she kept her eyes on the villagers. She wanted them to look in her eyes and see her desperation, her helplessness and her grief. Everything.

She also demanded they see her anger, her rage and her blinding desire for this nightmare to be done.

*Everything!*

She wanted this over. From the sickening despair she'd felt when her brother confessed what he'd done to the fatal knowledge he'd gambled away their home. The laird would banish them to a war-torn country with nowhere safe to go. She refused for it to happen.

These villagers thought to fight? She would fight twice as hard. Her brother had paid with his life; she'd paid with her fear, and kidnapping and weeks of desperation. She was *owed*.

With wide movements, she took another step. She didn't care that the Englishman and Caird watched her anger. She didn't care if she looked more maddened than the madman!

'Are you just going to stand there?' she called. 'Watch his sword slice into our hearts? Murder us until we nae longer breathe?'

The elation of finding the jewelled dagger, the spiralling hope then horror as she watched her brother die. His eyes widening in pain before growing distant and shutting for ever. Terrified, but determined to retrieve the dagger, only to enter Caird's room instead.

Another step. Uneven surface. She looked down to see her left foot on a thrown blade. She didn't care if her feet took her directly in the path of a sword pointed to her. As long as she held one as well.

She heard voices then, Caird's, the Englishman's, but they were distant, too far away to make any difference. She grabbed the blade.

The cold blade's power felt *wonderful*.

She smiled, and knew there was a fierce light in her eyes. Raising the blade over her head, she cried, 'Are you going to follow his orders? How does your Scottish blood flow? For truth or lies? For your families or for this Englishman?'

Remaining still, the villagers stared. She wouldn't let them see her eyes close never to be opened again. Not if she could help it.

She swung to face Caird and the Englishman. They had shifted. Now, they stood in a crooked triangle, with her at the head. Her dagger pointed at them both.

With an intelligent light in his bulging eyes, the Englishman looked almost gleeful. It didn't matter. She knew she was more crazed than him and she *relished* it.

Caird was speaking his words again. Over and over until they resembled: 'Doona, they'll kill you, doona, they'll kill you, they'll kill you.'

Trying to make her see reason, Colquhoun? Didn't he know? She'd been born making mistakes. All of it was her fault...and his. Caird, who had thrown a dagger at her, touched her, kidnapped her, kissed her, called her names, apologised, made her *care* for him.

Caring for this man, knowing there couldn't be more, *shredded* her soul. He faced their enemies and risked his life. He could die right in front of her. Just like her brother.

The hornets flared and stung inside her. It was a mistake; she didn't care for him. She couldn't care for anyone any more. Not her family, her brother, Caird.

She. Was. Done.

'You are wrong, Englishman,' she said. 'I'll not be giving you the dagger and jewel.'

Grinning now, the Englishman slipped a hidden blade out of his belt. It was so small, it would only hurt Caird, but it was sharp enough to kill her. She had no skill.

The crooked triangle put Caird too far away. He couldn't stop them without hurting her and she was counting on his hesitation to save his life.

'These people owe me a debt. They will kill you, my dear,' the Englishman answered.

Caird could take the horse and flee before the villagers could react.

'They may owe you a debt, but by killing my brother, you owed me first,' she replied.

She was swift. The Englishman was swifter. Caird charged.

But not before the blade cut near her heart and the Englishman gave a harsh cry of pain. Not before she felt the strike of a fist against her temple and heard Caird's bellow.

Only then did darkness claim her.

## Chapter Twenty-Four

Mairead turned her face to the breeze to cool her overheated body. Cold warred with hot. The tight stickiness across her chest made her even more uncomfortable and she cringed to escape it all.

'You wake?'

Mairead opened sore eyes to see Caird hovering above her.

Before she could part her dry lips and mouth to speak, he lifted a cup to her lips. She drank the broth, but some liquid escaped and Caird's thumb wiped the rest away.

'Where?' she whispered as she settled back on the bed. She breathed deeply and felt the burn as she stretched the skin on her chest.

Caird sat on a stool next to the bed. His tangled hair partially covered one of his very grey eyes, but the reddish lock couldn't hide the deepened grooves between his brows or the lines on the sides of his mouth.

'You need rest.' Caird touched her hand. An order, but the relief in his eyes softened it.

'Tell me,' she whispered, moving her hand away from his touch.

Caird looked like he wanted to argue, but then told her of her collapse, her dagger wound needing stitches and of him tending her in a villager's home.

She didn't want to know of Caird's caring for her. 'The jewel. Where is it?'

'We have it,' he answered. 'The dagger's safe, too.'

After so long a struggle, she didn't feel relief.

'What happened to the Englishman?' She'd never forget his malice or his amusement. She had raised her dagger to kill him, but he'd struck first.

'Gone,' he said.

'How?' She tried to get up. Her brother's murderer was free. They'd *never* be safe.

'Rest easy.' Caird's hand on her opposite shoulder held her gently, but firmly. 'He is not here to threaten us.'

Not here, but they weren't safe. 'He's still a threat.'

Caird gave a curt nod and slowly removed his hand.

Her head and chest hurt, but mostly her body ached. 'How long did I sleep?'

'Two, maybe three...' Caird rubbed his face,

testing the beard there. 'Three days,' he finally answered.

Three days. She had too many questions. 'What happened to the villagers?'

'They're safe.'

Too much trouble, too many mistakes. 'What harm did I do? I shouldn't have rushed—'

'Shhh, there is much to tell you.' Caird shook his head. 'You saved us. If you hadn't risked your life, they wouldn't have helped.'

'Who?'

'The villagers, and…an archer.'

'I doona ken,' she said. 'The villagers helped us?'

'You questioned the villagers. With blade drawn you ran for the Englishman.' Caird reached for her again, but he stopped and laid his hand on the bed. 'You were *fearless*. An archer let loose an arrow. It sliced the Englishman's arm and stopped his blade slicing deep.'

Caird's grey eyes locked on her wound and his left thumb flexed. 'Angered by the arrow, he struck you in the head, and you…fell.'

'If the Englishman was injured, if you were there, how could he be gone?' she asked.

Caird's hands rested uneasily and he shifted on the stool. Patience. Mairead needed it. She'd lain here for days, her head wound far worse than the cut to her shoulder. But he had no patience. He still fought the rage that demanded he kill the Englishman. He tried to release the pressure by sword training, but he had no one to practise against and he felt crazed.

Only touching her calmed him. For three days, he had touched her constantly. He'd lifted moist linens to her lips, adjusted her in the bed and cooled her when she needed it. She could have died without ever waking. Now she was awake and she deserved answers. But she was alive and he fought the need to pull her close.

'We let him go.' Those shattered seconds after she'd attacked still made little sense. The Englishman had been hurt, but it was the sight of the arrow slice on his arm that made him furious. After he struck Mairead, he'd searched the crowd, daring whoever shot it to step forward. At that point, Caird knew he could have killed the Englishman.

But by then Mairead was hurt and his knees were in the dirt, his arms around her, his fingers trembling as he tried to stop the flowing blood. Only then did the villagers step forward.

'Why?' she whispered.

Caird heard the incredulity in her voice. The Englishman had killed her brother. How to make her understand he *had* to? 'If we'd killed him, we'd have more deaths on our hands. We doona know who he is or what power he wields."

Her eyes filled with tears. He didn't know what he'd do if they spilled.

Standing, he said, 'You need rest.'

'*Nae*, I have to know.' He could hear her tears weren't from pain, but from anger. 'You let him go. How could you do that to me?'

Accusation and shame. It had killed him to let the Englishman go. He had worried for days she wouldn't forgive him for letting him live. With her question, he knew he had been right to worry.

'I didn't want to let him go. I burned to kill him. Yet think, Mairead. The Englishman wanted the jewel for power. But for his own, or for a country? And which country? Our clans would not survive if there was more than the English involved. He had to be set free, but because he had nae help, he was forced to leave the jewel behind.'

'Who is he? At least tell me the name of my brother's murderer.'

'I doona know. Nae one does.' So many failings. He shook his head. 'A villager thought he knew.'

'Thought he knew?' she asked. 'How could he not be sure?'

'He was sure. I am not.' Sighing, he continued, 'The villager had interrupted a conversation between the Englishman and the thief. He'd opened a closed door just as the thief said "How". That's the only word he heard. From the way the thief said the word, he believes the Englishman's name is Howe.'

'"How" could be the thief asking a question.'

'Aye. I talked to all the villagers. There wasn't any more information. The man was most positive, but it's hardly proof.'

She bit her lip with indecision. His words had helped, but had not convinced her.

'This—' she began. 'Everything is confusing,' she admitted. 'What happened to this archer or the villagers?'

Her eyes glinting with tears scoured him. He deserved her accusations, her anger and he should remain to face them. But it was her confusion that held him still. Leaving now would only hurt her again. He *couldn't* hurt her again.

'The archer never stepped forward,' he answered. That was a mystery. There was no doubt the archer had his bow drawn before Mairead had attacked. The arrow was too quick. It had already been pointing their way, but who had it been pointed towards?

'Nobody knew who he was?'

Every word cut him. He thought he'd slain all the soldiers, but one had been lying in wait. 'Nae one ever saw him. He never disappeared, because he had never appeared to anyone. The archer was another reason I let the Englishman go. He still had someone to protect him. Someone, who could kill you.'

The archer was a lethal killer with astounding skill. A purposeful wound, not a death shot, and so precise it stopped the Englishman from gain-

ing full movement without truly hitting him or
Mairead. Her wound was deep, but not fatal.

Unable to stop himself, Caird gently brushed
the hair across her forehead. The bruise covered
the right side of her face and went across her eyes.

He was grateful she stayed still for his touch.
But her wary eyes did not calm him.

'The villagers all left.'

She pulled her head away. 'They lost their
homes?'

He clenched his hand. 'They lost their homes
when they allowed that man to buy them,' he said.
'In the end, they helped us and forced the Englishman to leave with nothing.'

Mairead looked everywhere except the Colquhoun who continued to hover over her. Who
seemed compelled to touch and care for her. She
was already flooded with guilt caused by her mistake and his care made her restless.

'There's more,' he said. 'It isn't safe for the villagers. Most have gone to Colquhoun land, but
a few families have left for the Buchanan keep.'

All the villagers gone, but not banned. He had
offered them protection with his own clan, even
after they harboured the Englishman. But why
did some families go to the keep? 'What have
you done?'

'The families, who have gone to the Buchanan
laird, had the dagger.'

'I thought we had the dagger.'

He shook his head. 'Only the jewel.'

'You've fought to keep the dagger and the jewel together. Now you just willingly let it go?'

'Aye, I let it go.' His brow furrowed. 'The dagger had protected the jewel. I had hoped to keep them together to gain answers.'

His troubled look told more than his words. He had let it go, but reluctantly. Which still begged her question.

'You have nae answers, so why did you relinquish it?'

He opened his mouth, closed it and kept his silence.

She'd been asleep for three days. Too much had happened.

By letting the dagger go, Caird endangered her family and there was only one reason for that. 'You did this for the debt. You put them in danger!'

'Nae!' he said abruptly. 'They know nothing except to give the dagger to the laird. To say it was for Ailbert.'

Her breath left her. With the silver and rubies, the dagger might be enough to keep her family safe. If it could be done quietly, maybe her family wouldn't suffer humiliation. She had no doubt the laird would understand the message. Ailbert had received many warnings. 'You trust these families?'

He gave a curt nod. 'They ensured the Englishman left the village and you have not been further harmed. They've proven themselves. They'll be safer with the protection of our clans; it's more than they had before.'

She felt no relief. The villagers were gone, which meant only Caird had been tending her. Unnerved, she seized on one thought.

Nothing had been resolved. They still had the jewel, her brother was still dead and the murderer was still free. Her mistakes would haunt her for ever. 'I need to get up.'

He pushed aside the stool to help her up. There was a slight sting, but it was bearable.

'They left clothing for you.' Quickly, he stepped away and she noticed the villagers had given him new clothes as well. The tunic and braies were clean, but ill-fitting for a man his size. They were, however, better than the ripped and bloodied ones he had been wearing.

Since her clothes were just as torn, she was grateful for the new gown. Nevertheless, accepting it made her uneasy knowing Caird must have requested it for her.

His movements unusually agitated, Caird picked up a pot. 'This is here so you can relieve yourself. I'll prepare food,' he said.

Laid about the room were linens, dried herbs and clothing. She was surrounded by the evidence of him caring for her. 'We need to go,' she said.

She couldn't be here any longer. Caird had cared for her and the Englishman was free. She hadn't killed him. Another mistake, another shame.

'In a day or so, we'll go,' he answered.

'But the risk—'

Grey eyes stormed green, his movement wild as the empty pot swung in his fist. 'You almost died!'

Stunned, she blinked.

Caird brimmed with ferocity and frustration and it was all suddenly pointed at her.

'Right in front of me—*for* me.' He waved the pot at her as if to hurl it. 'So you will eat and rest!'

Caird's breath was heavy. He had pulled himself to his full height, every bit of him intimidating and very magnificent.

Then his eyes darted to the pot in his hand as if surprised it was still there and set it down on a table.

'I'll get food,' he said.

It was Caird's sudden vulnerability that changed her emotions from accusations to something more insidious and painful. Grief, shame and guilt had been waiting for this moment. When anger wasn't her first emotion, when there were no distractions.

If Caird left the room, the tears would come. All her mistakes would claim her again. She could do nothing about those feelings, not alone.

'Doona go,' she said, taking the steps towards him.

He paused.

She held his arm and he looked at her hand.

She sensed he tried not to look in her eyes. 'You need to rest,' he said.

His touching, his wild confession. 'I didn't die,' she said.

A jerk of surprise under her hand, his eyes moving to hers.

Something was held in balance and she wouldn't look away. Grey eyes, flickering green, turning dark. A sound emitted from his chest before he took her in his arms and pressed his mouth to hers.

This was the kiss she wanted. Caird's lips firm, demanding, just this side of greedy. His hands, careful of her injuries, making sweeping circles along her sides to the small of her back. His kiss deepening.

She didn't heed her injuries, as she swept her arms up his chest, around his neck, and pulled herself closer to him.

Caird pressed kisses along the side of her jaw, down her neck, while his hands made small circles of heat along her hips.

'Aye,' she whispered, welcoming his kisses, his touch. This was what she needed. Caird taking. Forgetting her mistakes.

He pulled away.

'What did you say?' His eyes searched hers.

She stayed quiet, but she didn't close her eyes and she couldn't hide her feelings, not when all her emotions were clamouring at once.

'You're angry still,' he said, brows drawn.

She couldn't deny it.

Releasing her, he stepped back. 'You're hurting. It's too soon.' His breath was uneven; his eyes not hiding the evidence of his desire, but also his disappointment and resolve. Turning away from her, he said, 'You still need food.'

Mairead released a shuddering sound as Caird walked out of the room. Holding still, she realised, too late, that the distraction she sought was far more dangerous than if she'd just let Caird go. As if, by seeking his caresses, she had run against drawn swords to forget a thorn in her finger.

Caird's kiss made her forget anger and grief, but desire and need brought her closer to him. Her impulse to care for him, and his gentle touches only created something more between them. *Anything* more would be a mistake.

With the room empty, she stared at the pot he'd left, but had no intention of using it. It was time to feed herself and heal. It was time to leave Caird and all the madness between them.

For now, she was tired and needed to rest. Tomorrow, she would be home and she could begin to forget.

## Chapter Twenty-Five

Day came again and Caird was not comfortable. His feet hung off the edge of a too-small bed that had more gaps than rope and the mattress hadn't been filled properly, if at all.

But he wasn't moving. Not when Mairead curved so contentedly against him.

When he'd returned with food, she had been asleep in the bed. With no other place he wanted to be, he had lain next to her. Sleep had claimed him immediately.

It was the light in the room telling him another day had gone. Maircad's head was tucked under his chin and her breath was warm against his chest. The softness of her breasts gave to the hardness of his body; he could feel their bounty with each gentle inhale she gave.

Only when he held her, only in sleep, was she giving and soft. Her body was built for his fantasies but it was her bravery that left him awestruck. At some point, she had become a coveted dream.

A very cold dream.

Her feet were like ice and he adjusted to fit her more firmly against him. When he tucked her legs between his own, the curve of her hips matched his.

He could no more prevent the hardening of his body than stop his heart from beating. Days and nights of wanting were built within him.

His need for her now, like fire arcing through his chest, came not just from the wanting.

He'd almost lost her. Injured or not, he had to touch her, had to make her real to him. It had to be now.

Asleep, she was soft and giving. When awake, she was angry, and hurt, and denied they were different together.

Gently, slowly, conscious of her injury, he skimmed his fingertips along her shoulders, revelling in the softness of her skin before her gown impeded his direct touch.

Then his fingertips flattened to his palm as he caressed the curve and dip of her spine under her gown, felt the welcoming narrowness of her waist and the flare of her hip.

When his fingers swept lower, he stopped.

Mairead woke to warmth, to heat, to a determined caress across her covered skin. She held her breath as she waited for Caird's hand to continue, but he held still.

A tension thrummed through him, taut and full of need.

'You wake,' he said. Exhaling, he moved out of the bed.

Surprised, she turned.

The morning did not hide the tension in his shoulders as he went to the table still laden with food.

There was more of the vegetable broth he'd given her before, but also bread and cheese that he tore into hunks for them to share.

She was starving, yet wary.

Yesterday, when he'd left the room for food, she'd forced her grief back inside her, knowing soon she would be home, that only then she could let it free. But it still clamored inside her.

When Caird handed her some food, she took the offering, but avoided touching his fingers. His earlier caresses still felt like they skimmed across her skin. Those traces only increased her uneasiness, and she didn't know what more of his touch would do to her.

'We leave today,' Caird said, finally turning his gaze to her.

They had both eaten until there wasn't any more food and the break in the strained silence felt ominous.

When she saw his shuttered expression, she knew to ask, 'Where to?'

He walked to the far wall and leaned against it. 'To my brother and laird. A decision must be made about the jewel.'

This was why she was wary.

'I'm not going with you to see Laird Colquhoun. My home's not more than a short ride away. You'll be leaving me there!'

He shook his head. 'You will stay with me.'

Arrogance and kidnapping again. But this time, he had the jewel and her family had the dagger. They didn't need each other.

And it…complicated things when she was with him.

'Why do I stay with you?' She stood and brushed crumbs from her hands. 'I need to return to my family.'

'Your family is safe because they know nothing of the jewel. If you return, they'll know.'

She swept her arm, felt the pull of her injury and pressed her hand to the spot. 'I would never tell them.'

'Aye, and do you think the Englishman would care? He'd kill you first, and so you'll stay with me.'

His grey eyes searched hers until it felt like they could see every uncontrollable emotion inside her. She also knew if he kept watching her like that, her emotions wouldn't, couldn't stay inside her.

'I ken none of this. Haven't I hurt you enough? At the inn, in the forest, at the river and—' she gestured around them '—even here, I've hurt you. Let me go!'

'Aye, you've hurt me! But it'd hurt—' He stopped.

'But what?'

'We're different,' he said, pushing away from the wall. 'Even if you refuse to see it. We're different than we were at the inn, in the forest and it would hurt me more if something happened to you!'

'You think you care for me? Why? Because of a few kisses, because I saved our lives, because you tended a few injuries. You can't care for me. You doona know the truth.' She drew herself in, braced herself to admit her guilt, her shame, her *never-ending* mistake. 'Because I killed my brother.'

Mairead's eyes were tortured, showing the exact look he'd seen before she'd fled in the forest. Like then, he wanted to comfort her, but he knew she was a hair's breadth from running now. So, he willed his feet to remain still even though her eyes troubled him far worse than before.

'I killed him,' she continued, walking away from him and around the bed. 'It was all my fault. He wanted to wait for another market, another day to sell the dagger. To wait, just in case the man he stole it from would return for it.'

She laughed harshly. 'But I wouldn't let him. I couldn't wait. Impulsive you call me? Aye, I am! I was too eager to repair and hide my brother's gambling. Too desperate to end the nightmare before further damage could be done.'

She paced now. 'So he did it,' she continued. 'He went, even though he was being reasonable. Even though he knew it was dangerous. He did it for me! When they surrounded him, he never had a chance. I watched his agony, his death and knew it was *all my fault*! You want me with you to keep me safe. But you need to let me go. I doona think before I act and I make murderous mistakes.'

Caird held still, knew he had to hold still. So he watched pain and guilt tremble through her even when all he wanted was to hold her and fight all her fears.

But she was finally telling him what he needed to know to understand. She was giving him answers. So he did what he did best, and stayed quiet.

'You want the jewel, thinking to save Scotland?' she continued. 'Keep me with you and see how I interfere! How, somehow, I would cause more deaths, more war!'

Caird felt something unfurl in his chest. This was her secret she'd kept from him. She thought she had caused her brother's death. This was her pain and why she fought him. Why when he insisted they were different, she didn't accept him. Why she wanted to *forget*.

He could never forget why he wanted that jewel. 'You think I did this because of political reasons? You doona know why I risked this.'

'Did you kill your brother, too?'

He knew the pain she was in. When his had been fresh, he'd lashed out as well.

But he had brothers, a sister, the support of his clan. Her brother had died and she had no family with her now. By forcing her on this journey, he denied her the comfort she should have received. He deserved her hatred.

But she needed to understand more. He deserved not only her hatred, but his brother's as well.

At Dunbar, he had rescued Malcolm, but he could never forget the argument they'd had before his brother went. Nor would he forget overturning dead bodies until he found Malcolm buried beneath a corpse. Carrions were already picking the flesh of the body. Barely alive, his brother didn't fight when they picked at him as well. Malcolm lived, but he would never be the same.

'I didn't kill my brother, but I might as well have,' he answered.

Her eyes widened before she recovered. He didn't want her to recover, or to mantle herself in anger and guilt any more.

'Using that jewel was never about Scotland. After Dunbar, I just wanted the power to end the war. I wanted it for Malcolm. You saw his scar.'

He just held in his helpless rage. That *scar*. It was only thin because of the finest sutures and care. Some of it would even fade. Malcolm had been unconscious, but when Caird had seen it, the wound was wide open.

'I couldn't find him for days because he was trapped under a corpse. There were flies...' He shook himself. 'Carrions.' There had been other scavengers as well, human ones, for Malcolm's sword and boots had been taken. 'Nae, Mairead, I didn't kill my brother, but I will never forget he had gone to Dunbar alone. Because I refused to go with him.'

He could see Mairead's anger falter at his words. Horror and pity flickered in the dark depths of her eyes and her lashes were spiked from tears. Then she jutted out her chin and stopped the tears from falling.

'But he survived,' she said stubbornly.

She was stubborn, but she cared.

He could see that she cared. It was there in the trembling of her lips. It had been there before the village, when she'd let him hold her all night. When she'd told him she knew he'd come for her.

She had feelings for him, but she didn't want them.

'Aye, he survived,' he said. Somewhere in all

her hurt, he wanted her to *recognise* him, recognise them for what they were now. But she blindly held to her doubts and fears. 'And you're still nothing but a deceitful, lying Buchanan.'

Fury blazed in her eyes. 'How dare you!' She stepped forward, her hand rising to slap him. He didn't move, waiting for her to take the remaining steps. He deserved it.

He'd even welcome it. Maybe it would help release some of her grief. He wanted to share her grief because he wouldn't stand for anything separating them.

'Aye, a liar, Buchanan,' he repeated. 'You know we're different now than at the inn, than in the forest. You know we're different because you saved my life and told me of your brother, even though you didn't have to. You could have bargained differently with the Englishman. At the river, you recognised we were different when I swam the water to get to you! You responded to me, were giving yourself to me. Because you wanted me!'

'Lust is different.'

'From what?' he pressed.

'From this caring for each other,' she finished. 'You think I care for you because I saved you. You think you care for me because you tended me. But it cannot be that way, when I doona want it to be!'

'Care for you?' His feet took steps closer to her before he could stop them. 'Is that all you think I feel for you?'

His eyes searched hers as if he'd never seen her before. As if he'd never see her again. 'Clever Buchanan,' Caird whispered vehemently, 'haven't you guessed yet?'

Mairead's eyes, which had always shown every emotion if only he'd look, revealed her again. Because he no longer had his prejudices against her, he saw everything: guilt, anger, hurt, fear, desire. But it was her longing that tugged at him. In her longing he had his answer.

She wanted them different, but she didn't trust him. No, it was even more than that.

The Buchanan Clan were notorious liars and deceivers. They used it to their advantage and were proud of it. But for Mairead, all those lies and deceits went further. She'd never been shown trust. Not from her own family, her bereaved mother, her giggling sisters or her reckless brother.

Mairead didn't know the ways of trust. Nor the ways of love. And he did love her, but first she needed to accept the trust between them.

Love. Trust. Two emotions that took lifetimes to understand. He'd learned them from his clan, from his family. He had their love, trust and returned it. She did trust, but she didn't understand it, maybe didn't realise she gave it.

He had to get her to listen to him.

But there was only one time she listened, only

one time when she didn't fight or argue or pace away from him as if trying to escape.

And that was when he held her.

Held her...close. Her tiny frame and generous curves, lush and pressing against him. For a man his size, trained until his body gave not an inch, he wanted to be buried in every plush, giving bit of her.

When he held those curves, she listened. She didn't fight him or argue; she became soft and giving.

When he cradled her closer until she nestled into him, and their breaths were no more than shared gasps of desire. When he could do nothing but feel her soft lips give under his, knowing their kisses were all that he needed and yet only a fleeting taste. Then, and only then, she held still, she listened and she responded.

Her *response*.

A spike of lust so severe slashed through his body and he forced the air back into his suddenly empty lungs.

Love. Trust. They took a lifetime to understand. But his body wouldn't let him wait a lifetime to show her.

He knew it was imperative they start that lifetime together. Immediately.

It wasn't only his thoughts that made him certain. It was Mairead's own actions. For while he gathered his thoughts, his eyes kept steady on her. Every lush bit of her.

So his desire began with her pacing the small room and it strengthened when she reached one end only to spin to the other. Each spin giving him full, generous views.

His need increased as sunlight filtered through the window and highlighted her dark eyes that contrasted with her creamy skin. Highlighted the rose glow of her cheeks that bloomed in her agitation and, he knew with satisfaction, bloomed and unfurled when he held her.

His lust became greater still seeing her hair. Her hair that made the breath in his lungs burn quickly away with pure need.

Her hair. Unbound and wild. Brushed by his own hand while she healed, it was wilder than ever. The repetitive action had calmed him, but now each lock sprang around her head, defiant, defying and taunting him again.

She might not know what love and trust were, but he did. She might deny it all, but her responding body wanted them to be together. He had the proof with her hair. Her hair *beckoned* to be shown.

He could only comply.

If it killed him, he'd show her love and trust. And he would show her. *Now.*

Mairead couldn't stay still. She'd confessed her

mistake and her guilt but Caird hadn't reacted as she'd expected.

Instead of displaying horror and disgust, he had held perfectly still and silent while she laid bare her shameful mistake.

Then he'd told her of Dunbar and Malcolm. He'd confessed to his own mistake, confessed to his own guilt and shared it. With her.

It shattered what little hold she had.

Oh, how her legs trembled then, how she wanted to believe what she thought was in his eyes. But how could she? She'd made so many impulsive mistakes and everything she felt about Caird was impulsive. She couldn't trust herself.

Caird said he cared for her. But even in that she didn't trust herself. Because he sounded incredulous, angered and disappointed, too. So many emotions were displayed in his declaration, she didn't know what he meant.

And he didn't tell her. In fact, he didn't say anything. Absorbing her with his grey-green eyes, he'd become quiet.

Trying to avoid his all-too-knowing eyes, she paced and by the time she stopped she was as far from him as she could be in the room.

She stopped because she felt the change in him. Clear across the room. The way his gentleness and understanding turned to something more. Something like desire, but more than the familiar need. More than the whisper of wickedness that his steady regard usually gave her. Now it was darker and more elemental.

It wasn't whispering, wasn't beguiling or coaxing or beckoning.

It was heat and a sheer surge of power emanating from him. It stunned her.

Her feet stopped their pacing before the rest of her body caught up and she lurched unsteadily forward. When she felt his need battering against her back she turned, thinking she could change her stance and become steady again.

So she turned and was dizzy in that turning. Aye, she was dizzy because she wasn't more steady facing him. She was distinctly more unsteady, wavering and trembling.

Caird's three steps were all it took for him to be right up against her. That stopped her dizziness. When his eyes flared and his hands curled upon her upper arms, that stopped her unsteadiness.

But his touch and proximity did nothing for her trembling. Her trembling incrcased.

And his grey-green eyes that had been studying her, trying to find his precious answers, weren't doing so now.

Now his eyes were filled with desire and determination.

'We're different now, Mairead,' he said. 'I'm different.'

Grip tightening, he enfolded her in his arms until her cheek pressed against his chest. The only thing she could hear above the roaring in her ears was the consistent, battering beat of his heart.

'More different than you've ever known,' he said. She didn't only hear the words; she felt them. They rumbled deep within her.

She had never seen Caird like this, as if he couldn't restrain himself. Through her trembling, she shook her head to deny his words.

He sighed and she felt the rise of his chest and shoulders, felt the air shuddering into his lungs before he released it.

'Stubborn,' he whispered.

She felt that word, too.

He pulled away, just enough to look down at her, but not enough to stop his heart pressing against hers. It was beating as fast, and as hard, and as erratically as her own.

Because he remained silent she looked up to understand him. To see his eyes that displayed more emotion than was good for her.

'I'm taking, Mairead,' he said. 'I'm taking and giving.' His eyes were searching and finding every bit of her heightened colour and every wayward unruly lock of hair. 'And I'll take again,' he promised. 'Over and over. Until you realise. Until you have nae more doubts.'

She didn't know what she was supposed to realise, not when she was this close to him, not when she felt more than his heat, his breath, his heart.

She felt his want, his need, his desire. Felt him pull just enough to bring her up and closer to him.

'My words are—' he dipped his head '—going to fail me.' His lips brushed hers. 'So, I'm going to show you our trust.'

The persuasive pressure of Caird's lips slanting over hers sent a moan through her body that reverberated between them.

'Aye, show you,' he whispered. His lips and teeth sucked her lower lip into his. 'I'm going to show you trust; I'm going to show you care.' He repeated the action on her upper lip until her breaths were little pants.

'I have nae ale; my words will stumble.' His tongue swept across the seam of her lips. 'It may kill me—days of wanting, of needing and denying. Now you're stubborn and demanding my patience. Patience!' He shuddered. 'At this moment, I'm less patient and more impulsive than you.'

He increased the pressure of his kiss, just enough, coaxing enough, so when his tongue teased again she met his with her own.

Caird's hands gripped, loosened.

But he didn't deepen the kiss. Instead, his mouth hovered along her jaw, wended its way to her ear. 'At the inn, you responded like this. You're a maid, Mairead, but you responded.'

His tongue, flickering, made tiny movements along the shell and down behind it. ''Tis not usual to respond to me as you did.' Kisses along her neck, trailing down, increasing her trembles. ''Tis not usual how I responded to you. Despite the ale.'

He pulled away, his breath just behind her ear. Her eyes were closed; she was afraid his were open.

'That response was trust, Mairead,' he whispered. 'You came to my room to find the dagger and save your family. You were grieving and you kissed me.'

Trembling even more as she fought his words, Mairead gripped the back of his neck and splayed her fingers through his hair.

'It was lust. Like now,' she said, her voice broken by her breaths. 'I forgot everything else.'

He slowly shook his head. She hadn't opened her eyes, but she could feel his hair brush against her shoulders.

'It was trust,' he insisted. 'You trusted I'd care for you. So giving was your response.'

Her body was against him, but Caird held back until she felt she wasn't close enough. Finding purchase with his shoulders, she pulled and Caird shuddered out a sound, but he held firm.

A few breaths. A few heartbeats until he continued, 'Then you ran. You ran and I followed and I fought.'

Mairead couldn't make her legs cooperate so she could press more fully into him. Not when his lips reversed the trail along her neck, returned to her other ear, his tongue and breath both giving and denying contact.

'I fought to keep you near me. Even then at the campsite, I knew I couldn't let you go. That had nothing to do with the jewel, but with what I longed for with you.'

His mouth was kisses and words, but his hands, oh, his hands' caresses were both lengthy and fleeting, everything she needed and still not enough. Careful of her injury, he touched everywhere, but gave only whispers of heat.

'Did you know I'd come for you?' he asked.

She felt his need hard against her as his hands tantalisingly skimmed up her arms that were wrapped around his shoulders and neck. He brushed his fingers over her clenched hands only to sweep back down her arms, along her sides and swirl at her lower back. And again.

'Did you?' he repeated, stopping his hands.

She blinked. Had she? She remembered forcing the horse faster. She tried thinking. Caird stopped his hands and she needed them to move again. She'd known he'd come for her.

'Aye,' she answered.

A curl to his lips. 'It was trust.' His hands continued their hovering caress. Touching her, but only increasing the pressure inside her. He was making her *wait* as she answered his questions.

He should know she didn't like to wait.

She lowered her hands along his upper arms.

'It was your arrogance, Colquhoun. I knew you'd follow because you felt entitled to kidnapping me.'

'Stubbornness.' Caird's hands flexed at her waist, his breath hitched just at her jaw.

He caressed again, but his hands and lips no longer skimmed, they swept.

'It was trust that I'd follow,' he said. 'That I'd find you, protect you, keep you from harm.' Just before he reached her lips, he whispered, 'That blow to my chest I took purposefully.'

She shook her head, not listening to his words, only aware of the increased pressure of his lips and hands. Because with just the shake of her head, he increased his touch again.

She didn't think he realised it. But if denying him and caressing him made his control slip, she'd do it again.

'An accident only,' she insisted. 'You didn't care for my safety. You didn't want me fleeing and ruining our tale to your cousins. Your worry was for show.'

'I worried for you. Even then, and far too much.' Caird flexed his hands on her sides. 'Your trembles as I held you were real. I trembled, too.'

She shook her head as she gripped his arms, the leverage enough to pull him roughly closer.

His surprise was all she needed. She tilted her head until her lips were against his.

He held still. A heartbeat, and another.

'Your response,' he growled against her lips.

'To me.' A warning. 'Is trust,' he insisted as another sound, something primal, erupted from deep within him.

Gripping her hips, Caird kissed her.

Her breasts ached and she moved against him, tiny movements, which only increased the tension.

Another sound from Caird, him moving, a jolt to their bodies as his shins found the bed.

He pulled his head away, breaking their kiss, but not his intent. 'The flooded river,' he said hoarsely. 'You wanted me.'

She nodded, but he wasn't looking at her.

'Tell me,' he repeated.

'Aye,' she said, her voice not her own and just as breathless as his. 'Aye, I wanted.'

He swallowed. 'And how did you feel when I followed you? When I swam, when I ran, when I feared I wouldn't reach you?'

The icy water dragging her down. Caird too far away. But when she had been struggling to breathe, to survive, she'd kept her eyes not on the shore, but on him. She'd known he'd come for her.

She had never depended on anyone. Because she'd never had anyone like Caird before. There was only one word to describe how it felt. But could she say it?

When Caird was touching her and kissing her, she was helpless not to answer him.

'Wondrous,' she answered truthfully, impulsively. 'It felt wondrous.'

He nodded, satisfied. 'Trust is wondrous,' he said. 'When you put your back to mine against those soldiers. When I woke from my injury, knowing you had saved my life by mending me, by protecting me.'

Even as she protested, Caird lowered her down. 'It was wondrous trust,' he said.

Her feet touched the floor, but it was only so his fingers, his hands, quick, efficient, could unlace the cords of her old gown and push the torn and frayed material off her shoulders. Only so his palms and spreading fingers could tug the weakened fabric until it unravelled and fell in defeat around her ankles.

Gripping her transparent chemise, his eyes on hers, he ripped the garment in two. On a shuddered sigh, it billowed around them until she was completely bared to him.

'Mairead,' he said with reverence. His eyes didn't hold hers any more. Instead, they roamed over her body and she *felt* his eyes everywhere.

Under his gaze, her body didn't feel like her own. She took a much needed breath and his eyes stilled and rested on her breasts.

'Your skin,' he whispered. 'Against your dark hair and eyes, it's impossibly white, impossibly soft. I've only had a taste and I only want more.'

Her legs and limbs were shivering. She stood, but she felt as if she was moving in different directions at the same time. It wasn't only his touch, it was his words, too.

'Are you sure you had nae ale?' she asked.

'I do speak,' he breathed roughly. 'When I can't control, can't restrain, I speak words. Ale makes me so and apparently so do you.'

'I make you without control?'

'Constantly. More so than ale and I'm not used to it. Like now with you bare before me.'

As his arms and hands worked slowly, efficiently, Caird's gaze brushed upwards and stayed with hers. She blinked and his tunic was gone.

In daylight every scar, scrape and wound was shown in relief, but that wasn't what held her gaze. It was the breaths he took, the heightened colour of his skin, the sheen of sweat as he laboured. Laboured simply by looking at her.

Another blink, and another, his leggings and braies hit the floor.

In front of her, Caird stood naked. She'd seen him, but never—never—like this. Everything was different.

Because now it was daylight. And the sun wasn't as hot or warm or as magnificent as the man in front of her.

Still he didn't take; still he waited. She was beginning to realise what he meant by showing her trust would kill him. Because she felt that way as well, dying bit by bit, but also recreated. Reborn into something more. Something different.

Caird took the step necessary to hold her. When he did, the hairs on his arms brushed against the sides of her already sensitive breasts and she couldn't stand any more.

When he held her closer, it was shocking, surprising, overwhelming, everything and nothing she could expect.

The strength of muscle beneath heated skin, sinew binding and tensing from lifting her, beginnings of slickness encouraging her fingers to trace and glide.

She wanted to touch it all.

Caird held Mairead close to him. Her body everything he thought it could be, and more.

'I doona know the way of this,' Mairead whispered.

She tilted her chin to raise her eyes to him. He was left with shaking legs when he saw the desire and trepidation in her eyes. Just that look alone sent such a satisfaction through him, he immediately craved to hold and claim her. To take.

'Of this?' he asked, his fingers moving along her cheek. 'Or of what we have between us?'

She had more generous curves than any gown had outlined. More tempting skin than the sunlight revealed through her chemise. Her curves, her breasts, her hips spilled against him. And his hands and mouth felt unbearably greedy.

Calling on his last reserves of patience, he waited for her answer. 'Mairead?' he asked.

'Both,' she whispered.

A precious answer.

'There is nae way of this. There is only removing doubts. There is only us.' His finger tucked a curl behind her ear. 'What is it you want to do?'

'Touch,' she answered. 'Everywhere.'

'Impulsive.' His lips curved as the tension grew.

Now that she was given the freedom to touch, it was her eyes that roamed.

She laid her palms just below his chest and along the ridged symmetrical planes of his stomach. Her fingers traced around his wound. The fresh stitches were fine and holding. Around the area she'd burned, the wound was only faintly pink. It would scar, but it was healing.

She continued to gaze as her hands felt. Her fascination increased as she stepped closer to reach higher up the expanse of his chest and shoulders. Closer, standing on her toes, until she leaned against him and he grasped her hands. Held her. A pause, a breathless wait. She darted a look. His face was darkened with colour; his cheeks were hollowed as if he took a sword wound again.

Mairead's tentative touch was brief and the barest hint of time he craved from her hands. Even so, he couldn't withstand it. Not when he still needed to show her trust.

Releasing her hands, he vowed, 'Another time.' Then he lifted and lowered her to the bed as he knelt between her legs.

With her lying before him, he savoured her kiss-swollen lips. Greedy, his hands kneaded her generous hips and her outer thighs before caressing upward, until he covered and cupped her breasts. When she gave a sound of pleasure, he broke the kiss.

'Your *response*,' he said with a curve to his sensual lips. His hair, disarrayed and wild, fell forward with the tilt of his head.

He held her breasts in his broad warrior's hands. Her pale skin against his tan. Soft, unmarked against calloused and scarred.

'Now will you, Colquhoun?' Her hands clutched the linens beneath her.

'Soon, I'll take, Buchanan, I'll take until you're helpless to give. When you do… I'll take again,' he replied.

He adjusted himself between her, one leg closer to the apex of her thighs. Eyes locked with hers, his hands circled, cupped, kneaded. And again.

'Glimpses of your breasts, of wondering how they'd feel.' Circling again, cupping, kneading. A rhythm he repeated again. And again. 'Never enough.'

Her breasts filled with a sort of burning heat that wasn't pain, but something hotter, something searing.

'Now to see, to feel their weight in my hands.' He lowered his head, so his whispering words fanned across her and increased the pleasure and pressure. 'To almost taste them.'

The pleasure built as he hovered his mouth over her, as he continued his rhythm. She needed to move, tried to move, but his knee was there, blocking, forcing her to lift her hips up— She gasped. Not a barrier at all. Exquisite pleasure arced through her.

He held still as if she shocked him. Without raising his hands or his mouth, he slowly moved his knee.

'Not like that, not so soon,' he said against her breasts, but she sensed a new tension in him. Something feral. She felt that same tension at her breasts, and between her thighs. She was desperate to move again.

'What do you do?' she asked, wanting his knee to return. Her hands cupped his head to keep him there in case he moved that pleasure, too. Never had she felt like this.

'Showing you trust,' he said. 'And I can nae longer wait.'

He lowered his mouth and she felt the flicker of his tongue, the press of his lips on her breasts.

She gasped.

An answering sound from him. Hungrier, greedier kisses, everywhere she wanted and yet… never did he touch the tips.

She couldn't keep sounds inside nor her movements still. She wanted more.

Finally, agonisingly, she felt his breath against her nipples and she whimpered.

His mouth hovering, a curl to his lips, his hands stilled again.

'Your response, Mairead,' he said. 'Give me your response.'

Breath fast against her, he waited for answers she couldn't allow. Even now.

His brows drew in. 'You *doubt*.' Incredulous. 'You gave me trust, Mairead, more than I could ever hope.'

He breathed deeply, holding on to his slipping control as he moved his mouth away. 'When you told me I'd come for you.'

Caird gave her breasts more strokes, more slides of his fingers until she moved with and from his touch. Until she arched and tightened. She needed his lips, his mouth right where he poised it above her. And he was making her *wait*.

'You doubt,' he said, 'but against all odds I fought and won because you trusted me.'

Cupping her breasts, lifting them again, his mouth hovering at the tip, his breaths tormenting, he vowed, 'It was a precious thing. Your trust and your response. I'll show you.'

Mairead, her want sharp, felt the heady pleasure of his breath and roughened chin. Then finally, breathtakingly, his mouth covered the tip and rolled her nipple with his tongue.

Her breath stopped on a gasp.

Eyes locked with hers, his hand lifted the other breast to his waiting mouth. A longer wait. Then a sound before he sucked, and stroked, and pulled— more.

Pleasure ripped through her. Giving waves of release.

When Mairead's response eased and her breaths returned, Caird rested his head between her breasts and cupped his arms around her sides. Her body was sated, soft and ready for him.

He forced his breaths to return, for the pain of desire to subside. Mairead had given her response, but not her trust.

It wasn't enough. He needed to remove her doubts; he needed to show her more. Right now, he didn't know if he could.

Her touch. Tentative along his head, his hair, his shoulders. Pleasure easing his pain. Needing more, he held still.

Maircad didn't know the way of this. But Caird was showing her. His words and touch were intense and wondrous pleasure. Her body felt complete as he rested and cradled her against him. Impossibly, it also made her crave him more.

She couldn't crave more. Already she'd almost lost him.

'Were there many?' she asked. The soldiers, at the village. She'd never asked.

Caird turned his head, but kept it resting on her chest. He seemed to want her touch along his slickened skin, so she continued. As her fingertips circled back along his shoulders, his breaths eased.

'Harsh and hard odds, and at least one I missed,' he answered, a different tension in him.

He didn't tell her how many soldiers. She feared he didn't know because there had been too many to count.

'Does it pain you…your shoulder?' he whispered. 'With me, like this, is it too much?' He lifted his head.

'Nae,' she whispered. She hardly noticed it. Not now. Not when her heart pained her worse. The feeling was so fierce, she couldn't avoid it. It was fear at almost losing him. And yet, as she had stood there in front of the Englishman, she knew he'd come for her.

Caird watched as the light in Mairead's eyes changed. They were dark and fathomless, but the life within them gave shimmering light to their depths. Like a night sky with too many stars to count.

What he saw there gave him hope. Some conflict, some doubt was there, but she was starting to believe. Her eyes gave him strength to show her more, to make her bright eyes glaze with passion.

He wanted to bring her to that peak again. He knew her body was ready for him. But it wasn't enough, he needed her trust.

Adjusting himself, he started again. Trying to

be gentle, trying to coax with his hands, he kissed, he touched. But his ragged control slipped with a caress along her arm, a taste around her fingers, a breath against her wrist.

'Caird?' she whispered as she touched. Tentative caresses weakening…undoing him.

'Follow me,' he asked. Did she want words? They were burned out of him by her response, by her doubt.

He kissed along her bared shoulders, down the valley between her breasts and underneath.

His hands moved along her sides; his fingers feathered along her waist until he felt her hips. Then he moved his hands and mouth lower yet.

'What do you do?' she whispered, her hands tightening along his arms, refusing him.

'Showing you,' he said. 'Trust.'

Reverently, savouring the texture and taste of her, he continued his kisses along her stomach. He stroked the softness and heat of her skin. He had to give and show her patience, and it was breaking him.

Delicately, intensely, Mairead's hands eased and released their grip. Then, he heard her response above the sudden roaring in his ears, above his need for her.

Her response. 'Please.'

When Mairead's hands began their tentative caresses, Caird knew he could no longer be gentle. He was taking as his body demanded he do. The taste of her, the feel of her breasts and her release now drove his need.

He took her hands, so much smaller than his and pressed them above her head. Taking his other hand, he caressed and kissed along her hip, along her thigh. Her tiny movements encouraging what he desperately wanted.

Murmuring approval, he continued lower, widening his thighs and spreading hers. She was exposed, and he was more than ready to taste her.

Then, and only then did he release her hands and lift her to his mouth.

Her sounds of confusion turned to gasps of pleasure. Her hands caressed his head, his shoulders. His hunger, temporarily assuaged, only increased as he kissed her and kissed her more. He knew he wouldn't last.

But he needed her desire to bond with his, knowing he was on that cliff and it was imperative she was there with him.

Mairead couldn't catch her breath. Caird's hands and kisses were skimming across her bared skin. He was everywhere she needed, even as she craved more of his touch.

Then with his body brimming with need and pain, he stopped.

He was curved between her thighs and his arms embraced her hips. His forehead rested on her stomach, where his hair fanned out and covered what he had brought her to.

A precipice.

Her body clenched, and ached. It was nothing like before; it was more.

But if she was at the edge, Caird was still climbing the rocky crags.

His back and arms glistened with sweat that highlighted healing wounds and raised scars.

He whispered, too. Whispered as he gave a slow steady shake of his head. Answering or denying a question only he could hear.

She didn't know what to do; didn't know the way of any of it. Only, knowing his pain distressed her. With both hands she cupped his head, which stilled, and she caressed his hair, which clung to her fingers.

When she got to the ends, he raised his head.

She had never seen his eyes like this. It was as if he'd reached the top of the cliff, his battered hands on the ledge where she stood. A few loose rocks and he'd plummet, his control shattered— utter vulnerability and utter masculine power.

'Your response,' he whispered, his voice broken. His hands on the cliff, trembling.

'Give me your response, Mairead. Before I claim you. Tell me you have nae doubts. Give me your trust.'

Looking into his eyes, her body poised on the edge, she gave the only answer she could. 'Aye.' She licked her dry lips. 'Aye.'

His breathing changed, his eyes changed, his

body, if possible, became larger, more indomitable, more *there*.

A quick shake of his head. 'In this.' His mouth descended. A kiss below her navel, reverent and branding just as his hands slid along her sides, his thumbs wide cupping and caressing under her breasts before returning to her hips.

Head raised again, eyes searing, he demanded, 'Or. In. More.'

Greedy Colquhoun. Still never assuming, still never jumping to conclusions.

Still hanging on the cliff.

Then she understood only she had the power to lift him. That here, now, he gave her that power.

Licking her lips again, conscious of how open she was to him. How bared she was to his gaze, to his kisses. She knew her answer. She had doubts still, but not about Caird. Lying here now, with him, she wondered how she ever doubted.

Then she remembered...he was Colquhoun, and she was Buchanan. So because it was him, she answered the only way she could.

'In this...' she began.

Grey eyes swirling green, swirling surprise, vulnerability, pain and doubt.

'In more,' she continued, keeping her eyes steady on his. Willing him to understand more than her words. 'In. All.'

Caird's head fell to her stomach, his breath

harsh bursts across her thighs, his fingers flexed at her hips.

She smiled. Because a Buchanan had bested a Colquhoun.

Again.

Caird wanted to roar at the feeling of victory and rapture that swept through him.

Victory. But his body didn't think so. His body was still in torture. He was right. Earning her trust this way nearly did kill him. If she had denied them, he had vowed he wouldn't claim her.

The risk was great and too dear. It was more than any battle he had ever fought. Mairead had to have understood this. Had to have known. Yet she had tortured him more.

Deceitful, clever Buchanan.

He should have expected that, but she'd given her answer.

Adjusting himself higher, he gloried in the dark mischievous light of her eyes, just as he knew he'd have them glazed again. And he would glory in that more.

'I have to have you ready,' he promised. His mouth descended, his hands caressing.

A kiss for every pulse she gave, until he again adjusted between her thighs. His hands lifting her, his mouth and tongue and heat and breath shredding her understanding of desire. A sharp kiss, a gasp of sound. She was almost…there.

Breaking the kiss, his lifted his head. 'Soon,' he said, a plea, a vow.

His eyes on hers, then on his finger that slowly, agonisingly teased her entrance where she ached the most.

'I have to claim you now,' he said. 'Here, do you understand?'

She stilled, she watched, she felt.

'When I do, it will hurt.' Another finger replaced his first. A little deeper, a little wider. 'But like this, you'll give yourself, you'll follow me.'

His eyes remained riveted on his fingers. He released his touch, but not his eyes. By using his fingers to prepare her for him, she knew he would soon take her maidenhead and it would hurt.

But it could be nothing to the torrents of pain flowing over Caird's entire body. His face was drawn, his cheeks were hollowed, his breaths were ragged.

She knew that pain would only go away if she followed, if she gave. Because it was him, she did. With both hands she caressed his jaw until he looked at her.

'You need to take, Colquhoun.' She brushed her fingers delicately against his lips. 'I want you to take.'

She cupped his face and brought his lips to hers.

This kiss was forgiveness and desire. Grateful because he did take then. Just as he kissed her, and kept on kissing her until her body moved beneath his, and he adjusted his body to hers. She felt the pressure, a slight pain, but then—wonder.

When he moved, she moved with him. Giving him the trust and the care he had shown her. She gave because it was him and it was all she could do.

His lips released from hers and his movements increased. Until their sounds and strength and need bonded and he surged within her, taking and giving with everything he was. And she did what he asked her to do.

She followed him.

## Chapter Twenty-Six

'I still believe it was deceitful of you to get me to agree to this,' Mairead argued. Again.

She was making a mistake. But this time Mairead knew the enormity of her mistake and still she made it.

She couldn't seem to stop herself.

However, for this last mistake she made, the Colquhoun was partly to blame. He just needed to agree with her.

Yet, Caird remained silent. As was his lifetime habit of control.

They'd travelled for days now, so she'd asked him about his need for silence and she understood now. Accepted it because she knew he couldn't remain silent.

And she liked that she was responsible.

What she didn't like was agreeing to take the jewel to Caird's brother, Bram, the Laird of Clan Colquhoun, only to be told he wasn't on

Colquhoun land. That he was, in fact, on Fergusson land. Which was miles south. It would take a sennight or more to reach it.

As a result, she was only getting further away from her family. Her distress seemed to pain him, which she accepted as a partial apology. But he wouldn't be swayed in letting her go.

In truth, she was beginning to believe if Caird was burdened with the jewel, she would be, too. That wasn't all his fault. She also wanted the jewel's mystery solved.

So they travelled south. At least now they had ample supplies, and were well rested. But as long as they travelled, they remained vulnerable. Caird never said, but he continued to sharpen swords and his eyes constantly scanned the terrain.

Yet, for every moment he watched, there were other moments where he touched. One horse carried the supplies, while they rode the other. Caird took every opportunity to caress, to kiss. Her body and skin were so sensitive, that only his look would send her blushing and wanting again.

Since that day in the village, she'd only encouraged their frequent stops.

'I'm beginning to think you've been deceitful in other ways as well,' she continued, trying to keep her thoughts together, something which wouldn't happen if she thought about Caird's caresses.

She felt him tense at her observation. He might not talk much, but he was a good listener.

'In what ways?' he asked.

'You have too many secrets.'

'Secrets?'

'Aye, like the one where you said the wedding celebrations were for your sister, Gaira, but you wouldn't tell me her husband's name or why the celebrations were weeks after the wedding or why the celebrations weren't on Colquhoun land.'

She straightened, warming up to her point in this conversation. 'You also won't tell me why Bram is on Fergusson land, or why he wasn't attending the celebrations with you.'

They were getting close to Fergusson keep. She was running out of time for answers.

She wanted answers and she was reflecting again. Which meant she'd spent too much time with this Colquhoun.

She exhaled, knowing she had to say the last bit again. Had to make him understand. 'And it's a secret you keep from me about why your family hates Buchanans so much. Why Malcolm hates me in particular.'

That secret hatred was the reason she knew her travelling with Caird was a mistake. She would always be Buchanan and Caird's family could never accept her. Although she and Caird shared something wondrous, she couldn't see them sharing a life together.

Caird stopped the horse and she felt his fingers skim down her jaw and lift her eyes to him. She liked it when he did that. She didn't like the doubt in his eyes.

'We're different, Mairead. This is different,' he said. 'I thought there was trust and…care between us.'

'There is,' she agreed. It was wondrous and overwhelming at the same time.

'Then trust in this. They are not my stories to tell. They are Gaira's and Malcolm's, and I cannot tell you without them agreeing.'

Mairead heard the pain in his voice. She knew Caird hadn't kept all his secrets. Since they'd left the village, he had told her how his sister, Irvette, had died during the English massacre at Doonhill. He hadn't been there and none of his family could prevent it. She still had many questions but he couldn't talk of it more.

Now, he asked her to go in to the unknown and trust him. But her trusting him didn't stop her reflecting and worrying. And her not doubting him didn't mean she didn't still doubt herself.

'I doona know the way of this,' she said. 'Can you tell me something? So that—'

He sighed. 'It pains me not to tell you. But there were promises. I can answer some of your questions, but not all. Gaira's wedding occurred in April before Dunbar. There wasn't time to celebrate. Since Bram had…concerns on Fergusson land and because of their loss, the Graham clan requested to hold the celebrations there.'

This was more than he'd given her before, but it wasn't enough. She didn't know what Bram's concerns were and she didn't know who Gaira had married or why it was a secret. But if Caird was answering some of her questions, she had to ask the most important.

'What of Malcolm?'

Caird stayed quiet and she felt him weigh her words. When his left thumb flexed she knew he'd decided.

'Know that what happened to Malcolm and my family happened many years ago,' he said. 'It was permanent.'

He looked over her shoulder, but she saw the regret and grief before he hid it from her. 'Malcolm may— It will take a long time for Malcolm to accept you. But my clan and family will accept you, on that you can trust.'

'How do you know?' she insisted.

Caird's lips curved before he looked down at her. 'They'll accept you because of Gaira's story.'

'Ach! Gaira's secret you mean.' Mairead looked forward again and clamped down on the hornets beginning to swarm inside her. He told her much, but she didn't know Gaira's story, or Malcolm's and Bram's. She was tempted to use her elbows on the arrogant, overbearing Colquhoun. Very tempted. But then she realised something.

'For one clan, you have many secrets,' she said.

Caird didn't say anything, but he started the horse again.

'To keep these secrets, you must have to avoid telling the truth,' she pointed out.

Caird made some sound in his throat, but she didn't know if it was confirmation or denial.

She didn't care. She knew the truth and she understood it very well. She was Buchanan after all.

'Secrets, lies, deception,' she continued. 'I think you Colquhouns must be masters at them. Maybe you could even teach me your tricks.'

Caird gave a choked huff and she knew she surprised him. And when Caird laughed? He overwhelmed her.

Mairead settled against him with at least one reflective worry gone. Clan Colquhoun wasn't going to be as overbearing and oppressive as she thought. 'We need to stop for the night,' he said, slowing the horse.

She didn't protest. It was early yet, but they had run out of food and would need to trap more.

'There are few trees here. Are you going to show me something new?'

'Aye, and I think we'll be walking far tonight.' She heard the teasing smile in his voice.

'I hope you'll keep up this time,' she retorted.

They had done this for days now. Taking walks with him showing her new ways to find trails and trap food. At first, he had taken care not to tire her, but she loved to walk Buchanan land. She wasn't surprised to find he liked to walk as well. For her, it was a chance to keep occupied, for him, a chance for reflection. They had entered into a companionship she didn't expect and she didn't trust herself with.

She was being impulsive and she'd keep making mistakes. Like travelling south with this man and blindly trusting it would be fine. Caird seemed sure, but she wasn't.

Because as much as Caird said he trusted her and cared for her, he never said he loved her. He never said what would happen once Bram decided what to do with the jewel.

Then there was Malcolm. Caird had all but admitted Malcolm might never accept her and they were close brothers.

Also, she didn't know if by some future act she wouldn't hurt him. She hurt everyone she loved. She didn't, couldn't, trust herself.

Still, she impulsively rode with him. Soon, she'd discover if it was another mistake.

The sounds of the village reached them before they crested the hill. The homes were scattered before becoming tightly packed. The single road was riddled with people and livestock. But it wasn't the noises, the homes or the people that caught her eye. It was the contrast.

Stacked neatly around dilapidated homes and

poorly clothed people were great sheets of thick thatch, bright rushes, freshly carved wooden beams and giant bolts of new wool.

The entire village looked as if a wealthy bene-factor had come through and discarded much-needed supplies. Instead of using them, the villagers seemed to be going out of their way to ignore them.

Scampering children used them for their games, shepherds navigated animals around heav-ily laden carts and some villagers leaned against stacks of thatch as if they were boulders. One large-boned robust woman walked over a bolt of green wool as if it wasn't even there. Mairead longed for a fitted gown with no holes. If it rained again, the wool could be ruined.

The keep rose in the distance, low buildings around it, many people, maybe a hundred, in front. As they approached, she saw various tents, and soldiers, who were either idling or training.

Soon it became apparent why there were peo-ple and soldiers outside. The gates were closed.

Caird had told her that Bram had concerns on Fergusson land. But if he was barred from the keep, it seemed Bram had more than a mere con-cern on his hands.

With no room to manoeuvre, Caird slowed the horses and helped her dismount. They had pushed the last of their journey and her legs were un-steady and sore.

Someone took their horses as Caird took her hand and led her towards the gates. She wondered at the futility of it.

'They're closed.' She pulled up her gown, which only made it gape more. The villager's gown hadn't fit.

'Hmm.' Caird pointed. 'And my brother trains before them.'

Even if Caird hadn't pointed, there would be no missing his brother. If Caird's hair showed slight red only in the brightest sunlight, Bram's would show red even at night. Its intense bright colour waved down to his shoulders. For ornamentation, a small plaited strip fell far over to the middle of his chest.

He was one of the few training, but as they approached, he lowered his sword and gave them a smile. Despite his commanding presence and build, he looked tired. His fine clothing was unkempt and filthy. Bram handed his sword to a soldier, who left the crooked circle they'd made.

'I had not expected you here so soon,' Bram said as they reached him, 'but I welcome the company.'

Caird returned his brother's hug.

'Have you heard from the north?' Caird asked. He had left the elders in charge when he travelled to Graham land.

'I'd received a message two days past. All's well.'

Caird gestured at the men outside the closed gate. 'What happens here?'

'I've been waiting,' Bram said.

'All this time?' Caird asked, incredulously.

'Aye, our brother has turned as weak as a Buchanan.'

They all turned at the voice.

Malcolm approached, his eyes not hiding his contempt for Mairead.

Bram scowled. 'It is not weakness, but tactics.'

Malcolm shrugged. 'Starving a woman, and her annoying siblings, is hardly a battle worthy of the Colquhoun Clan.'

'You lay siege here?' Caird looked aghast at his brother. 'Against children?'

Caird didn't know what to expect as he approached the Ferguson keep. Gates closed and soldiers idle certainly wasn't one of them. He even spotted Colquhoun's best craftsmen here playing dice. Now this? Bram was the better natured of the siblings, quicker to laugh than his sister. He was here to make amends to the Fergusson Clan, not torture them.

'Tactics, not a siege.' Bram's eyes darted to the keep before returning to Caird's. 'And not only children. There is a woman.'

Caird looked pointedly at the partially wooden keep. As he stared, a lean figure emerged at the top of the gates.

The distance wasn't far. With shorn hair and

wearing a tunic and leggings, the person should have been a young man. But the wind left no doubt a woman stood there.

'That lass bars you?' Caird asked.

Bram quickly swung around and became almost deathly still. The camp stilled, too. 'We will come to an understanding soon,' Bram whispered, his eyes never leaving the woman's.

Caird watched Bram's assessment change, his demeanour switch from congenial to predatory. He had seen his brother like this when he hunted bigger game. Only then did Bram become silent… and deadly.

But it was clear the woman was no prey. Her shoulders were back and her eyes bore down on them. They both held themselves like two hunters waiting to strike.

'I allow this respite, for now.' Bram's eyes never left the woman's, as if they silently communicated. 'I'll not have more reason for her…them… to hate me.'

The figure descended as quietly as she had come and the camp exhaled a collective breath.

'Perhaps, but vexing all the same.' Malcolm turned to address Caird. 'You have arrived, but it has been longer than a fortnight.'

'How went the celebrations?' Caird asked.

'You were not there, and I was amply occupied,' Malcolm said, shrugging. 'John and…' Malcolm's eyes darted to Mairead '…the groom won most everything. How did you fair?'

'We still have it,' Caird said.

Malcolm's eyes changed. 'It wasn't returned to her brother? How surprising.'

'What is this you speak of?' Bram asked.

Caird was surprised. 'You have not told him?'

'I did not know which tale to tell,' Malcolm said calmly.

Caird ignored Malcolm and turned to Bram. 'I have private news only for my brothers' ears.'

'There is nowhere for my men to go. I'm afraid this is it for privacy,' Bram answered.

Caird knew this was not nearly private enough, but his brother was entrenched. He could delay no longer. 'I have the—'

'Wait,' Malcolm interrupted. 'You tell this in front of her?' He nodded in Mairead's direction.

'Aye,' Caird replied.

Malcolm's demeanour blackened as he addressed Bram. 'I want it noted, my *laird*, I protest this tale told in front of her.'

Caird didn't know how Bram was reacting to this conversation, but he didn't have time to mend Malcolm's feelings. 'She has my trust,' Caird announced.

'So be it.' Bram's eyes travelled from Malcolm to Caird. 'I want this tale told.'

'It is neither tale nor legend,' Caird replied, and

then he spoke of the jewel. Malcolm remained silent, as did Bram. Surprisingly, so did Mairead.

As he listened, Bram's expression changed, and when Caird finished, Bram only replied, 'So close.' But he said it softly, almost to himself.

The siege and unrest were now apparent on Bram's face, the jewel's responsibility seemingly ageing him between breaths.

Giving his brother time to assess, Caird looked around them. Everything appeared the same, but he knew everything had changed for Bram and his clan.

When Caird made the gesture to open the pouch at his waist, Bram stilled his hand. 'Nae, not here. In fact, I doona want to see it.'

Mairead had been silent as Caird told his version of their journey. He left out many details, but never, she was beginning to understand, the important ones.

Yet now, Bram didn't even want to see the jewel?

'Why?' Mairead asked before she could check her response. They had risked their lives. The least he could do was look at it. 'You have to see it!'

Bram looked to Caird. 'Impulsive female.'

Caird nodded.

'But yours,' Bram said.

'Aye,' Caird answered.

'What?' Mairead blurted out.

'Never!' Malcolm said, his casual stance gone.

Incredulity and anger tightened his body. 'She's a Buchanan!'

Bram stilled and turned to her.

Reeling from Caird's declaration, Mairead braced herself. Bram was laird. He could make decisions regarding her life. 'I am Mairead, of Clan Buchanan,' she said, hoping her voice could be heard above the roaring in her ears.

Had Caird just declared to his brother they were betrothed? They had only talked of caring and trust. Was he now proposing marriage? His family hadn't accepted her!

His expression inscrutable, his gaze swinging from Caird to Malcolm, Bram replied, 'I see.'

Mairead glanced at Caird, who watched his brother. Mairead didn't need to turn to see Malcolm. She could feel the sharp look he placed between her shoulders.

'And you're here now, with these matters,' Bram said.

The laird made decisions, but he didn't know everything. 'Aye, but reluctantly,' she answered.

'Nae doubt,' Bram agreed as he glanced at Caird. 'But on everything?'

Blushing, Mairead glanced to the gates. The woman had returned. Mairead felt as if she was intently listening to this conversation. She hoped she couldn't hear her humiliation.

'Nae,' she answered. 'Not reluctant on everything.'

'I didn't think so.' Bram turned to Malcolm. 'She is Buchanan, but she risked much with Caird. Some debts can be forgiven.'

'Do you expect me to accept?' Malcolm asked.

She didn't understand any of this, but she knew by being here she brought discord to this family. She was making a mistake, just as she feared. She couldn't do it.

'There's nothing to accept,' Mairead said. 'We brought this jewel here for the laird to decide. I can return to my home. Any debt to me for my troubles was already made in payment to my clan.'

There, she had said it and she did it without her voice breaking.

Caird made a gruff sound next to her and she glanced at him. Was *amusement* in his eyes?

'There, now!' she gestured towards the arrogant man. 'Caird doesn't deny the deal we made. I'll be gone soon, just as I tried to be weeks ago!'

Bram made a sound, too, and it sounded like a swallowed chuckle. 'Nae,' he said finally.

'Nae?' she questioned, irritated. 'You cannot deny payment. I earned it. Since it's already in Buchanan hands, I'd like to see you try to get it back!'

'Nae, Buchanan, you keep your payment. Your story tells of much valour, honour and bravery.' Bram's eyes softened. 'Such a journey also tells of my brother's desire to marry you.'

'Nae!' Malcolm cried.

'What?' Mairead gasped at the same time. 'We do what?'

Caird turned to her. 'We marry.'

'I agree,' Bram said, patting Caird's shoulder. 'Soon. Today.'

'How could you?' Malcolm moved in front of Mairead and closer to Bram. 'You cannot wish this!'

'About this marriage?' Bram said. 'Or our sister's? It has taught our clan much.' He glanced to the closed gates and to the woman watching. His frown increased. 'And keeps on teaching us,' he said slowly.

'You compare Gaira's marriage to this?' Malcolm paled, his scar standing in stark relief. 'Knowing I still haven't accepted hers?'

'As laird, I order it.' Bram's face became forbidding. 'You must remember this.'

Malcolm's eyes went cold. 'I remember...*everything*!'

Bram reached for Malcolm's shoulder, but he shrugged off the comforting hand.

'Wait!' Mairead cried out. 'I doona understand this.'

'You won't until you are married,' Bram said.

'I trust her,' Caird said, his voice rough; he didn't like this edict.

'But it is not our tale to tell,' Bram said. 'I'll have them sisters first.'

Bram stepped towards Malcolm. 'You need

time, Brother. So it is you who will be taking the jewel to where it belongs.'

Caird shifted and Bram's eyes went to him. 'Do you have objections?'

Caird's eyes lingered on Mairead. She couldn't comprehend everything he was silently asking her, but she did understand most. He worried for his brother, and worried for her. But would he let the jewel go after all they did to secure it?

Caird released her eyes and looked to Bram. 'Malcolm should have it. He should find where it belongs.'

Her jaw dropped, just as Malcolm's defeat quickly turned to derision.

'There is nowhere it goes then,' Malcolm answered. 'It is homeless, just as I am.'

Bram made a sound deep in his chest. 'You are not without a home.'

'Nae?' Rigidity returned to Malcolm's shoulders. 'You say this as you send me on a fool's errand to remove me from this clan.'

'It's not like that,' Bram said. 'Later, we will talk of the jewel.'

'It's exactly like that.' Malcolm stepped back. 'Despite this talk, I will choose what to do with the jewel.' Not waiting for approval, Malcolm turned to leave.

'Malcolm!' Mairead called, not knowing what she wanted to say.

He stopped and looked over his shoulder.

Mairead felt helpless again. She could sense Malcolm's pain and it hurt. But she couldn't apologise because she didn't know what to apologise for. But she wanted to say…do…something.

Malcolm glared at Caird. 'You didn't tell her?'

Caird gave a quick shake of his head.

'Your adherence to rules, and promises, and vows,' Malcolm sneered. 'Well, know I'm about to break every one of them. Tell her!' He gestured to Mairead, but didn't look at her. 'Tell her every blood-ridden drop of it.'

When Malcolm turned to leave again, they let their brother go.

Seeming to get his emotions under control, Bram addressed them. 'I will go after him,' Bram said. 'But I have more to say.'

Mairead waited for the truth to finally come out, for some sense of reality.

Bram clasped his hands behind his back. 'My stay here may be extended.'

Caird shifted. 'You already appointed me in your absence.'

'Aye. But negotiations have taken longer than expected.' Bram shrugged. 'The hunting is good here though.'

Bram's favourite pastime was hunting, as was all varied and leisure activities. Here, there were only responsibilities. The skills his brother did have, his renowned diplomacy and profit-making abilities, were clearly scorned by the keep's mistress and villagers. Bram belonged on Colquhoun land.

'You are my older brother and Laird of Clan Colquhoun,' Caird insisted. 'It's not like you to remain idle for this long.'

'Not idle. You'd be pleased to know, I've been gathering answers. This clan has been much abused. I could not force myself on them again.'

'Your diplomacy has not worked here though; they bar you.'

'Aye, but not for long. Negotiations are about to change.' Bram looked to the keep.

Caird recognised his brother's resolved tone. He'd argue no longer.

'I will leave you to talk now.' Bram lips curved. 'Just stay far away from the keep's walls.'

When Bram left, Mairead knew the world was different. She just didn't understand to what extent.

'What is the meaning of all this?' she said. 'I doona ken. I cannot marry you. Your clan will never accept me.'

'My clan just did,' he said. 'They will accept Bram's word and they will accept mine. It's those secrets, Mairead. You will know them now.'

'What of the jewel? Why did you let it go?' she asked, too flustered to disagree with the other part.

His brows drawn, his eyes questioning. As if

he wanted to say something and then thought better of it.

'I only ever wanted the jewel for Malcolm. To never have a repeat of Dunbar. He is owed the right to have it. Bram and he will talk and they will find its true path.'

'It didn't look like they would talk.'

His lip curled. 'They will talk. Whether Malcolm will listen, or whether Bram will finally reveal why he denied his brothers' fighting in Dunbar, I doona know.'

'You won't have your answers.'

'Not for now,' he said. 'But as always, my brothers will have my loyalty.'

Rules, adherence. For loyalty to his clan, he would let the jewel go. But that still didn't explain why he looked to her when he did it.

'You look doubtful,' he added. 'The jewel has been dangerous for us. It has repeatedly threatened your life. Can you think of nae other reason why I'd willingly let it go?'

Had he thought she'd protest? She had only ever wanted the dagger.

'You sent the dagger to my clan,' she said. 'But I doona know if it is enough, or if the laird will allow them to stay.'

He tilted his head. 'I sent a letter with the dagger giving them sanctuary on Colquhoun land. I also sent a letter to Colquhoun elders to send a chest of silver to your laird. One or the other will be there before the English.'

She'd forgotten how rich the Colquhouns were. But still it was a debt she couldn't repay, and her clan… 'You'd allow the Buchanan laird to claim both?'

'I requested the chest to be used first, and that we would expect the dagger when we return.'

'Return?'

'Aye, in the letter I explained much, Mairead. They know you are safe, that they are safe as well.'

She blinked, breathed in deeply and took some steps, but she couldn't pace. They were alone, but not far away were men and soldiers. She had to stay and face Caird.

'What of Malcolm?' She locked her knees and tried to still the tiny trembles in her body.

'Why are you questioning?' he asked.

Her throat suddenly dry, she licked her lips. He was taking away all her arguments against him, until she was only left with accepting him. Could she?

'Mairead, you are throwing questions, like obstacles, at me. Why now?'

She feared she felt something more than trust and care with Caird. She couldn't have something more. Especially now, when she knew she couldn't stay with him. After everything he had risked for his brother, she wouldn't come between them.

'I won't come between brothers,' Mairead said.

Caird looked over her shoulder. 'We all have our own paths, our own purpose in this. Malcolm must have his own.' His all-too-knowing eyes returned to hers. 'This cannot be why you question me.'

'I'm Buchanan,' she said. She did, indeed, feel like she was throwing obstacles against him.

'It couldn't be more wondrous,' he said. 'Lying, taunting, beckoning and deceiving me since that night at the inn. But all of it, all you have done was with purpose.' He took a step towards her. 'Now, I want that purpose to be with me.'

'Did Gaira marry a Buchanan? Is that why nae one will say his name, and why you are so certain in this?'

He gave a curt shake of his head. 'You won't get that secret so easily. But know that Gaira's marriage is…complicated.' He gave her a knowing look. 'And I believe I'm finding out that marrying a Buchanan will produce its own demands.'

She swallowed. 'Do I have nae say in this?'

'You always did.'

Oh, those beautiful grey eyes storming with green. They were beautiful, but there were dark shadows beneath them and his cheeks were hollowed from the lack of food. They'd had little rest since he'd tended her. Yet, he was giving her a choice. How much it probably pained the arrogant Colquhoun to concede anything.

And how much she loved that he conceded to

her. Loved. Now she realised why she threw obstacles at him. Because she'd made another mistake.

She loved him.

She must. But loving him, staying with him, would mean another mistake. She'd only hurt him. Anguish, shame and guilt lashed at her. She hadn't the strength for anger.

So the words that needed to be said couldn't be simply thrown at him. They had to be wrenched from her, like that knife she'd buried inside her.

'How can I do it?' she whispered.

Caird held still, but she knew he felt her words.

'Mairead?' he asked, not saying anything more, but not needing to.

She blinked away the threatening tears. She wanted—needed—to see him clearly. He had to know; he had to realise.

'I make mistakes. I make them constantly. Impulsively. With Ailbert, with everything. I doona trust myself; I never have! So how could I with you?'

Caird's eyes closed and his left thumb flexed. And again.

She said something he didn't like, but she didn't know what and she wasn't done with what needed to be said. 'You're asking for me to trust you, I do, but how can I be with you, marry you, knowing I'll just hurt you?'

When he opened his eyes, he looked pained.

'Are you saying that what has kept us apart is not your trusting me?'

Trusting him had never been an issue. How could she not trust an arrogant, all-knowing Colquhoun? 'Mostly.'

Caird's eyes turned from hurt to incredulous. 'Then this fighting me has been because you doona trust yourself…with me?'

She nodded her head. 'I may hurt you. I have feelings. I doona understand them, or if they're real or just me being impulsive again. That's when I make mistakes. We went through so much and it could be you or—'

He held her to him. 'Does this feel like a mistake?'

She was engulfed in Caird's warmth, comfort, scent, which had always felt right. 'None of this feels like a mistake,' she answered truthfully. 'But that may be my mistake.'

'You think I doona make any?' he answered.

It was her turn to be quiet.

'I've risked your life many times since we met. I regret all those mistakes. I know there is still a murderer out there, who, even if we nae longer have the jewel, may come for our lives. I was careless with the defeat of the soldiers. One archer was left free. Those days of caring for you, I never knew if an arrow would come for us.'

It would always unsettle him that the archer and the Englishman were free. He didn't have the answers he sought and they would always be in some danger.

'They were circumstances you couldn't control.'

'I could have controlled my blindness with you. Seen who you were long before we ever reached the river, the cave, the village.'

'The jewel was important. You were worried about your brother.'

'You make excuses for me, but none for yourself.' His eyes were insistent. 'We'll make mistakes, both of us, but we'll learn. Mairead, you have to forgive yourself. Your brother's death wasn't your fault.'

Grief, quick and fierce, pierced and freed itself from her heart. She buried her face in Caird's tunic. She wouldn't be able to hold her tears in. Not now.

Warm arms folded around her. 'Not your fault,' he whispered as her tears coursed silent and unstoppable. But Caird was there giving comfort and strength, and when she could, she raised her face to him.

'I can't think—'

'Not now.' His hands cradled her face; his thumbs brushed tears she couldn't seem to stop. 'Not now, but give it time. Let's learn this together.'

Trying to make her tone light, she asked, 'Are

you saying you've forgiven yourself for how you treated me?'

He huffed and rested his hands on her shoulders before they slid around her again. 'Nae, but I'll learn to cherish you and protect you. And that means your family as well.'

'My family?'

'Aye, your mother and giggling sisters. We'll see them, Mairead, as soon as we can travel.'

She felt those words and she realised the truth of it. This man was dependable like a mountain. If he said they'd see her family, they would. She had fought it long enough, and, wrapped as she was within his arms, she didn't want to fight it any longer.

But something inside her still resisted him so she shook her head. 'I may hurt you.'

'Stubborn,' he said, his voice gruff with emotion. His arms tightened and drew her to him. 'There's only one way to hurt me now, Mairead. And that's if you keep us apart.'

She felt those words and they wrapped warmth deeper than Caird's arms. They wrapped warmth around her very heart.

He pulled slightly away and lifted her chin with his finger until their eyes met. 'But I need answers,' he said.

Greedy Colquhoun. She gave a quick nod.

'Is it possible,' he said, 'I didn't need to show

you…to the extent I did…the trust you have for me?'

She blushed, as she always did remembering that morning at the village. When Caird had shown her, in the most giving way possible, how she'd trusted him all along. Keeping her smile hidden, she gave a quick shake of her head.

He swallowed, hard, as if afraid of the next answer. 'Then we merely had to talk about your doubting and trusting yourself with me?'

'Maybe,' she answered.

He groaned. She smiled; she couldn't help it. Caird's face looked both pained and relieved.

'Mairead, you almost killed me that day. My body still hasn't been set right. It's the reason we've been—' He stopped, and she could have sworn he blushed.

Caird hadn't had enough of her that day and she hadn't had enough of him. She welcomed his touches and kisses and honeyed words.

'Do you mean you would have left me alone on the journey here?' she asked.

'Aye! That day at the village, I would have shown you our trust, Mairead, but not to the extent… You were a maid; it was too much. After, you needed rest. Instead, my body wouldn't let me stop touching you. I may never stop touching you.'

Mairead couldn't believe his confession. The day at the village had been wondrous as had every day after that. Because she had been with him.

Something eased within her; the final defence against him had always been herself. Now, with his confession, that barrier was gone. Because she just had proof she could trust herself with Caird. With that trust, she could love.

'Ach, then that's two mistakes I didn't make,' she said.

'Two?'

'Aye. The first is going to your room at the inn,' she confessed and revelled in the warmth of his gaze.

'And the second?'

'When I wasn't exactly truthful—' she made sure to lower her voice as she trailed her fingers up his chest '—about my trusting you.'

'Deceitful Buchanans. All of you.' He gave her a squeeze. 'If I didn't love you—'

She started. 'Love?'

He looked down at her. 'Aye, love. Clever Buchanan, how could you not guess? It's always been love. Our caring, our trust. Those feelings you have and doona trust yourself with? I have them, too. It's love. And I trust it most of all.'

Her tightly wrapped and warmed heart soared even as she emphatically shook her head ensuring he saw her denial at his words. Oh, she did love this man. But he had to know he was marrying a Buchanan.

'You doubt it's love?' His brows drew together then rose in realisation as his eyes gleamed with determination. 'You're not going to make me *show* you, are you?'

She smiled. She couldn't help it. Even though she was supposed to be the better liar.

And because it was him, she answered the only way she could. 'Ach, I believe I have some doubts.'

\* \* \* \* \*

# MILLS & BOON®

## Buy A Regency Collection today and receive FOUR BOOKS FREE!

Transport yourself to the seductive world of Regency
with this magnificent twelve-book collection.
Indulge in scandal and gossip with these
2-in-1 romances from top Historical authors

Order your complete collection today at
**www.millsandboon.co.uk/regencycollection**

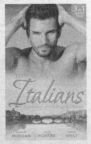

# MILLS & BOON®

## Want to get more from Mills & Boon?

Here's what's available to you if you join the exclusive **Mills & Boon eBook Club** today:

✦ *Convenience – choose your books each month*
✦ *Exclusive – receive your books a month before anywhere else*
✦ *Flexibility – change your subscription at any time*
✦ *Variety – gain access to eBook-only series*
✦ *Value – subscriptions from just £3.99 a month*

So visit **www.millsandboon.co.uk/esubs** today to be a part of this exclusive eBook Club!

# MILLS & BOON®
## HISTORICAL

**AWAKEN THE ROMANCE OF THE PAST**

## A sneak peek at next month's titles...

### In stores from 2nd October 2015:

- **Christian Seaton: Duke of Danger** – Carole Mortimer
- **The Soldier's Rebel Lover** – Marguerite Kaye
- **Return of Scandal's Son** – Janice Preston
- **The Forgotten Daughter** – Lauri Robinson
- **No Conventional Miss** – Eleanor Webster
- **Dreaming of a Western Christmas** – Lynna Banning, Kelly Boyce & Carol Arens

Available at WHSmith, Tesco, Asda, Eason, Amazon and Apple

*Just can't wait?*
Buy our books online a month before they hit the shops!
**visit www.millsandboon.co.uk**

**These books are also available in eBook format!**